PÁDRAIG KENNY

Chicken House

Scholastic Inc. / New York

Library of Congress Cataloging-in-Publication Data available
ISBN 978-1-338-27755-5

10 9 8 7 6 5 4 3 2 1   19 20 21 22 23

Printed in the U.S.A.   23
First edition, April 2019
Book design by Maeve Norton

FOR CAROLINE, LOCHLANN,
SADBH, TADHG, AND TEAGAN

THE LAWS OF MECHANICS

1. Only licensed and registered engineers have
    the legal right to animate mechanicals.

2. It is forbidden to confer life and sentience
    upon any raw material that conforms to
    the standard agreed dimensions of an
    adult or "proper" human being.

3. All mechanical devices conferred with "life"
    must be so created using the principles of
    Gross Systematic Propulsion and the
    mechanism of glyphs.

4. It is strictly forbidden to confer life upon a
    mechanical using the principles of Refined
    Systematic Propulsion or "Ensoulment."

CHAPTER 1

Snow was falling from the night sky, and all the world was cold and hushed except for the regular metallic squeaking of Jack's joints. Christopher glanced at Jack, but the mechanical looked straight ahead, oblivious to the sound. Absalom was walking a few feet in front, his thin black coat billowing around him.

Squeak squeak.

Christopher willed the sound to stop.

Squeak squeak.

Absalom wheeled around, raising his tall, spidery frame up to its full height.

"I thought I told you to oil him before we left the yard," he said, glaring down at Christopher.

"I did, Mr. Absalom."

The truth was, in all the panic of their hurried departure, Christopher had completely forgotten to oil Jack's joints.

Absalom scowled at him.

"He did. He even checked me for loose rivets," said Jack.

"Fix your hair," said Absalom, flapping his hand at Jack,

who pulled down the edges of his wig and grinned at Christopher. Christopher smiled weakly in response. Ever since Absalom had informed them that there might be the possibility of an actual sale in Aylesbury, he'd felt an awful, cold sinking sensation in his chest.

Absalom hadn't made a real sale in quite a long time, except for his scarecrows, which were frankly embarrassing concoctions. The most recent had walked out of its field and was found three months later, ten miles away, facedown in a river.

But this time, Absalom had told them, "the stars were aligning." A sale was most definitely in the cards, and after a bit of gleeful capering around his office he told Jack to replace his regular red hair with a brown wig "because nobody buys gingers, awful sickly-looking things." Jack didn't mind. He was secretly delighted at the possibility of being sold, although Jack being Jack, he was too hardheaded to show it. Even so, Christopher had caught him grinning to himself on the way over in the truck.

Christopher stole another anxious glance at Jack as they walked along the street. He was grinning to himself again, but this time he noticed Christopher watching. Christopher looked away quickly.

"What's wrong?" said Jack.

"Nothing," Christopher replied.

Absalom's mood was improving. He looked up in amazement at the falling snow. "Beautiful. I couldn't have planned it better if I'd arranged it myself."

He signaled them to stop halfway along a row of redbrick houses, clasped his hands together, and grinned at the two boys.

"Here we are. Number ten is the abode we require. Remember what we practiced, Jack."

"Yes, Mr. Absalom."

"Christopher."

"Yes, Mr. Absalom?"

"Stand up straight, look smart. Remember, you're assistant to the greatest engineer in all of Britain."

"Yes, Mr. Absalom."

The door they faced was dark green with a dull brass knocker. Absalom straightened himself up, took the knocker, and gave it three confident raps. He spoke to the boys without looking at them:

"Smile, lads."

There were a few moments of silence broken only by the soft fizz of falling snow, then the sound of a bolt being thrown back. The door opened, and Absalom smiled his broadest smile.

A man in his thirties with a curly mop of hair poked his head out.

"Yes?" he said.

Absalom gave a small bow.

"Mr. Chapman, allow me to introduce myself. I am Mr. Gregory Absalom, a creator of rudimentaries, mannequins, mechanicals, and machines of varying sentience, variety, and vivacity."

He snapped his wrist and a business card appeared in his hand. Before Mr. Chapman knew what was happening, he'd taken the card and was looking at it with a dazed expression. He looked up, his head bobbing, eyes blinking, as if he'd just been punched.

"I'm . . . I'm sorry, what's this about?"

Absalom clasped his hands together in a gesture of prayer and took on a somber cast.

"Word has reached me, sir, of your personal tragedy. Please accept my sincerest condolences, late though they may be."

The man's face whitened. "Who told you? How is that any of your . . . who told you?" he demanded.

Christopher felt suddenly nervous. He tried to catch Absalom's eye, but the engineer was too busy fixing the man with a look that was both sympathetic and predatory.

"I have friends in the village, Mr. Chapman. They came to me out of the kindness of their hearts, and they told me of your predicament."

Mr. Chapman looked at him with wide eyes, resting his hand on the frame of the door as if he was trying to steady himself.

"How long has it been, Mr. Chapman?" asked Absalom, his head tilted, eyes soft and moist with well-practiced compassion.

Mr. Chapman trembled for a moment. "Six weeks," he said, his voice suddenly hoarse with grief.

"And he was your only child."

Mr. Chapman nodded.

Christopher felt blazing hot spots on his forehead and cheeks. He'd presumed that this was just a normal sale. He hadn't realized what the circumstances were, and now he was furious with Absalom for trying to take advantage of this man. He was about to step forward and say something, but Absalom, without even looking at him, deftly raised his right hand and put just enough pressure on his chest to halt him in his tracks.

"Very sad, very sad indeed," said Absalom, sighing and shaking his head—Christopher saw the sly glimmer in his eyes. "What would you say, sir, if I told you I could alleviate your pain and grief in some small measure?"

Mr. Chapman's eyes grew wide and defenseless. Christopher knew the poor man was now right where Absalom wanted him.

Absalom flourished theatrically in Jack's direction.

"May I present a top-of-the-range model. One of my finest creations, if I may be so bold."

Jack stepped forward and smiled at Mr. Chapman. He tilted his head, just as Absalom had taught him, and gave Mr. Chapman a hopeful, humble look. Christopher felt sick.

"Jack, we call him, but of course his appellation is a movable feast, should you make the decision to purchase. He comes complete with all the attributes of a boy of his apparent age. A sense of fun . . ."

Jack smiled and gave a little jig while he rocked his elbows back and forth like a music hall comedian.

". . . an intelligence far beyond that of his contemporaries . . ."

Jack put his hand to his chin and squinted sagely into the sky. "Three hundred and ninety-five times six hundred and seventy-two is two hundred and sixty-five thousand four hundred and forty."

". . . along with splendid mobility and articulation."

Jack did a cartwheel followed by a handstand. His joints squeaked, and Absalom took the opportunity to give Christopher a sour look. Christopher glared back at him, and Absalom's expression disappeared as he once again turned and smiled at a stunned Mr. Chapman.

"As you can see, sir, he is a most estimable model, a miracle of engineering, and I can assure you, a most affordable price should you make the decision to purchase."

"Thomas, who is that?" A voice drifted from inside the house. "Who's at the door?"

There was a long wintry silence before a woman appeared from behind Mr. Chapman, her hair straggly, her eyes vacant and shadowed with lines of sleeplessness.

"Who is it, Thomas? What do they want?"

Mr. Chapman looked anxious. "Nothing, Ruth. Go back inside. It's no one."

Absalom moved with the whiplash speed of a rattlesnake. "Mrs. Chapman," he said as he moved toward the threshold. "I was just offering your husband my most sincere condolences. From what I've heard from our mutual friends, your son, William"—Christopher saw Mr. Chapman flinch; his wife's hand went to her mouth—"was a most eminent and decent young man."

Absalom finished the sentence with a crack in his voice and dabbed at his eyes with his hankie before continuing.

"I was just showing your husband our latest model, one that I hope might offer a suitable approximation of your son, one indeed that might give some small measure of emotional fulfillment and sense of family at this most auspicious time of year."

Jack was walking around on his hands. Mrs. Chapman looked at him with a kind of nervous astonishment. She bent down to have a closer look.

Jack flipped back onto his feet and looked at Mrs. Chapman for the first time. He walked toward her, a look of genuine sincerity on his face.

"This is Jack, Mrs. Chapman," Absalom said gently. He ushered Jack forward by the shoulders.

A great hush descended again. In the background, Christopher could hear the low murmur of a mournful wind.

"Ruth . . ." said Mr. Chapman.

His wife didn't seem to hear him. Her head was quivering, and she bent even lower as Jack approached.

"One of my finest creations, Mrs. Chapman. A very subtle mechanical approximation of humanity both in form and content. Jack can be a worker, a friend, a companion . . ."

Absalom paused as Mrs. Chapman's eyes widened.

". . . a son."

She gave the smallest of whimpers. Mr. Chapman lowered his head and let out a plaintive, "Ruth, please . . ."

Jack stepped closer, and Christopher's heart lurched when he saw the look of agonized hope in her eyes. Absalom spread his arms wide and said:

"As the snow falls, think on this; how good and proper and right it would be to have a family together at Christmas. The putting up of the tree, the smiles, the anticipation, the scent of orange and spices in the air, the melodious comfort of carols. And who better to share all of this with than one's own progeny, to be together as a family unit, bound by love, by joy, and the anticipation of a visit from Father Christmas himself."

Absalom began to casually fire off his prices, outlining various options for renting or buying. Christopher tried to dampen the hot, sickening anger he felt. He looked at Mrs. Chapman's eyes, brimming with tears and hope and pain. Mr. Chapman had his head bowed, as if he'd already surrendered to the inevitable. Absalom's voice was becoming more high-pitched, like he couldn't quite believe what was about to happen. His nostrils were flaring, as if he could smell money about to change hands. The sight filled Christopher with disgust.

It took one word to bring it all crashing down.

Jack stepped forward and smiled hopefully.

Just one word.

"Mummy?" he said.

It was as if the snow around Mr. Chapman had suddenly turned into a violent spinning vortex. Christopher had never seen rage like it.

"No!" Mr. Chapman screamed.

He kicked Jack full in the chest, and Jack hurtled backward into the snow, hitting the ground with a metallic clatter.

Mr. Chapman pulled his wife inside and slammed the door in Absalom's face. In the silence, the snow hissed down around them.

CHAPTER 2

Back in the truck, Jack took off the brown wig, reached under his seat, took his usual ginger hair out, and fixed it back on his head. Once he was happy it was in place, he wriggled a little, shoved his hand under one of his legs, and frowned.

"I think I've dented my bum."

This made Christopher snort with laughter. Jack joined in. The two of them giggled while Absalom wrestled with the steering wheel as he violently pulled the truck onto the road. The two boys were still giggling. Absalom couldn't take it anymore.

"And you!" he snarled, turning to Christopher, who stopped giggling abruptly.

"Me? What did I do?"

"Nothing, that's what you did. Nothing."

"What was I supposed to do?"

"What I trained you to do. Assist me in making a sale, that's what. Do some patter, add in observations, make grand claims for the merchandise."

"His name is Jack," said Christopher. He looked at Absalom.

11

Their eyes locked. They would have continued that way if Jack hadn't interrupted and pointed out something rather more pertinent.

"Mr. Absalom, the road."

Absalom whipped his head around just in time to turn the wheel and stop them careering into a ditch. He swore, and they continued their journey through the dark, the agonized swish and groan of the wipers counterpointed by Absalom's muttering.

The mounds of scrap in the junkyard were disappearing under layers of snow when they arrived back, and Round Rob was waiting for them just outside Absalom's shed-cum-office. He still looked as frightened as when they'd left a couple of hours ago, but when he spied Jack in the passenger seat the look on his face turned to one of relief. Manda was also with Rob, holding his hand. Her teddy bear was hanging from her other hand.

"He didn't sell you," Round Rob said to Jack as he waddled toward them as fast as he could. It was more a statement of relief than an observation. Jack shook his head. Rob smiled and rested a hand on his ample chest. Rob was shorter than Christopher, and he was round and squat. The trunk of his body was made from an old cooking pot—the one advantage Absalom found in his construction was that Rob could be hired out for proper children to roll him down hills at festivals and fetes.

Christopher spotted the strands of fraying blond hair that spilled over Rob's right eye, and he felt a strange pang of guilt.

Manda ran to Christopher and hugged his leg. Christopher chuckled. "We weren't gone that long, Mand."

"We were worried," said Manda, looking up at him. Her grin was as crooked as ever, and the brown curls on her head didn't sit quite right. Her left eye was also larger than the right, and her right leg was shorter than her left—a source of frustration for Christopher, who kept asking Absalom when he was going to get her a proper leg. Absalom would always fob him off with what he thought was a witty comment about it taking so long because he could never decide whether to get her a shorter left leg or a longer right leg. Then he'd deliver his trademark cackle, and Christopher would turn away in disgust.

They all turned at the sound of Absalom slamming the truck door. He headed toward his shed, coat rippling in his wake.

"What happened, Mr. Absalom?" Rob piped up.

Absalom wheeled around. "Absolute and utter disaster, that's what happened, Robert. And it's all thanks to these two."

"That's not true," shouted Christopher. "We didn't even know what you were up to until we got there."

"And a good thing too," said Absalom, wagging a finger. "Otherwise you would have been moralizing, young Christopher. Moralizing as usual when the one thing you forget is that—"

"Business is business," interrupted Christopher.

"Exactly," said Absalom, still too angry to notice the sarcastic tone in Christopher's voice.

Their standoff was interrupted by a great rhythmic clanking sound, and Gripper strode into view from behind a pile of junk.

Absalom liked to refer to Gripper proudly as his "firstborn." He was the oldest in the yard, even older than Manda. He was also the largest, standing over eight feet tall, with a barrel chest that tapered to his waist. He had tree-trunk-wide legs and great clodhopping feet. His huge arms were a muscled collage of wires and rivets and piping—they ended in gigantic clawed hands that served as both shovels and miniature crushers. His lower jaw was made from what looked like the triangular cow catcher of a steam locomotive, making his chin jut out and giving him a dull-witted look. It was illegal to create adult-sized mechanicals who were self-aware. Absalom had built Gripper to such extreme dimensions because he reckoned it meant that he fell outside the legal definition of what was adult-sized and "proper." He reasoned that creating something as "exceptional" as Gripper meant that he couldn't be prosecuted for breaking the law.

Most mechanicals had their propulsion and consciousness glyphs carved onto their skulls, but Gripper had the large curved symbols all over his body—something as large as he was needed more magic to power him. And yet, despite his appearance and the suggestion of fierceness, Gripper's dark eyes had warmth and kindness in them. He may have been the oldest of Absalom's creations, but in many ways Christopher thought of him as the most innocent.

Gripper ground his jaws together with a hoarse metallic scrape. To the untutored this was just noise, but not to Christopher and the others.

"Mr. Absalom tried to sell Jack, Gripper," answered Christopher.

Gripper looked at Absalom and "spoke" again.

Absalom looked at him incredulously and pointed at Jack. "Well, what do you think happened?"

A cowed Gripper took a step back and held his hands together against his chest in a penitent fashion. Absalom turned toward his shed, then stopped halfway, glared up at the sky, and turned back to Gripper.

"I'll need you tomorrow, to help clear some snow."

Gripper nodded slowly.

Absalom looked at Christopher. "It'll be a way of making money," he sneered.

Christopher sighed and followed Absalom into the shed, only to find his master had stopped and stiffened just inside the threshold. There was a brief pause before Absalom raised his arms in an expansive gesture of welcome and said, "Estelle!"

Absalom moved farther into the shed and Christopher squeezed in behind him. Estelle was standing by the table. Like Christopher, thirteen-year-old Estelle was proper. She was wearing an old herringbone coat at least a size too big for her. Her oval-shaped face was framed by her dark hair, and she was glaring at the engineer.

"I've done what you asked, Mr. Absalom," she said.

Absalom eyed her for a moment. Estelle was calm and serious, and was never easily unnerved. *She's like a real grown-up*, thought Christopher with admiration, *even though she's only a year older than me.*

"Thank you, Estelle. As ever I am filled with appreciation, and I know without even looking that your work is of the highest quality, as always."

Estelle stepped forward and sighed. "Four yards of skin. That's four shillings."

Estelle held her hand out. Absalom looked at her palm and then looked her in the eye with a sly, calculating look.

"I thought we'd agreed on three, Estelle."

"It's a shilling a yard. It's always a shilling a yard," she replied, not moving her hand.

Absalom sighed and reached into the pocket of his moth-eaten, oil-stained waistcoat and took out a small purse. He counted the money out into Estelle's palm, making a show with his quivering fingers, as if handing the money over was causing him great pain.

"Thank you, Estelle," he said. His voice was tremulous, almost self-pitying.

Estelle merely grunted, pocketed the money, and headed for the door.

"You're welcome to stay," Christopher blurted.

Estelle looked at Christopher and frowned.

"It's a cold night," said Christopher. "I thought you might . . . that's if it's okay with . . . Mr. Absalom?"

He looked at his master hopefully, but Absalom had lost interest and turned to sort through the junk on his table.

"Thank you, Christopher," said Estelle. "But I've got somewhere to stay."

"You still lodging with old Mrs. Barnaby, Estelle?" asked Absalom without looking up.

"That's right," she replied.

"Lovely woman, respectable, very fine manners. Surprised you can afford her class of lodgings."

Absalom smirked to himself, his lips pursing, as if he was trying to contain his laughter.

Estelle clenched her jaw and gave him a murderous look that he didn't notice. She turned and walked out the door, letting in a chilly gust of wind before slamming it behind her.

Christopher frowned. "You should pay her more, Mr. Absalom."

Absalom grunted. "She does fine work, and I look after her and she knows it. She also gets the honor of working for a master craftsman like myself."

Christopher raised his eyebrows at the words *master craftsman*. He very much doubted that a real master craftsman worked in conditions like this. The table wasn't the only mess—the whole interior of the hut was crammed with junk, everything from stroller wheels to empty cans. There were old washbasins, the shells of clocks that had been gutted for their springs and wheels, sheets of metal, copper wiring, and the smell of oil, rust, and Absalom's sweat. Anything that wasn't jammed onto a creaking shelf was left in a pile on the floor.

On the left-hand wall there was a large painting, hanging at an angle. It was yellowed and grubby with spots of mold, but if you looked closely you could see it was of a man in eighteenth-century dress. He was standing with both hands on the pommel of a walking stick, and beside him there stood a wooden boy. The boy was covered in carved runes and glyphs. Absalom had rescued the painting from a rubbish tip. Sometimes he would stand under it with his hands on his hips, smiling up at the man in the painting as if he knew him and was greeting him like an equal. Occasionally Absalom would refer to himself in the same breath as some of the great engineers of the past. Christopher looked him up and down. He didn't look much like a legendary engineer.

"What are you going to make next, Mr. Absalom?" Christopher asked.

Absalom had picked up two eyeballs from the table, and he gave them both a vigorous polish on his waistcoat. "Oh, I don't know. I think I'll take it as it comes this time. I shall let the muse transport me wherever it may." He gave a wave of his hand around the room. "I've had a new consignment of heads, one of which will be the crowning glory of my latest creation."

Christopher looked around the room. There were more heads scattered around than usual, but they were a dull gray and looked badly molded and scuffed. A few had dents in them, and knowing Absalom as he did, he knew they'd still have dents in them once they were up and walking about. He felt a twinge of sadness at the thought.

Absalom's ill temper seemed to have waned, but Christopher could still see a trace of resentment in his eyes over the botched sale.

"You should get to bed, my boy. Get everyone inside the workshop. We've a big day tomorrow."

"Yes, Mr. Absalom," said Christopher.

CHAPTER 3

Jack, Rob, Manda, and Gripper were waiting for him outside.

Together, they made their way toward the workshop, which lay directly across the yard from Absalom's shed. The snow was thickening, and the piles of junk were being buried beneath a smooth white blanket.

Halfway to the workshop, Christopher heard a terrible squeaking noise, followed by a dull clang. He turned around to see Round Rob's body spasming toward the workshop—minus Round Rob's head. The body suddenly accelerated forward, spun around twice, and then hit the ground. Christopher sighed. Rob's head was always coming loose. Sometimes the others would take bets on how long his body could keep going without a head. The record was thirty seconds.

Christopher walked back past the body and picked up Rob's head. Gripper had already scooped up the rest of him. Round Rob smiled, but Christopher winced at the lock of hair that still hung down over his eye. For some reason, he found that more distressing than Rob's head coming loose.

Estelle was inside the workshop, gathering her tools together in a canvas satchel. The new skin she'd made for Absalom was stretched across a metal rack. Christopher could tell by the slight glimmer in her eyes that she was pleased with it.

Sometimes Christopher saw that same look when she was making her mixture in the workshop's large black pot. She would bend over it, the almost heart-shaped curve of her black hair framing her face. Her lips were always tightly pursed as she concentrated, her eyes dark and intense as she gazed into the pot, mixing and melding, folding the white mixture in and over and on itself like dough, until suddenly, and without warning, it would develop a fleshy pallor.

The trick was to take it out of the pot at just the right point. Take it out too early and it would liquefy and loosen and spill all over the floor, returning to the color of milk. Take it out too late and it would become a gloopy substance bobbled with lumps and bumps.

Christopher didn't know whether it was through instinct or sheer repetition, but she knew the right moment every time, without fail.

"Looks good, Estelle, but not as good as your best work right here," Jack said, jutting out his chin and presenting his face to her, pinching the skin on his right cheek and wiggling it.

Estelle gave the tiniest smirk and shook her head. "Good night, Jack." She hoisted her bag of tools up onto her shoulder and left the workshop to a chorus of good-nights from the others.

Christopher went and took out his own toolbox from under his bed. He fixed Rob's head back onto his body, and when he was happy with the fit he picked up his scissors and cut the offending ringlet that had been hanging over his eye. Round Rob thanked him and gave one of his embarrassed but grateful smiles. Christopher then oiled the hinges on Jack's arms and told everyone to be careful in the snow in case of rust. Jack gave him a mock salute. Christopher took a look at Manda's short leg next, and made a face when he saw some of the corrosion on her knee joint. He made a mental note to nag Absalom about it, again.

Meanwhile, Gripper was swinging back and forth from the rafters like a gorilla. Christopher told him to come down, as he didn't think the beams could take much more punishment. Gripper let go and landed with a crash. Christopher scolded him, but he could see Gripper was pleased with himself and was fighting the urge to do a Gripper grin.

Exhausted, Christopher sat on his bed and started to take off his boots.

"I think I *have* dented my bum," sighed Jack.

"Told you, I'm not looking at it," said Christopher.

Round Rob sniggered, but Jack was frowning.

"What's wrong?" asked Christopher.

Jack looked a little guilty. "I was kind of hoping that I'd be sold."

Round Rob gave a little panicked whimper. They all turned to look at Jack. Christopher was taken aback.

"Why?" asked Christopher.

Jack looked at the floor. "I dunno," he said. "I suppose . . . I suppose I just want to be proper, like you. I'd like to know what it's like to breathe and to have real skin. Proper skin. I want to know what it's like to be small and to grow, and to keep growing." Jack looked straight at Christopher now. There was a fierceness in his gaze. "I want to be like you and experience normal but important things."

Christopher was lost for words. He suddenly felt uncomfortable and found he couldn't look Jack in the eye.

"Important things like knowing what it's like to have a mum and dad," said Jack.

"I don't have a mum and dad," mumbled Christopher. "Not anymore."

"You know what I mean," said Jack.

"Tell us what it was like, Christopher. Go on, tell us," said Rob.

"What was what like, Rob?" asked Christopher.

"Having a family," said Rob.

Christopher felt all their eyes on him. He was used to their questions about his past, and he didn't mind telling them the stories, but sometimes it just felt a little strange.

"I don't remember that much," he said.

"But what you do remember is good. I like it," said Rob, his eyes shining.

Manda had perked up. Even Gripper seemed interested. Christopher sighed.

"There's just snippets I remember, like little pictures."

Manda lay on the floor now, with her chin in her hands. "Tell us again, Christopher. Go on."

They were all begging him now. Christopher shook his head and smiled. "All right, all right," he sighed, quieting them.

Christopher sat on the edge of his bed with his hands under his thighs. He gazed at the floor as he tried to conjure up images from the past, willing them gently to the surface for fear he might push too hard and lose them.

He saw a woman's face. She was in a kitchen, and she was smiling. He felt the familiar warm glow bloom in his chest.

"Mum had blonde hair," he said. "It was soft, really soft, and it . . ."

The woman turned. Her hair shimmered and rippled smoothly like a wave of light. Christopher swallowed.

". . . it was like honey and it lit up the room."

"Was she pretty?" asked Manda.

"Very," Christopher said with a smile.

"Very," sighed Rob.

Even Jack seemed entranced.

"She used to bake the best cakes," said Christopher. He could see her now in her apron, checkered red and white, her hair shining, streaks of flour on her cheeks and nose. He smiled to himself.

"And your dad?" asked Rob.

Brown eyes, thought Christopher. He had brown eyes, but that was all he remembered, so he did what he always did and he made the rest up. There was the usual stuff about how good his dad was with his hands. He made things out of wood. Toys and tables and chairs. He had a workshop.

"But not like Mr. Absalom's. Better," suggested Rob.

"Yes," said Christopher. He smiled at the look of wonder on Round Rob's face, but he felt the tiniest pinch of guilt.

Christopher told them how strong his dad was, and how handsome he looked, and how he kissed him good-night on the forehead every night and told him bedtime stories.

"Like you do now," said Manda.

Christopher nodded.

"Tell us about the house again," said Rob.

Christopher looked at him and smiled, but the smile was just to hide the sharp spasm of pain he felt. There was that heat again. The sudden shock of a flame licking the air in front of him, ferocious and orange, and the smell of smoke, the crackling of burning wood, the roar, the terrible roar of air being eaten . . .

Christopher squeezed his eyes shut for a moment and sucked in air as if he was trying too hard to remember. There was a brief pause as the others waited.

"Not tonight," he said. "Maybe another time."

"Is it hard to remember?" said Rob sympathetically.

"Just a little," said Christopher.

Very, he thought. *So very hard to remember so very little, and for so very little to hurt so very much.*

"We'll never be proper," said Jack gloomily.

"But we can be better," said Rob brightly. "Just the other day Mr. Absalom said he'd get me a new torso."

Jack and Christopher exchanged a look. Rob didn't see it.

"He says that a lot, Rob," said Jack.

"But as soon as we make money," said Rob.

Jack tried to look optimistic, but it wasn't easy.

"Just think," said Rob. "A new torso. Maybe even new legs. We could all be upgraded. Zephyr grade maybe, or even a Pilkington."

"Pilkingtons don't last," said Jack.

"A Hockney Mark Two then," said Rob.

"I saw a Cormier Original once," said Jack.

"Did not," said Manda.

"Did too," said Jack. "Me and Mr. Absalom were in East Grimstead in a shop, and a girl came in with her parents. She had golden ringlets, perfect hair. She was dead pretty."

"It wasn't *her*, was it?" asked Rob.

"Ellie Lockwood? Yes. Mr. Absalom said it was."

"It was never, it was never Ellie Lockwood," gasped Manda.

Ellie Lockwood was the most famous mechanical in all of Britain. They said she was fifty years old, but looked like she'd been made yesterday. She went to all the best parties and she was in all the newspapers. It was said she'd even met the king.

"Did her hair look real, Jack?" asked Rob.

Jack nodded.

"I bet her eyes match," sighed Manda.

"They're blue too," said Jack. "She has the best skin. They say she can blush."

"I can blush," said Rob. He clamped his mouth shut and started to make squealing sounds.

"You don't have any breath, Rob," said Christopher.

Rob stopped what he was doing. "Oh, right, I forgot."

Manda giggled.

"Imagine being like that. Top of the range, and with parents and all. The nearest thing to being proper," said Jack.

Christopher saw the dreamy look in his eyes and felt bad for saying what he said next:

"They weren't her parents, Jack. They were her owners."

Jack looked slightly annoyed. "I know that, but still . . ."

"Top of the range," sighed Rob.

No one said anything. A gust of wind gently rattled the door.

"We should get some sleep," said Christopher.

"You mean *you* should get some sleep—we don't need sleep," said Rob. He raised his right eyebrow, which promptly fell off. He tried to lean over and get it, but couldn't reach, and he toppled over and started to roll around. Manda started to laugh, as did Gripper, who clapped his great clanking hands together with delight. Jack righted Rob and picked up his eyebrow and handed it to him. Rob held it out toward Christopher in the palm of his hand with a hopeful look.

Christopher rolled his eyes good-humoredly and dug around in his toolbox for glue. He quickly reattached Rob's eyebrow and patted him on the head.

"We'll get you new eyebrows soon," he said.

"Cormier class," said Rob. "All fluffy. Nice enough to run a little comb through."

Christopher grinned. "Yes. Cormier class. Absolutely."

Round Rob settled into his spot among the junk pile. Manda went to her chair, Gripper sat back against the wall, and Jack leaned nonchalantly by the door and listened to the wind.

Christopher pulled his blankets tightly around himself and lay facing the wall. A vision came to him, a vision of flames and smoke, and he screwed his eyes shut in an effort to banish it.

"I'll tell you what, though," said Jack. "That Ellie Lockwood fancied herself. She had airs and graces. Ideas above her station."

Christopher said nothing. The flames fizzled out into blackness. Sleep came.

In the darkness there was a warm light. He could feel himself rushing toward it. The light became golden, the world became green.

He was in a garden again. The sun was low in the sky. He could hear a bird singing as he sat on the grass. He could feel the dull ache in his hip from where he'd fallen. He wiped a hand across his face and it came away wet with tears. He looked around him quickly in a panic, but the vision of green and gold was beginning to fade. He cried out and reached blindly with his hand. A shadow fell over him and someone called his name.

CHAPTER 4

The next morning Christopher woke to the sight of the junk-yard smothered in snow. He looked up into a powder-blue sky flecked with fine wisps of cloud. His hands tingled and his breath frosted in the air as he walked across the yard. He felt alive and whole, part of everything, as if he'd stepped into a living painting.

Absalom was in his shed. He was back to being the expansive, chatty, and cunning Absalom they all knew so well.

He gestured out the window.

"Told you, my lad, didn't I? Told you we'd be busy. We've already gotten one call about clearing a road. There'll be more. A full day's pay for a full day's work. Time for you to marshal the troops."

Absalom turned to his workbench and started to pocket screws and a screwdriver.

"Mr. Absalom?"

"Yes, my lad?"

"I was thinking about my parents. Do you think they suffered in the fire?"

Absalom froze for a moment. Christopher expected him to say something dreadful, but his tone was surprisingly light and cheerful.

"You shouldn't worry your young head about such things." Absalom turned to face him. "The lady from the orphanage assured me of one thing—theirs was a merciful passing from this world to the next, quick and painless. May they rest in peace."

"But how did she know?"

Absalom reached for a box of bolts. "There were witnesses, obviously. The very same people who pulled you from the fire."

"Why don't I remember any of it?"

Absalom looked out the window for a moment and nodded slowly to himself. "A consequence of a blow to the head, I should think. That's what the doctor said anyway."

"I think I can only remember my mother, and I know I remember being here . . ."

"And what beautiful memories they must be," said Absalom, spreading his arms wide as if addressing a crowded theater.

"But I wish I could remember more. I wish I could be certain of more."

Absalom nodded, in an effort to look earnest and reasonable.

"So do I, lad. So do I," he sighed.

"Will I ever get the memories back?"

Absalom flapped his hand and went back to looking at his bench. "Who knows? Who knows?"

"I'd like that. Although sometimes I think I can see—"

"Look, Christopher, my lad," said Absalom a little spikily. "We really need to get to work today and I don't have much time for idle chitchat."

"All right, Mr. Absalom," said Christopher with a nod.

Absalom smiled at him, but Christopher could see by the tautness of the leathery skin on his face that it was a strained smile.

"You're my favorite, you know that, don't you?"

"Yes, Mr. Absalom."

"Good lad." Absalom patted his coat pockets, shoved a tool-box under his arm, and headed for the door. He ruffled Christopher's hair on the way out. "The very best."

In the passenger seat of the truck, Christopher looked out at the snow-covered humps of fields and the fretwork of tree branches, gray against the sharpness of the pale-blue sky. The frenetic snowstorm of the previous night had been replaced by a hush and a stillness that blanketed everything.

They passed a large factory. Black smoke belched out of its chimney stacks. In the distance, Christopher saw the sun glint off several rows of metal, no doubt mechanicals working outside while their companions kept the wheels of industry going inside.

"It'll take a while for this snow to shift," said Absalom. He gave a little self-satisfied chuckle.

Christopher looked at him, hunched over the wheel, eyes wide and money-mad, his whole being oblivious to the cold.

"Is it true that you and Jack saw Ellie Lockwood?" asked Christopher.

"What's that?" snapped Absalom, barely paying attention.

"Jack says you and he saw Ellie Lockwood in East Grimstead."

He frowned. "We may have. I don't really remember."

"They say she's a Cormier Original."

"People say a lot of things. She may have been a work of supreme craftsmanship. I can't remember. The only proper craftsman, like myself of course, that I ever came across was Richard Blake. Now there was a master. Proper articulation in his models, well balanced, fluid movement, and a near seamless capacity to carry themselves off as proper people."

28

Christopher thought about this for a moment. He'd heard all the stories about Richard Blake. He was considered by many to be the greatest engineer since the end of the Great War, and he was celebrated all over as the true heir to the great Philip Cormier. Blake had dined with kings and queens, and it was said he'd even advised the prime minister himself.

"Is it true what they say about his father?" asked Christopher.

"Is what true?"

"That he was killed by a mechanical?"

"Charles Blake was a good engineer. Although not as good as he thought he was, and he perhaps pushed his limited talents a little too far in the service of his country."

"It *is* true, then?"

Absalom licked his lips and swallowed. His voice went a little bit quieter. "Certain engineering practices and artifices are now quite rightly banned because of what Charles Blake did."

"You mean Refined Propulsion? Ensoulment?" said Christopher.

Absalom wrinkled his nose. "Maybe it's best not to talk about such matters."

Christopher sat back in his seat and frowned. He decided to try another subject.

"Is it true Richard Blake went mad?"

"He didn't go mad. He just disappeared," said Absalom. "People like to say he went mad because they like to think that genius drives you mad. Well, if that's true, then why am I still the resolutely rational man you see before you?"

Christopher didn't answer.

"Now, Mr. Cormier, on the other hand, he went quite mad after the incident that ended with Mr. Blake Senior's demise. How could he not? After all, he played a major part in that dark enterprise." Absalom's voice went low again. "That's why Refined Propulsion is banned."

Christopher nodded. Estelle had told him some of what she knew about the whole terrible episode. Rumor had it that Philip Cormier had discovered a new method for giving a machine consciousness. He called it Refined Propulsion. He used words like *psychonic adhesion*, *quintessential transference*, and other fancy terms, but really it just meant transferring a soul into a machine. Cormier had enlisted the help of Charles Blake, and during the public demonstration that had followed, dozens of people had been killed by the mechanical, including Charles Blake himself.

"That's also why Cormier went into self-imposed exile in Ironhaven," Absalom continued. "They say he melted down most of his greatest works. Smashed them to bits, disassembled them, smelted 'em and all. That's why Cormier Originals are so highly prized. Never underestimate the value of the work of a madman."

"I heard stories that he made adult models."

Absalom shook his head and gave a scornful look. "No one has made an adult model since the time of Runcible—it's against the law."

"But maybe by accident. That could happen, couldn't it?"

Absalom said nothing. His grip tightened on the wheel and he stared at the road ahead. He narrowed one eye, dragged the back of his hand across his nose, and gave a very loud sniff. Christopher looked at him for a moment and tried to gauge the best way to proceed.

He wanted to be careful, but the words were out of his mouth before he knew what he was saying:

"What about Proper Edward?"

Absalom turned on him with such fury that he almost sent the truck into a tailspin.

"I told you! What did I tell you!" he roared, spittle flying, his face flushed, eyes bulging with terror.

"I'm sorry."

"Not a word about that, I said. You say *nothing*. It never happened."

But it had happened; Christopher had been there. It was over a year ago now. Absalom had been preparing his scarecrows for the season and had cobbled one together from old parts he'd scavenged over the course of the winter. It was at least six feet tall, and he had it slouched in a chair in the workshop, its head lolling back over the headrest. Its mouth was jagged and crooked, and its copper elbows and knees stuck out through the holes in the clothes he'd given it. Absalom had just been making the final touches and was screwing the last nuts and bolts into place when it moved. This wasn't unusual for a scarecrow, but what was unusual was the fact that it said, "Hello."

For a moment, Absalom had been stunned. Scarecrows didn't engage in conversation; they weren't made to. The best they could manage was gibberish and absolute nonsense. The others had watched and presumed it was just a temporary defect, but then the scarecrow raised its head, looked around, and asked a question:

"Where is this?"

Absalom's legs had looked like they were about to buckle. His right hand went to his mouth, and he uttered a muffled, "Oh merciful . . ."

Christopher had been the first to reply. "This is the workshop," he'd said.

The scarecrow had looked at him guilelessly, like a child. "The workshop," it said to itself. It looked at the floor, then it looked at Absalom and smiled. That was when Absalom finally cracked.

"Jack! Get the manual!"

Jack did as he was told and dragged the large leather-bound

manual out from Absalom's desk. It was the standard text that all engineers used: *Runcible's Manual of Glyphs, Signs, and Symbols for the Animation of the Inanimate.*

Absalom had pored over it feverishly while the scarecrow looked around and continued smiling. He looked at the ceiling. He looked at the floor. He looked at each of them in turn and smiled and said, "Hello." They were all immediately taken with him.

"What happened, Mr. Absalom?" Christopher asked, as Manda and Rob shook the scarecrow's hand.

"This is a very subtle and precise craft, my lad," Absalom had replied, his voice tight with panic as he flicked through the manual's pages. "One does not reduce the act of making art into short condensed sentences. It's much more complex than that, and it would require too long to explain."

"You don't know, do you?"

Absalom threw his head back and gave a howl of frustration.

"I think he knows what he is," said Christopher, looking at the scarecrow.

"I can see that, lad," Absalom had shot back, nodding furiously.

"And he's adult-sized," said Christopher.

Absalom had flapped his hands around violently to show that he couldn't care less.

"That means he's not legal, Mr. Absalom," said Jack.

Absalom roared at him. "Thank you, Jack! Thank you for that most pertinent and timely intervention regarding the legal status of our new friend here. Where indeed would I be without the benefit of your voluminous legal knowledge."

"I was just saying," Jack muttered.

Eventually, Absalom had left the workshop, issuing strict instructions not to let the scarecrow out under any circumstances.

"And one more thing," Absalom had said, turning in the doorway. "Do not, I repeat, *do not* give it a name."

They'd all nodded solemnly in response. Jack even crossed his heart.

They'd called him Proper Edward.

It was Rob who suggested the name, "because it sounds grown-up, and he looks kind of proper, like a real adult."

The name had stuck, despite the fact that "Proper Edward" was not really proper, like a human.

They decided to see if Proper Edward could walk, and Jack and Christopher had taken him by his hands and helped him off his chair. Proper Edward had tottered and wobbled, like a newborn foal just learning how to stand.

"The workshop," he'd said as he wandered about. He looked around in awe at the most mundane things. They'd told him their names and he repeated them back and grinned.

"Christopher. Rob. Manda. Jack."

He looked down at Rob. "I like you, Rob."

"And we like you, Edward," said Rob.

Manda had clapped her hands with delight at this, and even Jack looked pleased.

For the next three days Absalom had barely come near the workshop. Christopher had no doubt that he was trying to formulate a plan to get rid of Edward, but he didn't see how the engineer could accomplish this—especially as Gripper refused to harm the scarecrow. In the meantime, they'd accepted Edward into their family.

Unfortunately, it soon became apparent that Absalom wouldn't have to worry about trying to figure out how to get rid of Edward. Whatever he'd unwittingly done only seemed to have a certain life span. After the first day, Edward had started to find it harder to move around. His movements became slower and more sluggish. After another day, his speech started to go. The gaps between his words became longer, and it had been like watching a toy winding down. Christopher and Jack had exchanged worried looks, but Rob and Manda had been oblivious to the changes.

On the third day, Edward sat back in his chair. He wouldn't move, no matter how much Manda and Rob pulled at him, and soon his head had started to loll back to its original position. He looked up at the ceiling and continued smiling until the end. The last words he said were, "This . . . . was . . . . . . ni . . . . . cccccccccccccccceee . . ."

His smile had been the last thing to go.

Rob had taken it the hardest, and cried for days afterward.

Christopher turned to Absalom, who was hunched over the wheel, wriggling uncomfortably.

"Sorry, Mr. Absalom," Christopher said again. "I shouldn't have mentioned it."

CHAPTER 5

They arrived at their destination twenty minutes later. Their job was to clear the road to a small village. The main road had been cleared as far as a forked junction about two miles from the village, but they had to remove the remaining snow. Absalom was already relishing the prospect of marching in and relieving the inhabitants of a substantial fee for the privilege of regaining access to the outside world.

A very steep hill led down to the blocked road, which was the right-hand part of the fork. They careered down the hill with nerve-shredding speed, juddering and bouncing violently. Christopher was gripping the sides of his seat, but Absalom seemed oblivious to any possible danger.

They reached the bottom of the hill and the truck was parked with a great shrieking swerve that made even Gripper bellow in panic. Absalom hopped straight out of the cab and was shouting orders before they had time to recover.

Two men with shovels were waiting for them: a young man in a woolen jacket that looked too big for him and an older man wearing a peaked cap and a waistcoat. Amazingly, he had his shirtsleeves rolled up. "We're all that could be spared," the older man told Absalom. Absalom negotiated a price with him.

It was graying over, lending a predawn gloom to the proceedings. This only made Absalom more agitated. He shouted at the mechanicals to hurry up. They started to get to work by the right fork. Round Rob wasn't much good at shoveling snow and Manda was a lost cause—she'd already ambled across to the other side of the road by the left-hand fork, where she was happily singing to herself while making a snowman. Jack and Christopher made steady progress, but Gripper did most of the work, shoveling great handfuls of snow and throwing them over a nearby hedge.

The morning became afternoon and the gloom thickened as the day wore on. Absalom started pacing, barking orders at the mechanicals and the two bemused men.

Christopher took a moment to lean on his shovel and look around him.

The fields were a glowing white against the lead sky. Several fat-chested crows glowered insolently at him from the branches of a nearby tree. The only sound was a distant moan, as if the universe was dreaming, punctuated by the soft, steady chuffing sound of spades in snow.

"Are you still disappointed that you weren't sold?" he asked Jack.

Jack frowned. "Sort of, sort of not."

Christopher was heartened by his answer. "I hope nobody ever gets sold, because someday I'm going to become an engineer and I'm going to earn enough money to buy all of you. That way we'll all be together."

"Always?" piped up a voice from nearby.

Christopher turned to see Round Rob looking up at him hopefully. He was knee-deep in the snow, and Christopher smiled at him.

"Always," he said.

Round Rob grinned and went back to his ineffectual shoveling.

Jack was still frowning. "You have to study to become an engineer."

"Then I'll study," said Christopher.

Jack looked over at Absalom. "If you study you'll be legitimate. Not like Mr. Absalom."

Christopher looked over at Absalom, who was now leaning back and looking at the sky with his hands on his hips. His operation wasn't strictly legal, but it was well known that the Agency wasn't as bothered about non-licensed engineers as they used to be.

"It takes a long time to study properly."

Christopher shrugged.

"We could be sold before then. We could wear down."

"I won't let that happen," said Christopher defiantly.

Jack regarded him for a moment, and he looked as if he was thinking about how to respond, when a small voice in the distance called to them:

"Look what I made."

Christopher turned to see Manda stuttering toward them. As usual, she propelled herself by throwing her right side forward. It required great effort, and Christopher could hear her joints squeaking from where he stood. He heard another sound as well, but he was only dimly aware of it. He looked over at the stumpy snowman, with its wonky black eyes and smile.

"Very good, Manda. That's the best snowman I've ever seen."

Manda grinned, and as she threw herself forward again, her teddy bear fell from her hand and onto the road.

"Manda, Ted," said Round Rob, pointing, but she didn't hear him—she was still beaming from the compliment, and the sound Christopher had heard in the distance was getting louder. She'd already taken a couple more steps before she realized what had happened to her teddy bear, and that was when Christopher recognized the sound. He turned to his left to look.

A car was cresting the brow of the hill.

Manda was turning back to fetch her teddy bear from the middle of the road.

Christopher's first attempt at a warning was a strangled yelp. He felt his legs lock and his throat constrict. Round Rob's mouth was wide open in shock. Jack hit Christopher's arm. "She's going to . . . she's . . ."

Christopher put his head down and bolted toward Manda. It was almost impossible for his feet to get a proper grip on the slippery road. He cursed the patches of snow and ice. He cursed the driver of the car for not turning on his headlights. He tried to shout again, but the effort of running meant he barely had enough breath to raise his voice. Behind him he could hear shouting, and above it Absalom's hysteria-tinged voice: "No, Christopher, no!"

Manda picked up Ted and turned to see the car. It was halfway down the hill now, hurtling downward at an insane speed, the steep incline giving it more and more momentum. She turned from looking at the car, almost in slow motion, the expression on her face transforming from horror to guilt as she saw Christopher bearing down on her.

Christopher gave a roar of rage and frustration in the hope it would give him more strength, but he was struggling to run and keep his balance at the same time. He could hear clanking and squeaking behind him. Was it Jack?

He shouted at Manda to get off the road. She turned to look at the car again, as if she'd lost the use of her legs. Christopher gave another incoherent roar and managed to cover the distance left between them, so that now he was right on top of her. He grabbed her arm and swung her round with such force that she was propelled back in the direction he'd come from. She went flying off the road. Christopher was barely aware that he'd done it with such power that he'd ripped her arm from her socket. He saw Jack stumble toward her as she lay on the ground. He looked at the arm in his hand; he heard the roaring sound, the beeping horn. He just had enough time to turn and see the car rushing toward him, the white, terrified face of the driver over the steering wheel, the car turning, but not enough. Christopher felt an eerie calm. *It's going to hit me.*

A bang.

A screech.

Christopher's world turned over and over, white snow, gray sky, white snow, gray sky.

Crows shrieked and took flight. There was a burning—a pain—a skidding spinning world . . .

Blackness.

I'm dead, thought Christopher in the dark. *I'm . . . de—*

When Christopher woke, he found himself looking up at the ceiling in the workshop. The only light in the darkness came from a small gas lamp in a corner. It was night, but he had no idea what day it was.

This has happened before, he thought.

He blinked and tried to speak, but he could only manage a dry croak that echoed back at him in the emptiness.

There was no one else here.

This has happened before.

"Stop it," he moaned to himself, and he was surprised by the sound of his own voice. He turned his head to the right to get his bearings, but his vision was suddenly riven with lightning flashes of imagery.

Round Rob's crying face, his hands on Christopher's chest.

Don't die, Christopher, he sobbed. *Don't die.*

Jack standing over him, shock and utter confusion on his face, and something else. Fear.

Fear?

Look at his arm, Jack said.

"No," said Christopher.

Look at his—

"No!" he shouted.

Silence all around him. Christopher steeled himself. He could feel it like an itch. He didn't want to do it, but he had to. Just to see.

Just a quick look.

It couldn't hurt to look, could it?

He raised his left arm. He could feel a low burning sensation in it. He was wearing fresh clothes. His shirt cuff was unbuttoned. He rolled it back along with the jumper, slowly, carefully. He looked at his arm.

He blinked to be sure he was seeing what he was seeing. The flesh on his hand was pale as far as the wrist. The flesh above his wrist was slightly darker and not as smooth. He pulled his sleeve up farther. The dark patch stopped just below his elbow. It was a crude oblong shape, but there was no mistaking the fact that it was a different shade from the rest of the skin on his arm. Now he found the strength to sit up, and he sat on the edge of his bed, staring at his arm. A sob came, but it sounded as if it belonged to someone else. He didn't understand, didn't want to understand.

And yet . . .

As if they had a life of their own, the fingers on his right hand went to his forearm. He dug his nails in where the darker skin began above the wrist. He clenched his jaw and squeezed his eyes shut. He jammed his fingers in deep, gave an angry scream, and ripped back the skin on his forearm.

And revealed the gleaming chrome beneath.

No blood, he thought.

Of course there's no blood, silly, said a voice inside his head.

No blood, because I'm not . . .

His legs didn't feel like part of him, and he had to drag them across the floor as he made his way toward the door. Tears came.

Tears? How can I cry? How can I cry if I'm not . . .

He almost fell on the door and leaned against it with his right forearm. He caught another glimpse of his left arm. His stomach roiled, and he felt the urge to be sick.

He pulled at the handle, but the door wouldn't budge. He pulled again with as much strength as he could muster, but it still wouldn't give. The door was locked from the outside.

He started to pound on it with his fists. "Mr. Absalom!" he howled. "Mr. Absalom!"

There was no response. The silence mocked him and despite his fear, Christopher felt a sudden scalding rage that lent him strength. He hurled himself at the door and gave a roar of animalistic fury.

There was only one possible question on his mind.

Only one.

Christopher screamed.

"Who made me, Mr. Absalom?! Who made me?!"

CHAPTER 6

A terrified Absalom stood behind the table in his shed. He looked fearfully at the door, wringing his hands.

Christopher's screams of rage carried through the night and across the junkyard. Everybody in the room could hear them. Estelle was packing up her things. She looked nervous and slightly ashamed. Manda was crying, and Round Rob was giving Absalom a run for his money in the hand-wringing stakes. Only Jack was reacting differently; only Jack's eyes were cold and distant, as if his mind was elsewhere.

"We should do something," said Estelle.

Absalom's head started to bob up and down. "That's right, we should, we should. We should stay in here and not go outside, that's what we should do."

Estelle frowned at Absalom, who immediately went on the defensive.

"It's the best thing for all concerned."

"Why?" said Jack. He blinked as if waking from a dream. "Why is it the best thing for all concerned?"

Absalom looked at him as if he were a stone that had some-how learned to speak.

"Because it just is, Jack."

Jack looked at him incredulously.

Absalom started to fumble through his coat. "I suppose you want to be paid, Estelle."

They were all stunned. Absalom never offered to pay without being asked. Estelle just looked at him.

"What?" she said.

"For his arm," said a distracted Absalom. "I'm sure you did a fine job."

"No!" Estelle shouted.

Both Absalom and the others were gobsmacked by Estelle's furious reaction. Absalom tried to say something.

"No," Estelle said again; this time she was trembling with barely suppressed rage.

Absalom's mouth fell open, and his eyes darted up and down in panic as he looked at Estelle. "You won't tell anyone, Estelle, will you?" he begged, his hands working against each other, over and over.

"Why? What if I did? And who might I tell?" said Estelle.

Absalom licked his upper lip and swallowed. "No one, why there's no one at all, no one at all who might be interested . . ."

Estelle's eyes darkened with malevolence.

"No one who might be interested in an unregistered mechanical?"

"Stop it, Estelle! Stop it right now!" Absalom shrieked.

Jack saw the fearful glances from the others. Absalom was biting his thumbnail now, his eyes darting between them. No one made a sound. They could still hear Christopher's cries drifting across the yard.

Round Rob looked toward the window. He whispered, "He's not proper. I thought he was proper."

"So did Christopher himself, apparently," said Estelle, glaring accusingly at Absalom.

"We should let him out," Jack said.

"No!" Absalom shouted.

"Jack is right," said Estelle. "We should let him out."

Round Rob nodded, and even Manda made a little pleading sound.

Absalom looked at them all as if they were mad. "We can't let him out."

"Why not?" asked Jack.

"Because . . . because . . ." spluttered Absalom. His clawed hands clenched and unclenched in front of him, as if the answer was there waiting to be gouged out of midair.

"Because *he'll* go to prison," said Estelle, pointing at the engineer.

Absalom gave a whimper and looked at her. Estelle's eyes were dark and angry. Jack saw Absalom give a little stumble forward, using the table to stop himself falling. The sight of an unnerved Absalom gave Jack a vicious little thrill of pleasure.

"That's not going to happen, Estelle," Absalom said, jutting his jaw out defiantly. "I've done nothing wrong."

"You should let him out, then," said Estelle.

Absalom shook his head violently and turned his back on her like a sulking child.

"Where did you get him?" asked Estelle.

"From the orphanage."

"What orphanage?"

"Bartleby's."

"You told me it was Saint Gabriel's."

"No, no, I distinctly said Bartleby's."

"Who brought him here?"

Absalom narrowed one eye. "A nurse . . ."

"Who? What was her name?"

"Her name . . . her name was . . . was . . ."

"You told me it was two nurses, Mr. Absalom," said Rob, all wide-eyed and innocent.

"Robert!" snarled Absalom.

Estelle snorted. "You're a liar. You were lying all along."

"I never lie," said Absalom, raising his index finger to the ceiling and waggling it. "I am, at all times, an ethical, good, moral man. Absalom Mechanicals is the finest—"

"How can he not know what he is?" demanded Estelle.

Jack smarted a little at the "what." *It's "who,"* he wanted to say.

"How can he not know?" Estelle repeated.

Absalom wouldn't look at her. Estelle narrowed her eyes.

"Have you been patching?"

Absalom pulled his collar up in a feeble attempt to hide his face.

"You have, haven't you? You've been patching. You, who haven't even got the skill to stick arms and legs together."

"Now how dare you, Estelle. How dare you," said Absalom, rounding on her. "I am a master craftsman. My reputation—"

"Where'd you get them? Where are they?" Estelle demanded.

"What's patching?" asked Round Rob.

"Nothing, Robert, nothing. Ignore Estelle, lads. The fumes and chemicals of her barely acceptable work have finally gotten to her and driven her insane."

Absalom looked at her with an expression of victory, but Jack could see the glimmer of doubt in his eyes, and the uncertainty in the way he clutched his hands together.

45

"How does he go?" Estelle said; her voice was low and steady.

Absalom flinched as if he'd just been slapped.

Estelle closed her eyes. She rubbed her forehead. "Oh, Mr. Absalom," she sighed, like a disappointed parent who'd just caught her child doing something he shouldn't have been doing.

Absalom stammered. "I didn't . . . I wasn't . . . I never—"

An explosive wrenching sound from outside interrupted him.

Rob ran to the window and looked out. "Gripper's just taken the doors off the workshop. They're coming this way."

Absalom squealed, ran to the door, and threw himself against it.

"We can't let him in," he shouted.

Estelle sighed. "Don't let him out, don't let him in. Which is it?"

"This all ends now. This nonsense. I won't put up with any more of it!" Absalom shrieked.

Estelle's voice was calm and ever so casual. "What are you going to do when Gripper comes bursting through the door?"

Absalom looked at her; his head gave a little shudder. He stepped away from the door, and Jack almost had to stifle a giggle when there was a knock on it and Absalom jumped. Estelle opened the door, and Christopher stood outside, Gripper towering behind him.

"Who made me, Mr. Absalom?" he said as he stepped inside and closed the door behind him.

Absalom retreated backward, shaking his head and looking at the floor.

Christopher kept advancing.

"Who made me?"

Absalom shook his head.

"Who made me?!" Christopher screamed.

There was a pause. Absalom finally raised his head and looked at him. His chin wobbled and he gave an apologetic shrug. His voice was a cracked whisper.

"I don't know," he said.

Jack believed him. He had never seen someone look so utterly lost.

Christopher turned to Estelle.

"Did you know?" he said.

Estelle shook her head.

"Did anyone else . . . ?"

Christopher looked around the room at the others. They shook their heads. Manda stepped forward with her bear clutched to her chest.

"I never knew you weren't proper, Christopher. Honest. But I don't care. I don't care at all, because you're still you."

Christopher seemed to nod gratefully, but Jack could see the dark, haunted look in his eyes. It was as if another Christopher had taken his place. He was a broken boy with a piece missing. Jack wanted to say something, but he wasn't sure what. He lost his chance, because in the next moment yellow lights slithered across the ceiling, and there was the low hum of an approaching engine.

Estelle ran to the window.

"Oh no, oh Lord, no," Absalom moaned, and he backed away even farther into the shadows.

Estelle's face was whiter than usual as she turned to them. The words she spoke sent a chill through Jack.

"It's the Agency," she said.

Jack ran to the window. A bronze-colored van was pulling

into the yard behind Gripper. There were no markings on the van, but there was no mistaking its official look. He'd never seen one before, but he'd heard enough stories about them. Two men got out. Both of them wore the regulation macs and brown hats. One of them, a tall slim man, said something to his hulking companion, and they started walking toward the shed.

"Oh no, no, no," Absalom gibbered.

"Shut up," Estelle hissed. She grabbed Jack and pushed him toward the back of the shed.

Manda and Rob started flapping their hands almost as much as Absalom. Christopher stood with his shoulders slumped, looking at the ground, as if he'd already accepted defeat. Jack wanted to go to him, but Estelle was still pushing him backward toward the shelves.

"What are you doing?" he squealed.

"I know what's going to happen. Trust me," she said fiercely.

Before Jack could say anything else she'd wrapped her right arm around his head and pulled.

Jack only had time for one muffled "No" before he found himself blinking at her at eye level. She was holding his detached head up to her face. Out of the corner of his eye he could see his body slumped on the ground. He hated being like this, and he was about to protest about the indignity of it all when Estelle cut him off.

"Shut up and listen. I'm going to put you on that shelf," she said, jerking her head toward the back of the shed. "You're to be our eyes and ears."

"But—"

"We need to know what's going on. And Mr. Absalom's not going to tell us."

She plonked Jack, or rather Jack's head, on the shelf. From

48

his vantage point he could see the others looking panicked and terrified.

There was a knock on the door, and everyone whipped around. Estelle gave Jack's head one final look. "Remember *everything*," she whispered fiercely. She bent down to stuff his body under a pile of scrap. When she was finished, she stood up and walked back toward the center of the room.

There was another knock, and a muffled voice called through the door:

"Mr. Absalom? Mr. Gregory Absalom? Could you open the door, please?"

There was a pause. All eyes were now on Absalom.

"Why?" he said weakly.

There was another pause, and this time when the voice spoke, its tone was casual, but with an unmistakable undercurrent of dark intent.

"Mr. Absalom, I really do advise that you open this door as quickly as possible."

Absalom went to the door and fumbled with the handle. He opened it to find the two men standing there. There was a brief moment while they took in what was before them, then they moved quickly into the shed. The slim one was wearing a trilby. He appeared to be in charge, and he brandished a black wallet with an identity card. He was brisk and businesslike in his tone.

"Mortimer Reeves, senior officer from the Agency, responsible for the investigation and regulation of all authorized and unauthorized sentients."

He pocketed his ID before Absalom could say anything and issued orders to his companion.

"Take the mechanicals outside for questioning. The girl too."

Reeves turned to Christopher, who still looked lost and broken. The agent gave a sudden smile, and Jack couldn't help but notice how small and perfectly even his teeth were, and how cruel his smile was.

"And him, of course. Take him."

CHAPTER 7

Reeves stood with his hands in his pockets and regarded Absalom with a slightly amused expression. He motioned for him to take a seat at the table. Absalom sat and tried to avoid his gaze, but he couldn't sit still. He shifted in his chair, his eyes darting back and forth as he looked at Reeves and away again. If Jack's head had been attached to his body, his limbs would have been tensing.

Reeves slowly and deliberately stepped away from Absalom, until he was standing under the mildewed portrait, his lips pursed.

"Runcible, the first engineer," he said, nodding at the picture. "Do you know what made Runcible truly great? Shall I tell you?"

Absalom stole a quick glance at Reeves, but Reeves didn't even turn around.

"Runcible systematized a series of magical glyphs that could confer sentient life on certain mechanical objects," Reeves continued, without waiting for an answer. "This method was referred to as . . . ?"

He turned his head sideways and looked in Absalom's direction. Absalom fiddled with his fingers in his lap. "Basic Propulsion," he said quietly.

Reeves's mouth twitched into a contemptuous smirk. "Very good, Mr. Absalom. Very good." He turned back to the painting and sighed. "Alas, Mr. Runcible's first efforts were met with a certain amount of mistrust and fear. The First, as they called his original creation, was taken from him and burned. Runcible, however, was not deterred. He created more so-called *mechanicals* and people began to realize their importance. They were used as labor and servants. Joshua Runcible changed Britain forever."

Reeves straightened the portrait before taking a handkerchief out of his pocket and gently dabbing at the paint, so Runcible's face could be seen more clearly.

"Unfortunately, some were still afraid. Adult models were particularly reviled, for fear they might supplant us. But a compromise was reached where the smaller, yet still quite industrious and durable, child models could be used in civilized society without offending public sensibilities."

Reeves pocketed his handkerchief and turned and grinned. Jack didn't like that grin. There was malice in it.

"But of course, you know all of this, Mr. Absalom, being, as you are, a member of an illustrious tradition."

Absalom swallowed.

Jack watched Reeves with a kind of queasy fascination. The man moved with unsettling precision.

Reeves removed his hat and placed it on the table. He then took off his jacket, folded it neatly, and placed it over the back of a chair. His hair was black and shiny and obviously Brylcreemed to his head. Nevertheless, Reeves patted it into place, first with the heel of his right hand, making sure not to touch it with his fingers, and then with the heel of his left hand. Satisfied that his hair was in order, he took a small note-book and short pencil out of the inside pocket of his smart, charcoal-gray suit, pulled the chair from the table, and sat on it with great delicacy.

"So, Mr. Gregory Absalom of Absalom Mechanicals." Reeves smiled. Absalom didn't appear to know how to respond. "Do you know what we do at the Agency?"

Absalom nodded.

Reeves continued as if he hadn't responded. "We are respon-sible for the regulation of the creation and use of mechanicals. We see that they conform to the industry standards, we see that each model is given its appropriate serial number, and we see that the engineers who create them are registered and logged as official engineers."

Absalom looked at the table.

"Were you trained and registered as an engineer, Mr. Absalom?"

Despite the tension in the room, or maybe because of it, Jack almost laughed. Absalom said nothing. Reeves leaned forward, his voice quietly sympathetic.

"Better to be up-front now. I can quite easily check our records back at the office, but, if you cooperate, then it might well stand you in good stead further down the line."

Absalom shook his head.

"What's that, Mr. Absalom? I didn't quite catch that. You'll have to speak up."

"No," whispered Absalom.

Reeves took up his pen and scribbled in his notebook, frowning and pursing his lips. He put his pencil down and fixed his hair in the same careful manner as before.

"Would you care to explain the rather large model outside?"

Absalom looked confused. "Gripper? He does . . . he's for heavy-duty lifting."

"I see."

Absalom became suddenly animated. "He conforms to industry guidelines, Mr. Reeves, I assure you. For starters, he really doesn't have the mental capacities to pass himself off as properly independent. Why, he's more like a child. And as for his size, I think you'll find in terms of *physical* appearance he is so far beyond the recognizable parameters for physical humanoid verisimilitude that he can in no way be mistaken for an adult human. In that respect, I do believe I have stuck well within the letter of the law."

Absalom had some of his old confidence back. He rapped his forefinger on the table to drive his point home, leaned back in his chair, and gave, if not a fully confident one, at least a tentative smile.

"Ah, the Filby precedent. I see you've read up on certain aspects of law, Mr. Absalom. What year was that again? Nineteen twenty . . ."

"Twenty-four," said Absalom, licking his lips and clearing his throat. He crossed his legs and laced his hands together on a bony knee and tried to look Reeves straight in the eye. "Nineteen twenty-four." There was a gleam in Absalom's eyes, as if he suddenly believed he might actually be able to talk his way out of his predicament. "So, you see, Mr. Ree—"

"Tell me about the boy," interrupted Reeves.

Absalom swallowed. "The boy?"

"Yes, the boy. Forgive me, I use the term *boy*, but we both know that he is in fact mechanical in origin. Hence my appearance here today in my official capacity."

Absalom took a moment, then leaned forward and gave one of his oily smiles. "I think you'll find, Mr. Reeves, that the boy you are no doubt referring to falls well within industry guidelines."

Reeves looked at him. Absalom tried to sustain his smile,

but something in Reeves's gaze started to erode his confidence. His smile became rubbery and loose. Jack allowed his eyes to flit quickly between Absalom's face and Reeves's. Reeves wasn't smiling.

"Are you saying you made him?" asked Reeves.

"Yes, yes I am," said Absalom, and he tried to force his smile back on his face.

"You're saying you made the boy . . ." He gestured with his pencil for Absalom to fill in the gaps.

"Christopher," said Absalom.

"You're saying you made Christopher. That you constructed him."

"Yes, I am," said Absalom, but this time there was a crack in his voice. He cleared his throat and shifted in his chair.

Reeves took a moment to look around him at the shelves and various bits of bric-a-brac on the shed floor. Jack could see the creeping disdain in his eyes, but the tone of his voice was still light and conversational.

"You created him and the others from these raw materials?"

"Y-yes," said Absalom.

Reeves's eyes fell on Jack's head. For one terrifying moment, the urge to blink returned. It was almost overpowering. Jack tried to keep staring straight ahead. After what seemed like an eternity, Reeves finally turned back to face Absalom.

"How is he animated?"

Absalom looked confused.

"How is the boy powered, Mr. Absalom?"

Absalom gave a nervous laugh. "Why, by Basic Propulsion, of course. I use Runcible's standard glyphs for the conferral of sentience and animation."

"Of course," said Reeves, tapping his pencil against his chin and regarding Absalom. "You're quite sure he's not powered by another method?"

Absalom barked with laughter at Reeves's suggestion. "Nonsense. What other method could there possibly be?"

"Tell me, Mr. Absalom, are you familiar with the methods, principles, and practices underlying the refined system?"

Absalom's head bobbled for a moment, as if he'd just been slapped. "What?" he said.

Reeves's smile became that little bit colder. His voice was soft. "Are you, Mr. Gregory Absalom of Absalom Mechanicals, familiar with the theory, systems, and practical application of the principles of Refined Propulsion?"

The color drained from Absalom's face. "I . . . I . . . please . . ." His voice was hoarse with fear. "Why are you asking me that?"

Reeves interlaced his fingers and lowered his eyes. He looked up again at Absalom, and his voice was still low and soft, but there was something dark in his eyes.

"Let me put it to you another way, Mr. Absalom. Is this boy animated by the principles and practical methods of Refined Propulsion?"

Jack felt a sudden hot jolt when he realized the significance of this statement. It could only mean one thing. His mind started to spin as he thought about the possibility.

Absalom shook his head. His eyes were wide and terrified.

Reeves sighed gently. "Tell me, Mr. Absalom, how is the refined system animated?"

"Buh . . . buh . . . by . . ." Absalom stammered.

Reeves nodded for him to go on. Jack's eyes were widening in disbelief.

"Buh . . . by the melding of a soul with the mechanical system."

A stunned Jack was barely able to take in what was being said.

"You don't think . . . do you think . . . ?" Absalom stuttered.

Reeves ignored him. He took a brisk breath in through his nose and turned back to his notebook.

"Where did you find him, Mr. Absalom?"

Absalom snorted and grinned, perhaps glad of the change of subject. His grin disappeared when Reeves looked at him again.

"Where did you find him?"

"I didn't find . . . I didn't. I made . . ." When he suddenly realized what he might be admitting to, he panicked. "I mean I made him, but not in the refined sense . . . I wouldn't . . ."

"Where did you find the boy?"

Reeves stared across the table at Absalom. Absalom tried to speak, but he could only make a strangulated sound in the back of his throat that Jack recognized as him trying to formulate an excuse. The engineer wriggled and squirmed in his chair as Reeves continued to look at him with his dark, piercing eyes.

There was a knock on the door that almost made Absalom fall from his chair in fright.

"Enter," said Reeves.

The other agent walked in and handed Reeves a scrap of paper. Reeves looked at it and nodded at him. "Very good."

The man left, and Reeves put the paper on the table and turned back to his notebook.

"Tell me about Proper Edward."

It was as if Absalom had been punched. Jack fully expected him to fly backward off his chair.

"Prop . . . prop . . . pop . . ." he stammered.

"Proper Edward," said Reeves, giving a gentle, encouraging smile.

Absalom was wheezing now. "I can explain . . . it was an accident."

"What was an accident, Mr. Absalom?"

Absalom stared at the scrap of paper. "Please . . ." he gasped.

Reeves placed his palms on the table. "Section one of His Majesty's code governing the creation and automation of mechanicals, subsection three, paragraph five, states that it is an offense to knowingly or unknowingly confer sentience upon any raw material, which, when built, conforms to the standard agreed dimensions of an adult human being. The committing of such an offense carries the minimum sentence of fifteen years in prison."

Absalom was gasping even more now, and his shoulders were heaving as he tried to catch his breath.

"An accident . . . I swear . . ."

Reeves leaned forward and spoke quietly. "Knowingly or *un*knowingly, Mr. Absalom. You know why it's not permitted to make adults, don't you?"

Absalom nodded. "It's wrong; it's not proper. People are offended by 'em."

Reeves leaned farther forward. "And I am offended by you, sir!" he roared.

Reeves was suddenly a snarling, raging devil, his eyes black with hate. Even Jack felt the full force of his outburst. "You, sir, are a charlatan and a liar! You make a mockery of His Majesty's laws and of the good name of Britain. Shame on you for your criminality! Shame on you for your lies, your deceit! You disgust me, sir. You disgust me!"

Reeves was shaking with rage now; the breath was heaving in and out of him so hard it made his nostrils flare like those of an angry bull. He started to calm himself steadily and slowly, taking deep breaths in and out. Eventually he was breathing normally. He straightened his shoulders and pulled prissily at the hem of his jacket. Then he patted his hair in his usual manner, the heel of his right hand, followed by the heel of his left. He gave a short, sharp satisfied "Ah" and shot Absalom a dazzling smile as if nothing had happened.

"As a senior Agency operative, I have the power to sentence you."

Absalom's head was lowered now, and his shoulders were shaking. It was clear that he was crying. Jack felt an odd mixture of contempt and pity for him.

"If you're truthful about the origins of how the boy came to be in your possession, then I can assure you I will be merciful with my sentencing."

"Found 'im," sniveled Absalom. "Found him in a ditch two years ago. He wasn't moving. I could see straightaway what he was. He was dormant, but I took him back here and managed to wake him."

"Where was this ditch, Mr. Absalom?"

"'Bout five miles from here, just outside Chippington," said Absalom, wiping his nose with his hand.

Reeves sat back in his chair. "Well now," he said quietly to himself. He leaned forward again. "And did he have any memory of how he came into being?"

"Nothing, just snatches of stuff that made no sense."

"But he's always thought he's a proper boy?"

"Yes."

"How did you convince him of this?"

Absalom looked furtive again. "I patched him."

"You *patched* him?"

"Yes."

"A man of your shoddy skills? You patched him?" Reeves shook his head in amazement.

Absalom lowered his head again.

"Where did you get the patches?"

"Black market." Absalom looked up; he seemed dazed. "I can give you the name of—"

"That won't be necessary."

Reeves seemed to be considering what he'd just been told. Then, with one swift elegant movement, he was up from his chair and in the process of putting his coat back on. He paused for a moment and looked down at Absalom. "My sentencing will be lenient. There will be no punishment for the potential harboring of a refined mechanical unit, but only if you promise never to tell another soul about what happened here today." He leaned down toward Absalom and spoke in an icy whisper. "No one must know, do you understand?"

Absalom looked up. His eyes were cloudy and his head was bobbling again. He somehow managed a nod.

Reeves straightened up and snapped the collar of his coat up around his neck. "Thank you, Mr. Absalom. You've been very helpful. I will reflect that in my sentencing."

He gave a quick bow and placed his hat back on his head. "When you feel sufficiently able, perhaps you could follow me outside."

CHAPTER 8

Once Reeves had left, Absalom sat and stared into space. After a while he gave a low moan and buried his face in his hands.

From where he was, Jack could see movement in the darkness outside the window.

"Mr. Absalom, I need some help," he said.

Absalom spun around so hard that he had to grab the table for support.

"Jack? But you . . ."

"Please, Mr. Absalom, hurry."

Absalom stumbled over to where Jack's head was, and after some fumbling and directions from Jack, he found the rest of him. He placed Jack's head back on his body and grabbed his shoulders.

"You didn't hear anything," he pleaded.

Jack shook his head sorrowfully. "I heard everything, Mr. Absalom."

He started toward the door, but Absalom jumped in front of him.

"I didn't know, I swear. I was trying my best is all."

Jack looked at him accusingly. "You knew he wasn't proper, Mr. Absalom, and you never told anyone."

Absalom tried to say something else, but Jack just pushed past him.

He opened the door and stepped outside. The glare from the van's headlights temporarily blinded him, and he held his arm up to his eyes.

"There's another one, sir," said Reeves's partner, pointing at Jack.

Reeves raised his head from his notebook, gave Jack a dismissive look, and waved the man away.

Manda and Round Rob came over to Jack, both looking frightened. Estelle was a few feet away, and a hunched Christopher was standing near the van. Gripper was by the shed, swinging his arms, watching everything and looking bewildered.

"He asked us questions, Jack," said Manda. "Rob told him everything."

"I did not!" said Rob. Jack could see the guilty look on his face. He smiled at him to let him know everything was all right.

"Don't worry, Rob," he said.

Absalom came out, leaning against the doorjamb, his long fingers trembling. Jack looked over at Christopher, who still hadn't moved.

Reeves cleared his throat and stood to attention, holding his notebook out as he read from it.

"Mr. Gregory Absalom, by the powers vested in me by His Majesty's government, I now sentence you for the crime of operating without an engineering license, and also for the particularly heinous crime of conferring sentience upon a mechanical unit that conformed to the accepted dimensions of an adult human being. I hereby compel you to hand over and/or dispose of all your assets within thirty days from this date or face the full rigors of the law. You are also banned from the construction of any mechanical device for the rest of your life. Failure to comply with this order will see you consigned to one of His Majesty's prisons for a period of not less than fifteen years. You will consent and comply with this order immediately."

Reeves nodded at his companion, who stepped forward and nailed a sheet of paper onto the door of Absalom's shed. Satisfied with this, Reeves put his notebook into an inside pocket of his coat and nodded in Christopher's direction.

"Mr. Dunlop, take him."

For a moment, Jack refused to believe what he was hearing.

Dunlop took Christopher under each armpit and started to drag him toward the van.

"NO!" Jack screamed.

Gripper leaned forward and let out a great bellow of rage.

Jack started to run toward Christopher. He was dimly aware that he had sent Round Rob spinning to the ground, but he didn't care. He had to get to Christopher. He had to stop them.

Dunlop spotted Jack rushing toward him. He unceremoniously pushed Christopher to the ground and started to reach inside his mac. Jack collided with him and the man pushed him back. Jack almost lost his footing, but he regained his balance and charged forward again.

Dunlop took a long metal rod from the holster on his right hip. There was a click, a sudden *FZZZCRAK* sound, a blinding blue shock of light, and Jack felt as if he'd been kicked in the chest. He went flying backward and hit the ground, skidding to a halt at Estelle's feet.

He tried to scream but he couldn't. The words wouldn't come. Estelle's face loomed above him, and Manda threw herself at him and started shrieking, "Jack! Jack! You killed Jack!"

Jack started convulsing, his limbs and head spasming wildly.

He was vaguely aware of Gripper's screams of pain and rage, another *SHRAKK* sound, and the fizzing of blue lightning and sparks.

He managed to raise his head far enough to see Dunlop forcing Gripper backward with the rod. There was another sudden *FRZZAK* and Gripper bellowed and flapped at the air with his claws. He had no choice but to retreat. The man casually reholstered his stick and picked Christopher off the ground.

Jack watched as Christopher was dragged across the yard toward the back of the van. His friend's eyes looked hollow and lost until he blinked, and it was as if a switch had suddenly been flicked. He started screaming. He tried to break free of Dunlop's grip, but the man was too strong. Christopher was kicking and screaming, trying to gain purchase with his heels and failing.

And in the midst of it all stood Reeves, quiet and still, his eyes dark and soulless.

There was one last scream from Christopher and then the doors of the van slammed shut on him.

Jack lay on the ground, his fingers spasming in and out like a crab's pincers. Estelle held his head. She was crying. He couldn't see Absalom. It was just as well. He hated him now, and once again his head juddered forward as he tried to speak. Round Rob was tottering toward them. The two agents were opening the doors of their van.

Reeves looked at them all one last time, then climbed into the passenger seat.

The van drove out of the junkyard and its lights quickly faded into the distance.

The only sound in the yard now was of sobbing.

The next morning, Jack was tightening a nut on his left hip with a wrench when Rob and Manda entered the workshop.

Gripper was standing, watching him. Rob immediately realized what he was doing.

"Why are you putting on a new pair of legs?"

Jack didn't hear him at first. He was too busy struggling with the nut. Gripper said something, and Jack looked up at Rob with an uncharacteristically angry frown.

"What?" he said.

"Why are you putting on new legs?" asked an unfazed Rob.

"No reason," said Jack. "It's just that the other ones . . ."

Rob and Manda both nodded.

"It was because of the stick from last night with the lecktristy in it, wasn't it?" said Manda.

Jack said nothing, but Rob could see his chin trembling.

"Estelle said the lecktristy makes things not work properly, and that your legs—"

Jack flung the wrench on the ground and roared: "It wasn't because of that, Manda! It wasn't that at all!"

Manda lowered her head and clutched her teddy bear to her chest. Nobody said anything for a moment, until Gripper made a gentle scraping sound with his jaws. Rob looked at him and then at Jack.

"Is that true?" Rob asked.

Jack just clenched his jaw and bent down to pick up the wrench.

"It was lecktristy," whispered an awestruck Manda.

Jack turned the wrench over and over in his hands without looking up.

"What was Mr. Absalom screaming about when he knocked over everything in his office? Refried repulsion?" Manda whispered to Rob.

Absalom had spent the night hiding in his shed. Then, just after dawn, they'd heard an awful commotion inside. Rob and Manda had heard him roaring and throwing things about.

This went on for half an hour. After that there had been silence.

"Manda . . ." said Jack, sighing with frustration.

Manda looked at him. "Are you going to shout at me again?"

Jack looked guiltily at her. "No, Manda, I'm not. I shouldn't have shouted at you in the first place. Sorry."

"'Pology accepted," said Manda.

Jack's eyes were dark and pained-looking, but he still managed a weak smile.

Rob looked at Jack's legs. Without even thinking about it, he held his right eyebrow in place with his index finger as he raised it.

"Are those your fancy legs? Are you going to a party?" he said.

Jack shook his head ruefully. "No, I'm not going to a party, Rob."

"Where are you going, then? You look like you're going somewhere."

Gripper stood up. He bellowed something and beat his chest three times with his right fist. *CLANK! CLANK! CLANK!*

"Really? Really really?" said Rob, spinning between Gripper and Jack so hard that he almost hit the floor.

Despite his earlier irritation, Jack managed to give a sly grin. Gripper bellowed again, even louder this time, and he beat his chest harder with his fist.

"Yippee!" yelled Manda.

Rob stared dazedly up at the roof, as if he couldn't quite believe what he was hearing. He grinned at Jack. "So what do we do? How do we . . . ?"

"We talk to him first," said Jack.

CHAPTER 9

"You listen here, Jack, my lad, this . . . you're not going any-where . . . I'll be damned if, if, if . . ."

Absalom had been pacing in front of them in the yard, but now he stopped and squinted suspiciously at Jack.

"Those aren't your legs," he said.

"They're his fancy going-away legs, Mr. Absalom," chirped Rob.

Absalom paced up and down even faster now, wringing his hands as he ranted.

"Well now, this is a fine how-do-you-do and no mistake! This is a proper way to show gratitude, isn't it? After all I've done for you. Well now, you'll be sorry," he roared, pointing his finger at them. "No one is to leave this yard. Absolutely no one. My word is final on this matter!"

Absalom straightened up, snapped his collar up around his neck, and gave them all a contemptuous sneer before turning on his heel and heading toward the shed. The shout that followed after him rang out across the yard:

"Gregory!"

All eyes went to Jack. Absalom froze. There was a stillness in the air, and slowly the engineer turned, a look of disbelief on his face as Jack spoke in a steady, even voice.

"We're going, Mr. Absalom. We're going to find Christopher and you can't stop us."

Absalom tried to say something, but the words wouldn't come. His breath frosted in the air and his shoulders went in and out like the wings of a bird.

Jack nodded at the others. "It's time to go."

Jack turned toward the truck and the others started to follow. He was surprised by the silence, and it was only when he opened the door of the cab that he heard a "Wuh . . . wuh . . . wait" behind him.

Jack climbed up into the driver's seat and was about to shut the door when Absalom grabbed the handle and held it open.

"You can't!" Absalom shouted. His eyes were wild and desperate.

"Yes, we can," said Jack.

Gripper helped Rob and Manda into the passenger seat, while Absalom gabbled at Jack.

"I won't allow it!" he shrieked.

Jack tried to pull the door closed, but Absalom held fast and was about to force himself into the cab until Gripper intervened by gently placing a giant hand on the engineer's chest.

"You can't do this, Jack. You belong to me."

Jack shook his head. "We belong to no one now, Mr. Absalom."

Gripper clambered into the back, and there was the familiar sinking sensation as the truck creaked under his weight. Jack concentrated, stretched, and gave a sigh of relief when his new telescopic legs extended far enough to reach the pedals. Manda clapped with delight. Absalom flashed her an anguished look and then looked pleadingly at Jack.

"Jack, please," he moaned.

Jack turned the key in the ignition, and the engine stuttered and rumbled into life.

"Goodbye, Mr. Absalom," he said.

As the truck moved off, the engineer made one final scramble to grip the door handle, but only succeeded in tumbling to his knees. He watched helplessly as Jack and the others drove out the gate. Jack looked in the side mirror and saw Absalom's forlorn shape, tiny, lost, and sobbing amid the mounds of junk, and he felt a momentary pang of guilt.

Jack could feel Rob looking at him as he drove. He turned briefly to see him biting his upper lip, then looking away hurriedly when he realized Jack had noticed.

"What is it, Rob?" asked Jack.

Rob buried his head in his shoulders and looked at Jack warily.

"Nothing," he mumbled.

Jack sighed. "Come on, Rob. Out with it."

Rob seemed to consider things for a moment, then he blurted: "Aren't you scared?"

Jack smiled. "Course I'm scared. It wouldn't be natural if I wasn't. If I had a heart, it would be hammering right now."

"But we have to do it anyway," said Rob defiantly, looking out through the windshield at the road ahead. "Because he's our friend."

Jack clenched the steering wheel. "Exactly."

There was a silence for a moment, which was eventually broken by a tiny voice:

"I'm not scared."

Jack grinned. "Good for you, Manda."

Manda gave her best "I mean business" look and scrunched her teddy bear tightly to her chest. Jack chuckled.

"So where do we start?" asked Rob.

"Adenbury," said Jack.

Rob gave him a confused look. "Christopher's in Adenbury?"

"No, silly, we have to pick someone up first."

The three miles to Adenbury seemed to fly by. Jack was being honest; he did feel frightened, but he also felt a strange rush of exhilaration the farther they went along the road. He felt in control and in charge, and the small life he'd known in the junkyard was gone. He could feel his life expanding, becoming part of something bigger.

The village was quiet this morning. The first person they met was a milkman driving his horse and cart over the bridge. The only other person who seemed to be up and about was the local postman, who gawped at them and almost fell off his bike in shock when he saw Jack driving the truck. Jack supposed they weren't used to mechanicals around here. Cars were probably a rarity here as well. Although he knew for a fact that it wasn't uncommon for someone like himself to drive around the streets of London.

They pulled up outside Mrs. Barnaby's guesthouse. It was a large solid building with a dozen windows. Manda was particularly taken with it.

"Is this where Estelle lives?" she said.

"Yes," said Jack.

"It's like a palace," she gasped.

Jack smiled as he parked the truck just outside the front gate. The road was quiet as they climbed out. Gripper made moves to follow them, but Jack told him to stay in the truck. They walked up a zigzag path of crazy paving made from creamy stone, Manda drinking everything in.

70

Jack knocked on the door. It was a deep burgundy and had obviously been recently painted. Rob nudged him and nodded toward his legs. It was only then that Jack realized he was a foot taller than he should be. He retracted his legs just before the door was opened by a sharp-faced maid. She frowned at them over a pointy beak of a nose.

"What you want?" she said.

"We've come to see Estelle," said Jack.

The woman looked from one to the other, and then to the truck, where Gripper made a moaning sound as he stretched. Her frown deepened.

"Where's your owner?" she said.

Jack opened his mouth to speak, but Rob cut across him.

"We don't have one anymore," he said cheerily.

Both the woman and Jack were about to say something, but Rob was off and running:

"We've come for Estelle to see if she can help find our friend Christopher. We thought he was proper, but he wasn't, and some men came and took him, and told Mr. Absalom that he had to give up his junkyard because he broke the law. That's Gripper in the truck, he's very strong. I once saw him lift a tractor. This is Manda, she's the smallest, and this is Jack— those aren't his normal legs, they're just his driving legs. I'm Round Rob, I'm *not up to much*, or so Mr. Absalom used to say, but you can roll me down a hill for sixpence and I won't complain."

Rob stopped just as suddenly as he'd started, and he gave the woman a big open smile. The woman gaped at him. Nobody said anything for a while.

"Is this a palace?" asked Manda.

The woman looked at them warily, then she jerked her thumb toward the back of the house.

"Out back," she said, and shut the door.

They all looked at Jack, who gave them a quick nod.

They walked nervously around the side of the house and into the backyard. There was a long, narrow shed filled with straw. A young goat was tethered to a post and a small mechanical boy was piling some vegetables into a cart.

"Where's Estelle?" said Rob.

At that, the boy looked up sharply and pointed toward the shed. They all stepped toward it, and it was Rob who first saw Estelle lying on the straw.

"Estelle!" he shouted.

Estelle sat bolt upright, bits of straw stuck to her hair. "What? What?" she said. She blinked when she saw her friends, and did a quick double take. Her face went paler than pale, then just as quickly it flushed to a crimson red. Her face was so red Jack thought her head might pop.

"What are you doing here?" she demanded, trying her best to assert her authority but failing, because it's hard to do such a thing when you're trying to get yourself up into a standing position from a pile of straw.

She brushed herself down, wrapped her coat around her, and cinched the old leather belt she used to keep it closed. Jack caught a glimpse of the moth-eaten jumper she wore, and he noticed there were holes in her (mismatched) socks.

"Well?" she demanded. She was trying to sound forceful, but her voice came out as a shrill squeak. Her color had calmed slightly, but she was still a very vivid tinge of pink.

Rob frowned. "Why were you sleeping on the straw, Estelle?"

"Is that your bed?" Manda asked.

"Were you playing a game of hide-and-seek?" Rob asked, with a big hopeful grin on his face.

Jack decided to intervene. Estelle's face was changing too

72

quickly for his liking, and she looked like she was about to explode.

"We came for you, Estelle. We want you to come with us and help look for Christopher."

Estelle gave them all a wary look. "Why?"

"Because you know stuff, and you're our friend," said Rob.

Estelle's shoulders relaxed a little, but she still seemed defensive and wary.

"I can't just go," she said.

"Why not?" said Rob.

Estelle looked genuinely flummoxed as she tried to think of an answer. "There's . . . work," she finally blurted.

"Is there enough?" asked Jack. "You're unlicensed, Estelle, and Mr. Absalom was your main customer."

"I do odd jobs around here," said Estelle, and as soon as she said it, Jack could see she regretted it. She shifted from one foot to the other and looked like she'd rather be anywhere than here, with everyone's eyes on her.

Jack looked at the boy filling the cart. He must have been at least fifty—it was obvious from the way the tarnished, bronzed metal of his body peeked out from torn flaps of skin on his face. He emitted a creaking noise when making even the slightest movement.

Jack looked back at Estelle; the expression of shame on her face was too much for him to bear. Jack felt sorry for Estelle, and he felt angry for her. It was clear what was going on here. Estelle couldn't legally look for work as a skin-maker. She was a girl, after all, and girls were prohibited from working in any part of the mechanical industry. She was doing odd jobs for Mrs. Barnaby to keep a roof over her head; the kind of work that only mechanicals would do. Mrs. Barnaby was obviously too mean to buy a new model.

"Come with us," he said.

Estelle looked unsure.

"Please, Estelle," said Rob. "What if my nose falls off on the way? Who'll stick it back on?"

Estelle looked at Jack, and he gave her an encouraging smile. It was decided. Estelle reached for her boots and sat down and started to put them on. "I'll meet you out front," she said. "Just let me get my things."

Estelle arrived at the truck a few minutes later with her satchel full of tools. Gripper took it from her and gently laid it in the back, then she squeezed in beside Rob and Manda in the cab. She still looked slightly flustered, and she pushed her hair back over her shoulders and shook her head in an effort to look imperious. Jack had never seen her so addled.

"So," she said, "what's the plan?"

Everybody looked at Jack.

"We haven't really got one yet," he said.

Estelle suddenly became the old Estelle again. Her voice was steady, her movements small and controlled.

"You don't have a plan?" she said.

"Not *yet*," said Jack defensively.

"Then why'd you come for me?"

"I thought you could help. Maybe give us some ideas."

Estelle turned away from him for a moment and squinted out the window.

"He'll be in London," she said. "They'll have him in the Agency's headquarters."

"Then we should go there!" said Rob.

"It's not that simple," she said.

Jack sighed and nodded in agreement.

Estelle clucked as she thought to herself. "We have to start

at the beginning. Why did they take him? What's so important about Christopher?"

"Where did he come from?" offered Jack.

"What makes one of you important?" Estelle asked.

Rob scratched his head. Jack frowned and then looked at
Estelle.

"How good a model we are."

"And what makes a good model?" asked Estelle.

"A good engineer," said Jack.

"Or a great one," said Estelle.

Jack sat back and thought about this, then he looked at
Estelle: "When I was in Mr. Absalom's shed, that man Reeves
was talking about Refined Propulsion." Jack almost couldn't
finish the rest, and he could feel all their eyes on him. "I think
Christopher has a soul."

Estelle nodded. Rob's eyes widened so much, Jack thought
they would fall out of his head.

"Cormier was the one who discovered Refined Propulsion,"
said Estelle.

"What's refried repulsion?" asked Manda.

"He has a soul, Manda," said Rob breathlessly. "Christopher
has a soul. He's nearly proper."

"He's Cormier class then, isn't he? He has to be," said Jack.
Estelle nodded.

"Have you ever seen a Cormier Original, Estelle?" asked Jack.

Estelle shook her head. "No, but only Cormier himself could
make a model as convincing as Christopher."

"What about a Blake?" said Jack.

"I've never seen a Blake, but I reckon you could spot one.
There's always something off, whether it's a joint, or an eye, or
the way they talk. Besides, Blake could never ensoul anything.
Only Cormier could do that."

75

"Cormier class," Jack whispered to himself, his eyes widening with delight.

"He might be one of the only ones left; that's what makes him so valuable," said Estelle.

"Are we going to London, then, to get Christopher back?" asked Rob.

"We can't just do that, Rob," said Jack. "We can't just ask for him back. Only his owner or engineer can do that, and no one owns him anymore."

Rob slumped back in his seat. Estelle looked thoughtfully at the dashboard.

"Can we just ask anyway?" said Manda. "If we sent Estelle in and she asked nicely . . ."

Jack shook his head sorrowfully.

No one said anything. Jack tried to think of something. He gave Estelle a pleading look as if she might be able to suggest an idea, but Estelle was busy looking out the passenger window.

"Then what do we do?" asked Rob.

"We go to London," said Estelle.

"But that's pointless without an owner or whoever made him. They'll just turn us away," said Jack.

"Not if we have his engineer," said Estelle, squeezing her lower lip thoughtfully between her thumb and forefinger.

Jack looked at her and shook his head in disbelief. "He wouldn't."

Estelle tilted her head and smirked. "He might. We could ask."

"Ask who what?" said Rob.

"Ask Philip Cormier to help us get Christopher back from the Agency," said Jack.

Rob frowned. "But how do we ask him?"

"Yes, how?" asked Jack, knowing full well what the answer would be.

Estelle turned to him and smiled, and because it was Estelle smiling, Jack almost keeled over.

"We're going to Ironhaven," she said, "and we're going straight to Philip Cormier's front door."

CHAPTER 10

"Don't think of it as a prison, think of it as home."

Prison, thought Christopher. This wasn't the headquarters of the Agency. Why had they brought him here?

They were standing on a wide, open plain. Mr. Reeves was looking up and smiling at the edifice that loomed above them in the morning light. It was a gray turreted monstrosity blistered with dozens upon dozens of windows. The windows were little more than slits in the lichen-covered rock. Great black streaks of damp rolled down from each window, and the horrid gaping hole of the black gate made it look as if the whole building was howling in torment. Christopher had also glimpsed a small tumbledown graveyard behind the building as they'd approached it. It was covered in moss and dotted with tombstones of soggy gray stone. Mounds of scrap metal were scattered around it.

"They call it the Crag," said Reeves, smiling to himself.

Christopher wasn't listening to him. He was too busy thinking about Jack and the others. There was an ache in his chest, and he swallowed painfully, willing the tears not to come. In an effort to hide his true feelings, he spoke, but his voice was barely above a hoarse whisper, and he hated himself for it when he heard how pathetic he sounded. Seeing the glint of sadistic pleasure in Reeves's eyes only made it worse.

"Never heard of it," he said.

Reeves bent down and gave him a patronizing look.

"You wouldn't have," he said. "The Crag is a very special type of facility. But like I said, you can call it home now."

Christopher looked at the grass at his feet. The blades were a pale green and mottled with brown spots, as if the foundations of the prison were poisoning the very earth.

Reeves leaned forward. "I said you can call it home."

Christopher's eyes flitted toward Reeves's face and away again.

"Say it, say the word," Reeves hissed.

Christopher closed his eyes. He thought of the junkyard. He thought of Jack and Rob and Gripper and Manda, and he stifled a sob.

"Home," he said.

"Say it again," whispered Reeves.

"Home," he said again, and this time he gave Reeves a look that he hoped was defiant, despite the fact that his lips and chin were trembling.

"Good lad," said Reeves as he ruffled Christopher's hair. Christopher felt a shiver of revulsion. A smirking Reeves didn't seem to notice. He turned to his companion.

"Mr. Dunlop, if you would be so kind."

Dunlop gave a grunt and produced a ring of keys from his mac. He inserted one of them into the large padlock on the front gate. The padlock opened with a great clacking sound. One in front, one behind, they escorted Christopher through the gate and into a large courtyard.

The courtyard was just as grim as the outside of the prison. The center was taken up with great mounds of gray tarpaulin, from under which scraps of metal and old wheels and tires spilled outward. The sense of the walls looming overhead, almost constricting the air around them, was overpowering here. Christopher's world was growing smaller and smaller. He could feel his throat tighten, and he felt a bout of dizziness.

But I don't breathe, he thought. *How can I feel dizzy?*

Dunlop took out his keys again and unlocked a metal door in the courtyard wall. He pulled it open with a wrench, and flakes of rust spilled from the edges. They entered a hallway, and Christopher smelled rot and damp and stone.

The corridor had a cement floor flanked by walls that were a sickly green. Paint was peeling off the walls in great swaths. Colonies of moisture droplets and fungus collected in random patches. They walked about fifty feet down the corridor, unlocking another door on the way, before they came to a set of double doors.

Reeves knocked before pushing them open, and they entered a large laboratory. The lab was cement gray with a strip of blue-and-white mosaic tiling stretching along the length of one wall. This same wall had a sink unit and some stainless-steel shelves bolted into it. There were several stained and rusty-looking surgical trolleys with various bits of copper, wiring, and sheet metal piled onto them. There was a large hydraulic press set in a far corner. What looked like a dentist's chair was situated to the left of the door.

There was a man in the center of the room. He had his back turned to them, and he was working on an intricate collection of silver wires and tubes.

"Well?" said the man, without turning around.

Reeves cleared his throat. "The device has been acquired, as per your instructions, sir."

The man flicked something, and a wire in one of the glass tubes sparked with blue light. "Very good," he said, and Christopher couldn't be sure whether he was referring to Reeves's words or his own work.

The man grabbed a rag from a nearby bench and started to wipe the oil from his hands. He was wearing a floor-length gray leather apron that looked completely at odds with his air of debonair poise. He looked to be in his early thirties. His features were finely chiseled and handsome; his well-coiffed hair was swept back over his head.

"Excellent," he smiled, "most excellent."

He strode toward Christopher with his hand outstretched. Christopher was so stunned by the gesture that he immediately raised his own hand. The man grasped Christopher's hand in both of his and shook it vigorously.

"Can I say how very pleased I am to finally meet you?" he said.

The man's smile was crescent shaped, all encompassing, dazzling. His teeth were perfect. His smile reached right up to the corners of his blue eyes, which shone with delight. Christopher was completely wrong-footed. He tried to open his mouth to say something, but the words wouldn't come.

The man went down on one knee before him, and his eyes roamed over Christopher's face.

"Remarkable, absolutely remarkable," said the man. "Were there any difficulties?" he asked Reeves, without taking his eyes off Christopher's face.

"No, sir. There was minimal resistance," Reeves replied.

"And the engineer?"

Reeves snorted. "If he can be called that. He has been dealt with. He believes he is now being kept under surveillance by the Agency. He won't be revealing what happened to anyone."

The man clapped his hands with delight. "Ha! Yes, the Agency. So the ruse has worked. Very good. Very good." His grin broadened as he inspected Christopher's face.

Christopher was confused. He felt dizzy. Who were these people, if they weren't from the Agency? He couldn't take in what was going on. None of it made any sense.

The man held up his hands in a gesture of placation. "You're confused, Christopher. I can see that. But all will become clear very soon."

"How do you know my name?" blurted Christopher.

The man stood up and smiled down at Christopher, ruffling his hair in a gesture of dismissal. He turned to Reeves.

"How old is he?"

"Twelve, allegedly. Older, of course," said Reeves.

"Of course," said the man, contemplatively stroking his chin. "And his memories?"

"There's been erosion, possibly through trauma. I suspect this has been followed by tampering."

"He's been patched, then?"

"So I've been told."

The man nodded. The discussion between the two men became a murmur in the background as Christopher's eyes darted around his surroundings. He felt a sudden scorching sense of indignation.

"Why am I here? Who are you?" he demanded.

Reeves blinked, and the man seemed surprised. This only made Christopher angrier.

"I'm sorry," said the man, "I should have introduced myself. I'm Richard Blake. Son of the late Charles Blake, and like my father before me, I am, and I say this with all modesty, possibly one of the greatest engineers of the age."

That broad smile again, as if Blake expected some kind of congratulations for his announcement.

"I want to go home!" Christopher shouted.

Blake's smile faltered. He looked disappointed. "But my dear Christopher, you *are* home."

Christopher stumbled backward, moaning, "I want to go home." Dunlop made to grab him, but Blake waved him away. Blake got down on his knees before Christopher and held him by the shoulders.

"Listen to me, Christopher. You're here now, and this is your new home. You're going to help us do something that will echo down through the ages. Do you understand me?"

Christopher looked at Blake, but he felt dazed, as if he'd been punched. It was all too much.

"What are you talking about?" he asked.

Blake squeezed his shoulders. "We're going to change the world, Christopher. You and I. We're going to change it for the better."

Christopher's rage was starting to fizzle out. He felt exhausted now, and the tears started to come. Blake's mouth opened in awe as Christopher started to cry, and once again his eyes roamed over his face, as if he were seeing a miracle.

"Remarkable," Blake gasped. "The mimetic capability to create tears. Fluidity and mobility of emotional transitions. These things have been beyond the talents of almost anyone for centuries." Blake stood up and shook his head in amazement. "Absolutely remarkable."

After a quiet discussion between Reeves and Blake, Christopher was escorted out the double doors by Mr. Dunlop. Reeves followed behind them as they made their way down the hallway.

Christopher didn't have to look—he knew Reeves was enjoying his discomfort. He could almost feel the horrid sliminess of his smile in the air.

They took a sharp right turn down a narrower corridor. There were a dozen metal doors on each side. Each one had a narrow, barred window at eye level.

Mr. Dunlop opened one of the doors and stepped aside for Christopher.

Christopher hesitated. He wanted to run, but he knew there would be no point. Dunlop's right hand went to his mac and he pushed it aside, resting a hand on the black stick holstered on his hip.

"That won't be necessary, Mr. Dunlop," said Reeves. He winked at Christopher, and Christopher suddenly felt the mad urge to rush him and claw his eyes out. But the feeling was gone in seconds and replaced by nauseous despair, along with the sense that he was being pushed forward by a force greater than himself. He stepped into the cell.

"There's a good boy," Reeves said.

Christopher felt the soft rush of air behind him, and then the sound of the door clanging shut. He turned to see Reeves's slyly malevolent eyes looking in at him through the small window.

"Home," he said, and then he was gone.

Christopher didn't know what to do. He felt numb. All he could do was stare mutely at that narrow rectangle, while around him there was nothing but suffocating silence.

He felt his legs give way and he collapsed onto the side of a steel bunk. Christopher thought about Jack. He thought about Round Rob and Gripper and Manda and Estelle, and this time the tears came with even greater force.

CHAPTER 11

The rain came down on Ironhaven.

Jack had never seen anything like it. As they drove, it loomed ahead of them, a great big hump of tangled towers and houses and pylons and trees and hills, all sleek and black and shiny in the approaching gloom of evening, and all of it made of metal. It was like the junk dumped in Absalom's junkyard, but junk that had found a pattern and purpose.

"Who made it all?" asked Manda.

"Mechanicals," said a grim-faced Estelle. Her look had darkened ever since she'd seen the first sign about a mile back. FLESH TURN BACK, it had said. This one had been followed by others, all badly painted and scrawled, but with similar messages: NO FLESH HERE; FLESH NOT WELCOME.

"Ironhaven was made by discards and deserters," continued Estelle. "Back in the old days there weren't any laws governing what people did with their mechanicals. They used to dump the old ones by the side of the road. Discards would just wander around until somebody either picked them up and used them or had them smelted down."

Rob shivered.

Estelle went on. "Mechanicals did what they liked here, and no one knew what to do with them. They started building homes and the town started to grow. Before the government could decide what to do, Cormier had moved in and proclaimed that Ironhaven was independent." They passed another sign: TURN BACK NOW FLESH! it said. Estelle glared at it. "Cormier banned all proper people from entering the town."

"Why didn't the government just stop him?" asked Jack.

Estelle shrugged. "Because he was Philip Cormier, the greatest engineer of them all. They didn't want to upset him."

"Why's that?" asked Rob.

Estelle looked at Rob. "Sometimes, Rob, when you have a temperamental child on your hands, the easiest thing to do is to give the child what they want."

Rob frowned at this and scratched his chin. After a moment's contemplation he nodded.

As they drove closer to the town, the rain became heavier until it became an impenetrable gray wall, and the sound of it thrumming off the cab roof was so loud they had to shout to be heard above it.

Jack marveled even more at the town as they got closer. There were trees here, but they were made of metal. They had iron trunks and tinplate bark and copperplate leaves. The houses, all sharp and angular, were almost piled one on top of the other, and yet looking at their construction and their placement it all seemed to make sense to his eyes. It was as if the town, despite its artificial nature, had grown from the soil.

He was distracted by Estelle bending her head low and moaning. He turned to her to see her rubbing her temples.

"What's wrong, Estelle?"

"Nothing, just keep driving," she snapped.

They drove on for a bit but didn't see anybody until they arrived in a narrow street.

"Stop here!" Estelle shouted. "I see someone."

There was a figure walking across the road, long and spidery-limbed. He turned to face the truck and Jack stopped a few feet in front of him. He looked at Estelle. She was rubbing her forehead now.

"Everybody out," she said.

They all clambered out of the truck, and the watcher in the road loped toward them. Even with the sound of the rain they could hear the clank of his limbs. Jack stepped toward him.

"Excuse me, do you know where we can find Philip Cormier?" he asked.

Jack could see the figure's long, mournful face and his large, round eyes. With a sinking sensation, he realized the mechanical he was addressing had no mouth.

"It's a Mute," said Estelle.

The Mute looked at them. His long legs were bowed and his back was hunched. His right hand was missing, and the rain plinked off his brass dome of a head. Nobody said anything, and the Mute continued to look at them with his doleful eyes.

"What's a Mute, Estelle?" whispered Rob, without taking his eyes off their observer.

"Mutes can't speak. They're used in factories, or by people who prefer to have servants they don't have to listen to. I'm beginning to understand why."

Jack shot her a look. He didn't appreciate the sarcasm, especially if it was directed at Rob, but Estelle wasn't paying any attention. She was too busy rubbing her temples again.

Jack stepped toward the Mute.

"Cormier. Do you know where he is?"

The Mute looked Jack up and down. His neck squeaked on its hinges. He slowly raised his right arm and pointed at a shack across the road. There was a soft orange glow coming from its interior.

"He's in there?" said Jack.

The Mute lowered its arm. It looked Jack up and down again, and slowly shook its head.

"But—"

The Mute raised its arm again and pointed toward the shack.

"I think he wants us to go in there, Estelle," said Jack.

"Fine," Estelle growled, and she stomped toward the shack, splashing up water as she went. As they approached, they could see a tiny figure outside the shack. It was an old doll, no more than a foot tall. She was walking back and forth, a ragged wet bonnet stuck to her head, and she wore an old soiled pinafore. She was saying "Mama" over and over again. She stopped for a moment and turned her head and looked at them. When she'd seen enough, she went straight back to marching back and forth and saying "Mama."

Estelle stepped toward the doorway of the shack. It wasn't much of a doorway, just a sheet of metal slanted at a precarious angle. Manda was gaping at a tree. She reached out and held a leaf between her thumb and forefinger. It was delicate and finely filigreed. "Oooh," she gasped, "it's beautiful."

"Come away from there, Manda," said a scowling Estelle.

Estelle banged on the door. Jack winced at the sound and her ferocity. He reckoned it was a bit more forceful than was required, but he was surprised when he heard a rather calm voice from within say, "Yes?"

"We're looking for Cormier," said Estelle.

There was no reply.

"Can we come in?" she asked, looking exasperated.

A boy poked his head out the door so suddenly that they all

flinched. Rob recoiled with such force that he had to spin his arms to keep his balance, and it was only the gentle hand of an attentive Gripper that stopped him from falling into a puddle.

"Did you know that the distance between John O'Groats and Land's End is six hundred and three miles?" said the boy.

They all just looked at him. He only had skin on the right side of his face, and what was left of it was peeling away. His head was scuffed and scraped, but his eyes were bright.

"Yes," he said with a smile.

"What?" said Jack.

"You can come in."

The boy stood aside, and Gripper held the sheet of metal to one side so the others could squeeze in. Estelle told him to wait outside. She took a deep breath and stepped into the shack.

CHAPTER 12

As they entered, the boy turned around and said, "Loch Ness contains more fresh water than all the lakes of England and Wales combined."

"That's really interesting," said Rob. "Isn't that really interesting?" he said, turning to his friends.

"Marvelous," said Estelle. She was wincing and rubbing her right temple with the heel of her hand.

"He's not here," said another voice.

They all peered into the depths of the shack. A lamp on a low table threw a soft glow around the interior. The voice belonged to a mechanical boy who was standing to the right of the table. He looked to be in reasonable condition, but he had several legs rather than two. He had two heads on either side of a chain draped around his neck. They were both similar in shape and look to the head of the Mute they'd met outside.

"This is Billy," said the boy with many legs, pointing to the boy with half a face. "He knows lots. He used to dispense facts at a carnival."

Billy gave a small bow. "Did you know that Big Ben started working on the thirty-first of May 1859?"

Rob shook his head in amazement.

"And I'm Sam Six Legs," said the other boy.

Rob's lips moved soundlessly, and his index finger jabbed the air as he counted the boy's legs. "You've only got five."

Sam smiled. "I used to have six. I'm hoping to get a replacement." He pointed at the head on his right shoulder. "And this is Tim." He pointed to the other head. "And this is Tom." He frowned, and his voice was slightly downcast. "Or is it the other way around? I can never remember."

Both of the heads rolled their eyes.

"Anyway," said Sam, brightening up and clapping his hands together, "what can we do for you?"

"We're looking for Philip Cormier," said Estelle. "Can you tell us where we can find him?"

There was the sound of an approaching "Mama, Mama" and the doll walked into the hut and continued to pace around.

"And this is Daisy," said Sam, with a big smile.

"Philip Cormier is known as the father of engineering, and is considered by many to be the greatest engineer of any age," said Billy.

Estelle winced. "Where is he?"

"In the iron house," said Sam.

"Mama, Mama."

"What's six times six?" Rob asked Billy.

"Thirty-six," said Billy.

"He's very good, isn't he?" Rob grinned at Jack.

"I knew that one," said Jack.

"Mama, Mama."

Estelle closed her eyes, as if she was having problems concentrating. "And where is this *iron house*?"

Sam and Billy pointed in two different directions simultaneously. Daisy was now walking in circles around Estelle, who looked like she was about to explode.

"Mama."

"Where . . ." Estelle began, but she stopped and grimaced as if in pain.

". . . Mama."

"Where is this—"

"There are five oceans," said Billy.

"Mama, Mama."

"Which is it?" said Estelle.

"Which is what?" asked Sam.

"The way to Cormier's house?" Estelle shouted.

Two arms immediately went up again. This time in two new directions.

"Mama, Mama," Daisy bleated, now looking up at Estelle.

"Why do you want to find Cormier?" asked Sam.

"Mount Everest is the tallest mountain in the world," said Billy.

"Mama, Mam—"

An enraged Estelle suddenly picked Daisy up and flung her out the door. She balled her fists together, crouched down, and roared:

"The trees are screaming!"

There was a stunned silence. The only sound was the rain falling on the tin roof. All eyes were on Estelle. Billy could be heard softly whispering, "The capital of China is Peking."

Estelle groaned and fell to her knees with her hands over her ears. Rob put a hand on her shoulder:

"What's wrong, Estelle?"

"It's the trees," said Sam. "Mr. Cormier made them. They make a sound that only proper people can hear. That's why you'll only get mechanicals in Ironhaven."

Sam started to rummage among some jumble in a wooden box. He took out a pair of earmuffs and handed them to Estelle. When Estelle looked up, Jack could see the agony in her eyes. Her skin had a gray pallor, and she looked nauseous. Estelle took the earmuffs and put them on, and immediately looked grateful. Her tightened brow finally slackened, and her face looked a lot less strained.

"We need to find Cormier," Estelle shouted. Jack signaled to her that she was shouting a little, so she lowered her voice. "We need to find his home."

Rob went outside.

"I can show you," said Sam. "But I have to warn you, he hasn't left his home in years."

"Why's that?" asked Jack.

Rob walked back in with Daisy in one hand and his other hand laid gently over her mouth as she continued her muffled "Mama, Mama."

Sam shrugged. "Nobody knows."

"Even I don't know. The square root of one hundred is ten," said Billy.

"We've been here a long time," said Sam. "We haven't seen him."

"There were plenty here before us too," said Billy.

"Not so much now," said Sam. "Some have gone. Some thought it wasn't worth it anymore."

"Some thought what wasn't worth it anymore?" asked Jack.

"Waiting," said Sam.

"Waiting for what?" asked Estelle.

"Waiting to be fixed," said Sam, and he shared a look with his friends that implied he couldn't believe he'd actually been asked that question. Even Tim and Tom rolled their eyes.

"That's why we're all here," said Billy.

"We came here to be fixed," said Sam. "Mechanicals used

to come from miles around. Cormier used to fix anyone who needed fixing. He wasn't just the most renowned engineer of all time—he actually cared about mechanicals."

"He hasn't been seen in years, but we wait anyway. Whales are the largest mammals known to man," said Billy.

"Take us to him," Estelle shouted.

"Do you know the way?" Jack asked Sam.

Sam nodded. "If I'm outside I can walk there. Just don't ask me to point out where it is." He tapped the side of his head and grinned. "I was hoping to get this fixed too, you see."

Sam led them outside. He told them it would be best to walk. The rain had eased off a little, and he led them down some cramped side streets. Rob marveled at how Sam walked. "You're like a centipede," he said.

As they made their way through the town they picked up stragglers along the way. Some mechanicals came out of their huts and houses and started to follow them like dark shades in the rain. It was as if they knew something was about to happen.

They finally arrived at the end of a street that opened out into a square. At the far end of the square was a large black wall with a gate in the middle of it. Both wall and gate were made from riveted steel.

"He's in there, behind that gate," said Sam, pointing in the opposite direction. "No one ever comes out, and no one ever goes in."

Estelle walked across the square and started to bang on the gate.

Sam looked shocked. There were some mechanicals hiding in shadowy doorways and corners behind them. They retreated slightly when they saw what Estelle was doing.

"I don't think . . ." began Sam.

But Estelle wasn't listening. She continued to hammer on

the gate with her fist, until finally she couldn't do it anymore. She stopped to rub her hand, and turned toward Sam. "Is there another way in?"

Sam shook his head.

Estelle looked at the gate, as if trying to discern whether there were any weaknesses in its surface. When she turned around she had a hungry grin on her face. She looked at Jack, and Jack read her mind. They both turned their eyes simultaneously toward Gripper.

Estelle moved aside, and she motioned toward the gate with her right hand. "Grip, if you wouldn't mind."

Gripper looked from Estelle to Jack. He turned to look back at Rob. In the darkness behind them, shadows shifted uneasily.

Sam looked on anxiously. "Is he going to—"

Gripper put his head down and ran full pelt toward the gate. There was an almighty clang as he hit it. Gripper bounced off, but there was now a large dent where he'd collided with the gate. He looked pleased with his first attempt, and set to work.

He jammed his claws into the edges of the gate and commenced peeling it back like the lid of a sardine tin. Wrenching, screeching sounds filled the air as Gripper ripped the gate apart, until finally there was a great serrated gash right down the center of it.

"Good on you, Grip," Jack shouted.

Gripper's jaw moved and he emitted a loud scraping sound.

"That's right, Grip. I couldn't have put it better myself," said Rob.

Estelle gathered them together, and she looked at Sam and the others huddling in the shadows. "Do you want to come with us?" she asked.

A hopeful but nervous-looking Sam shook his head and took a step back. "I've been here this long. I'd rather wait."

Estelle nodded to show that she understood. "Right, then," she said, and she marched up to the remains of the gate and climbed through it.

A rough path led to a sharp, angular building that looked as if it was made completely from metal. It was less of a house and more of a citadel. There were windows in the building, but there was no light coming from them. A steel staircase climbed to the front door. Estelle promptly stomped her way toward it and up the steps, the others running to keep up with her. Estelle got to the door and started to beat her fists on it as the mechanicals clanged up the steps behind her. Estelle kept banging for a solid two minutes before she stopped. She stood there exhausted, panting and pale.

"Can you still hear the trees, Estelle?" Rob asked.

There was no reply. Rob tugged at her elbow and shouted, "Can you still hear the trees, Estelle?"

Estelle turned to him and nodded. Jack could see her face. It was hard to tell where the perspiration ended and the rain began.

Estelle raised her hand again. Jack grabbed her arm.

"Let Gripper do it," he said.

Estelle stepped aside and Gripper rapped on the door.

BOOM. BOOM.

Nothing happened.

A couple of minutes passed and Jack nodded at Gripper. Gripper knocked again.

BOOM. BOOM.

Jack could see Estelle gritting her teeth—she was breathing hard. He had to remind himself that she felt the cold and the rain, and that the screaming trees must be maddening, despite the fact that her ears were covered.

Another couple of minutes passed.

"Maybe he's gone out," said Rob.

Jack was about to say something to Estelle when the door was opened with such violence that the shock of it almost sent Gripper reeling off the top of the stairs.

"Yes?!" shouted the man standing there.

He was tall and old and straggly. His unruly gray hair stuck out at every angle from his head and was matched in its utter untidiness only by his beard. He was wearing a vest made of crisscrossing leather strips, leather trousers, and large black boots. His arms were wiry and surprisingly muscled for a man of his age. He scanned them all quickly with his piercing blue eyes and shouted: "WHAT?"

"Mr. Cormier?" asked Jack.

"Who's asking?"

"We are," said Rob brightly.

"Who's *we*?" growled the man.

"Us," said an unperturbed Rob.

The man's face contorted into a snarl. "Go away, *US*," he said, and slammed the door shut.

Estelle blinked slowly. Then her face hardened and she started pounding on the door.

"Mr. Cormier! Mr. Cormier!"

The door flew open again.

"What?!"

Estelle snorted fiercely. "You are him, then."

Cormier glared at her, then he looked at them each in turn. "I said go away, but that obviously didn't work. I'm a very mild-mannered and polite man, so I'm going to say it again, but this time imagine I'm using swear words. GO. AWAY."

He slammed the door shut so hard this time that Jack felt a draft rush past him.

Estelle was furious. She bludgeoned the door again and started shouting.

"We need your help, Mr. Cormier. We came a long way, and we're not leaving until we speak to you."

The rain was coming down in torrents, and it was spilling and sloshing down the steps.

Eventually Estelle stopped her pummeling and just stood there panting, her wet hair plastered to her face as she clenched her teeth and seethed at the door.

"He won't answer," said Jack.

"Then we'll wait," said Estelle.

"We'll wait somewhere dry, then," said Jack.

"Here!" Estelle shouted, pointing at her feet. "We'll wait right here."

She turned back to glare at the door. Jack sighed and looked at the others, and they followed his silent signal to move away. *Perhaps we can go back and shelter with Sam and the others,* he thought. Cormier obviously wasn't the friendly type, but maybe they could wear him down. They started down the steps. Estelle shook her head furiously, and reluctantly started to follow.

As Jack stepped onto the first step, he heard a creaking sound behind him. He looked back to see that the door was slightly ajar. Cormier's eyes blazed out from the darkness within. He looked furious.

"You," he said.

Jack looked around. "Who? Me?"

"No," barked Cormier, and pointed at Manda. "You. Who did that to you?" he demanded.

Manda looked at herself, then back at Cormier. "Mr. Absalom."

"Mr. Absalom? Who's Mr. Absalom? No, wait, don't tell me, I can tell just by looking at you that he's an idiot. A complete and utter idiot. And you—" This time he pointed at Rob, who duly pointed at himself. "Yes, you. Your hair's a disgrace, and as for your legs . . . and your torso." Cormier frowned and looked Rob up and down. "Well, all of you, I suppose."

He pointed at Manda, Rob, Jack, and Gripper in turn. "You, you, you, and you, the big lump with the stupid-looking jaw, inside."

"What about Estelle?" asked Jack.

"She's not welcome," said Cormier.

"Why not?" said Estelle.

"Because you're Flesh, and Flesh can't be trusted," said Cormier. "And there's the other thing. I can smell it on you— smelting skin, chemicals. Shoddy craftsmanship is your parasitical game, I'll bet."

Estelle's pale face suddenly flared red. Cormier raised a finger and tilted his head in warning.

"Not a word," he said.

Jack looked at Estelle. She nodded to give him her assent, but still looked furious. Jack stepped back onto the top step and Cormier opened the door wider. Jack went first, followed by Rob, Manda, and Gripper. Cormier growled at Gripper about minding his paintwork, while Gripper tried his level best to squeeze through the door without destroying the frame.

Cormier gave Estelle one last scornful look, then he slammed the door.

CHAPTER 13

Jack looked at the closed door.

"Are you going to leave her outside?" he asked.

"Yes, I am," grunted Cormier, without looking at him. He pointed to their right. "Down that hallway. First door you meet."

Everybody looked at Jack.

"Well, go on, then," Cormier barked.

Jack moved first and the others followed. The inside of the house was as metallic and functional as the outside. Jack could tell instantly that Cormier didn't care much for how his surroundings looked.

They all trooped down the hallway and turned right through an open door into a large room. The room was dimly lit by a naked bulb. The walls had a metallic sheen that reflected some light. Bookshelves lined the walls, but there were more mechanical odds and ends on the shelves than there were books. A large table dominated the room, but even that had three crates of scrap on it. More crates and boxes crammed with various bits of metal were scattered around, and the faded red carpet was covered in oil stains.

Jack was about to say something to Cormier, but the engineer moved with a sudden fervor and grabbed Manda. He led her toward the center of the room.

"Right, then, let's have a look," he said.

He knelt in front of Manda and held his right hand out.

"Left leg."

Manda obeyed and started to lift her left leg. She couldn't raise it far enough for it to reach Cormier's hand.

"Disgusting, disgusting," Cormier ranted. "Barely any articulation. Right leg, then."

Manda lifted her right leg. It was easier to move, but not much. Cormier shook his head in disbelief.

"Criminal!" he shouted. He turned toward the door and roared, "Egbert! Egbert!"

He turned back to examine Manda, muttering and swearing as he did so. Jack was completely bemused but Rob was fascinated and had a small smile on his face as he hovered by Cormier's shoulder. He tutted in time with Cormier's outbursts, while shaking his head in disgust and stroking his chin at the exact same moments that Cormier did.

"Yes, Mr. Cormier," said a bright clear voice by the door.

Jack turned to see a rather tall and skinny mechanical, wearing a butler's bib. His face was long and tubular, his arms matchstick skinny, as were his legs. He had no skin, but despite this he had the kindest face Jack thought he had ever seen. His long fingers were interlaced delicately in a poised gesture of patience.

"I need some legs, Egbert," said Cormier, without turning around. "Good ones too. Maybe over a foot long."

"Very good, Mr. Cormier," said Egbert.

"And tea, and oil. Bring glasses," said Cormier.

Egbert gave a small bow. "Yes, sir."

"Don't forget the legs."

Round Rob pursed his lips and gave Egbert a very serious look. "Legs, Egbert," he said.

"Very good, sir," said Egbert, bowing to Round Rob. He turned and left the room, and Jack frowned as he watched him leave.

"He's adult-sized," said Jack.

"Course he is," Cormier said.

"But that's—"

"Illegal? Pah! I'm Philip Cormier. I do what I like, laws or no laws. Hand me that toolbox," he said, pointing to his left.

"Yes, sir," said Rob, immediately waddling to where Cormier had pointed.

Jack couldn't wait any longer. He was already losing patience. "Mr. Cormier—"

Cormier held up his hand and shushed him. "I'm working."

"Yes, Mr. Cormier, but—"

"How old are these legs?" he bellowed. "I've seen fossils that were younger."

Round Rob burst out laughing. Cormier glared at him, and then the most surreal thing of all happened. A wet, rolling guttural sound was emitted from the base of Cormier's throat. It became a kind of hacking growl, and Rob threw his head back and laughed even more. It took a few more seconds for Jack to realize that Cormier was laughing, and now he and Rob were engaged in a circular round of tit for tat laughing that he thought might go on forever.

Gripper looked at Jack. Jack looked at Gripper. Both looked as confused as the other, and finally the laughing fest between Rob and Cormier started to fade.

Cormier wagged a finger at Rob and growled: "I like you. You can stay."

Rob turned toward Jack and beamed.

The next few minutes were a confused blur for Jack. Cormier worked on Manda while Rob handed him his tools. He managed to detach her legs completely, and Manda was propped on the floor, looking like she was wading waist-deep in water. This didn't seem to bother her, and she gazed amiably at Cormier, who looked fiercely at her eyes and her joints and hinges.

Egbert came in with a box of legs and put them beside Cormier. He disappeared again, and then reappeared with a tray of tea things, a can of oil, and some large drinking glasses. He set them down at a table and proceeded to pour the tea into a delicate china cup. He brought it over to Cormier, who slurped it down in one go. He wiped his mouth with his forearm and handed the cup out for Egbert, who took it gently and placed it back on the tray.

"Don't forget our guests," Cormier grunted.

Egbert poured oil into the four glasses and walked around the room with them on a small silver tray. He handed a glass to Rob, who took it and started to drink with his pinkie finger sticking out. "Very nice, Egbert," he said. Egbert gave Manda a glass, and another to Gripper, who took one look at it, then swallowed everything in one gulp, glass and all.

Egbert offered one to Jack.

Jack looked dumbly at the glass and the tray.

"It's premium," said Egbert, with a broad smile.

Jack took the glass and held it up to the light. Egbert looked at him encouragingly. Jack started to drink it, and Egbert's smile broadened.

"I hope you enjoy it, sir," he said.

Egbert took the tea things and glided out of the room with more grace than one would expect out of someone so spindly and gawky-looking.

"There. Done," Cormier shouted as he stood up.

Manda now had two new legs of equal length. She looked at them with astonishment.

"Give us a twirl," said Cormier, making circles with his index finger.

Manda obliged. Jack felt the urge to step forward in case she fell over, as she so often did, but he was stopped dead in his tracks by the sight of Manda pirouetting gracefully. She stopped and gave a bow. Gripper and Rob clapped. Cormier threw his wrench and let it spin in the air before catching it deftly. He pointed it at Rob:

"Right, then, you're next."

Rob waddled forward, but stopped when he heard the tone in Jack's voice.

"Please, Mr. Cormier," Jack pleaded.

Cormier gave him a one-eyed squint. "What? What is it? Do you have something that needs fixing? Come to think of it, that head doesn't look like it's sitting right. Come over here and I'll—"

"No!" shouted Jack.

Cormier looked slightly taken aback.

"We came here to ask for your help," said Jack.

"Help with what?" asked Cormier suspiciously.

"Our friend . . ." Jack began. "That is, we found one of your Originals."

Cormier looked at him for a moment, then he snorted in derision, threw his head back, and gave another of his growling laughs.

"Nonsense. There's my bits and bobs, that's all I've got left. My bits and bobs. And they're all under this roof."

Jack positioned himself directly in front of Cormier. "That's not true."

Cormier looked both stunned and angry. "Who are you to tell me what is and what isn't true?"

"My name's Jack, since you ask, and this is Rob, Manda, and Gripper. We came here in the hope you might help us find our friend, who just so happens to be one of your Originals."

"Oh, really?" said Cormier, raising a mocking eyebrow. "I must have dropped one somewhere when I wasn't looking. So tell me then, who took your friend?"

"The Agency."

Cormier considered Jack for a moment, and then gave a low chuckle while stroking his beard.

"Well then, you'd better go talk to the Agency hadn't you?"

He turned away under the pretense of examining Rob, but Jack could tell he'd pierced through that thick leather hide of his. Before the engineer had turned away, Jack had spotted a glimmer of doubt in his eyes.

"We can't talk to the Agency, because we're mechanical, you know that," said Jack.

Cormier merely shrugged and harrumphed.

"I'd like eyebrows," said Rob. "New ones. Ones that don't fall off. Ones that make me look distinguished. Maybe pointy ones that I can rub hair oil in and make them even pointier, like a proper gent."

Cormier was examining Rob's knee joints, but looked up sharply.

"What did you say?"

"I said I'd like new eyebrow—"

"No, after that, you said you'd like to be like . . ."

"A proper gent." Rob smiled.

"We don't use that word in this house," Cormier said quietly.

"What? Gent?"

"No," he grumbled. "The P word."

He went back to examining Rob's joints. Rob looked at Jack, who frowned.

"You can stay the night, but just the night, mind," said Cormier. His voice was different now, quieter, and all the aggression seemed to have gone out of it. Jack was confused by the sudden change in his mood. "After that you can be on your way," he said, waving his wrench.

"What about Estelle?" asked Jack.

"Who's Estelle?"

"The girl you told to stay outside."

"Flesh? Flesh stays outside," said Cormier, suddenly rounding on him, his volatility reignited.

Jack felt a rush of something dark and angry. "Estelle," he said. "Her name is Estelle."

Without realizing, Jack had taken a step toward Cormier. Cormier looked him up and down.

"Besides, you're *Flesh*. How are you different?" said Jack.

Cormier sniffed. "I'm special."

Jack kept glaring at him.

"All right then. She can come in. One night. But then all of you are on your way." Cormier frowned. "As a matter of interest, how did you get here?"

"We drove," said Rob. "Well, Jack did. He knows how to. Plus he's got his special driving legs."

Cormier looked at Jack's legs in disgust and shook his head. "Who put those on you?"

"I did," said Jack.

Cormier turned away, muttering to himself. "One night," he growled to no one in particular.

Cormier tightened a few nuts and bolts on Rob, then proceeded to examine Gripper, scratching his head and uttering curses to himself as he did so. He then led them all back out into the hall. "There's a room upstairs on the left. You can stay there."

Cormier opened the front door. Estelle was sitting on the front step, facing out toward the town, her knees pulled up to her chin. The rain was still coming down in gray sheets.

"Oi, Flesh," said Cormier.

Jack ground his jaw and glared at him, but Cormier was taking no notice.

Estelle still had her earmuffs on, so Cormier tapped her lower back with the toe of his boot. She turned and gave him a murderous look.

Cormier didn't seem bothered. "Inside," he said, holding the door slightly ajar.

Estelle stood up and walked carefully toward the door, glowering balefully at Cormier all the way. The engineer held up his hand and motioned for her to stop right outside the door.

"Ah ah, you're dripping all over my floor. Give yourself a shake."

"I'm not a dog," said Estelle. Cormier raised an eyebrow. Estelle sighed and gave herself a half-hearted shake. Cormier grunted and stepped aside.

Estelle gave Cormier another cutting look, which he ignored.

"The trees," she said.

"What about them?" Cormier scowled.

"They're screaming," said Estelle.

Cormier muttered something and stepped toward a black

box, attached at head height to the wall just inside the door. He flicked a switch, and the change in Estelle's demeanor was immediate. She lowered her shoulders and breathed a sigh of relief. Her features became more relaxed, and she took the earmuffs off. Cormier turned to Jack and the others.

"I made the trees myself. They emit a frequency that only Flesh can hear. I've had a lifetime of people whining in my ear, so I'm used to it, but it keeps unwanted visitors away." He looked at Estelle. "Usually."

Cormier looked Estelle up and down and sniffed.

"Your friends were nice enough to stand up for you. I, on the other hand, don't trust you. I'll thank you to keep to the room upstairs. There's a small bed there. It's yours for the night." He turned around and swept his eyes over all of them. "And I want you all gone by morning. Egbert!"

Egbert arrived smoothly from down the hall, as if his feet were on casters.

"Show this lot to the spare room upstairs," said Cormier, jerking his thumb over his shoulder.

"Yes, sir," said Egbert.

Egbert glided to the bottom of the stairs and gracefully stretched out his hand to direct the others up. As Estelle took the first step, she found herself almost nose to nose with Egbert. She gave him a sour, mistrustful look. Egbert merely smiled.

The stairs were also made of metal, but they groaned rather distressingly when Gripper stood on them. They made their way carefully to the room, which was bare except for a bed with a mattress that sagged in the middle.

"Would madam like a sheet and some blankets?" asked Egbert.

"Madam would," said Estelle.

Egbert disappeared, and they all stood in silence and looked around the room.

"So, let's be honest. He's not going to help us save Christopher, is he?" said Estelle.

Nobody answered her.

CHAPTER 14

Christopher was brought to the lab at dawn, where Blake was waiting. After Reeves had left, Blake asked him to sit. A cold feeling spread across Christopher's chest as he settled back in the chair.

"How far back can you remember?" asked Blake, his tone friendly and casual.

Christopher looked at him. "Remember?"

"I want you to think back on your past."

"Why?"

Blake smiled. "Humor me."

Christopher eyed Blake with suspicion. The man was obviously after something, but for now Christopher felt he had no choice but to comply. Perhaps if he did help, Blake would let him return to his friends. He knew the thought was a desperate one, but he clung to it like a drowning man to a piece of driftwood.

He swallowed, shut his eyes, and tried to concentrate: "I remember . . ." A tongue of flame licked the air before him, and Christopher felt the acrid tang of smoke at the back of his throat. He opened his eyes, feeling his heart clench. He couldn't tell Blake. He couldn't go there: It was too painful. "The orphanage. I remember the orphanage," he said instead.

"What do you remember about the orphanage?" Blake asked.

"I remember everything," said Christopher. "The lessons. Mrs. Jessup the nurse. Mr. Jenkins the caretaker."

"And before then?"

Christopher's mouth opened, but he didn't know what to say. The fire alone flickered at the back of his mind—nothing else.

Blake's voice was surprisingly gentle and compassionate. "Your memories of the past. Those memories of the orphanage. None of those memories are real."

Christopher could feel the hot panic rising up inside him. The edge of his scalp was suddenly slick with sweat.

"But I can remember everything," said Christopher. "Everything about the orphanage."

"And before then?"

Christopher's mouth opened, but he didn't know what to say.

"I'm sorry, Christopher," Blake said, his expression one of genuine sympathy. "I'm only asking because we need to know everything about your past so that we can change the future."

Christopher shook his head. Deep down he was frightened. His insides were squirming with panic.

"That's just . . . You're talking rubbish. How can memories be false? I want to go home. I want to go home now."

Blake sighed and shook his head in exasperation. "Oh, Christopher, Christopher. What we're doing here is trying to uncover secrets. Your memories have been tampered with in order to hide something." Blake gave a tight, bitter smile. "Someone once told me that secrets are secrets for a reason. I tend not to believe that. I think secrets are there to be uncovered. Like buried treasure."

"You say *hide something*. Hide what?" Christopher asked.

Blake ignored the question and simply smiled to himself. He reached behind him on the table for something in a tin box: a small rectangular piece of metal. He showed Christopher both sides.

"What do you see?"

"Nothing, it's blank," said Christopher.

Blake reached inside his breast pocket and took out a black piece of metal shaped like a pen. He started to inscribe something on the small rectangle with this pen. When he was finished he held it up. Christopher could see the symbols he'd engraved. They glowed with a soft white light for a moment and then faded out, leaving just the elegant black script Blake had created.

"What do you see now?" he asked.

"Glyphs."

Blake smiled. "Very good, yes. Glyphs." He climbed down off his stool and started to look through another, larger box on the table.

When he turned back to face Christopher he had what looked like a metal marionette in his hand. Its head was smooth and featureless. He started to delicately inscribe tiny symbols on its skull.

"The secret of glyphs is in their combinations. Different combinations produce different results, different personalities and suchlike, and there are all manner of variations. There are sets of glyphs and subsets of glyphs. Certain subsets can be used to create memories. Now, your friends, they wouldn't have needed memories. They would have woken into the world with a clean slate, much like this."

Blake put his lips together and blew some of the steel

shavings from the head of the marionette; then he enclosed the head with his hand, closed his eyes, and whispered something. Light glowed from under his hand for a moment, and then it faded.

A few seconds after the light had faded the marionette's legs started to jerk. Blake smiled and put the marionette on the table. Its legs spasmed and went from under it. It clambered up, and then jerkily started to walk across the table, eventually finding a smooth rhythm.

"Stop," said Blake.

The marionette stopped.

"Sit," said Blake.

It sat on the edge of the table with its arms down by its sides.

Blake smiled and spread his hands out in front of the marionette. "Voilà. The rudimentary. The basic system animated in its simplest form." Blake seemed genuinely pleased with the result. His eyes were shining like those of a small child. "It never ceases to amaze me," he said, then shook himself. "Anyway, to work."

He was holding up the pen-shaped instrument again. He walked toward Christopher and stood near his head. He pushed a lever and the chair started to recline. As he sank lower, Christopher felt the panic rise in him again, and he tried to sit up.

"Shh," said Blake, laying a firm but surprisingly gentle hand on his chest.

He positioned himself behind Christopher and laid his right hand on his forehead, just below his fringe.

"You may have heard Mr. Reeves referring to something called patching."

Christopher nodded.

"Patching is a process that requires quite a lot of skill to be done properly. A high-grade mechanical may be patched and repatched to suit the owner's needs. The best way to explain patching is to demonstrate it."

Blake held the piece of metal in front of Christopher's eyes. Up close Christopher could appreciate even more the delicacy of the script on its surface.

"This is a patch," said Blake. "This one is interesting because I've modified it with very specific glyphs." Blake pressed down a little firmer on Christopher's forehead. "If you would permit me."

Christopher didn't think he was in a position to argue. He was also strangely curious, and nodded as best he could.

Blake pushed up the fringe of Christopher's hair and gave a little jerking motion with his hand, and suddenly Christopher's hair was rising from his head. Christopher twisted around in shock. "It's a standard feature," said Blake. His smile was almost apologetic. "Settle back."

Christopher tried to relax. He fixed his eyes on the ceiling, and he felt Blake's hand move to his skull, the slight pressure of the patch on his head. There was a small click, the sensation of a tiny added weight. Blake let Christopher's hair flop back down.

"Now," he said.

"Now what?" said Christopher.

"Do you remember that picnic you went on when you were five years old? You had Rusty with you."

Christopher frowned.

"Your pet dog."

Christopher looked bemused. "I've never been on a picnic, and I've definitely never had a d—"

There was a burst of golden light, the warm, green scent of grass. Christopher was on a hillside overlooking rolling hills bathing in a haze of sun. He was sitting on a blanket. The remnants of sandwiches were scattered around him. There was a bottle of lemonade by his side. Just by looking at it he could feel the tang of it on his tongue. He remembered the burst of flavor as he swigged it back and screwed his eyes shut against the brilliance of the blue sky and the sun, and he could hear barking—barking, as Rusty joyfully lolloped toward him, his tongue hanging out, his reddish-brown ears flapping. Rusty, *his* dog, running toward him, getting closer.

Christopher held out his arms.

There was a click and a deadly *whush* sound, and the world suddenly seemed to gray again before Christopher found himself back in the chair. The pang of loss was almost unbearable. He jerked forward and clenched his fists against his chest.

"What was that?" he gasped.

"Christopher—"

He spilled off the front of the chair and almost collapsed in a heap on the floor. "What was it?" he screamed.

"I'm sorry, it was the easiest way to show you," said Blake.

Christopher leaned forward and braced himself against the front of the chair with his right hand. The sense of loss was fading—he could still see Rusty, but the pang of grief that had been so sharp was dulling. It was like waking from a particularly realistic dream, when you carry the emotion with you into the waking world, until gradually it fades like a ripple vanishing in water.

"I'm sorry," said Blake. "I do apologize."

"Was it a dream?" asked Christopher.

Blake shook his head. "No, it was a memory." He paused in thought, frowning. "Or at least the imitation of one." He held the piece of metal up for Christopher to see. "A patch has inscribed upon it what you might call memories. Once attached to a mechanical, it gives them the illusion of having had a past. To give you an example of a practical application: As you know, some buyers seek mechanicals as child replacements. They may deem it necessary for the purchased device to have certain memories of their family. Their first day at school. An incident where they were stung by a bee and comforted by a parent, and so on."

Christopher still felt nauseous. He didn't like the way Blake was speaking, as if he were delivering a public lecture and expounding on his own greatness. The engineer looked at Christopher, attempting to feign concern, but Christopher could see something else in his eyes, a glint of callousness that told him that Blake only saw him as a means to an end.

"Are you all right?" Blake asked.

Christopher rubbed his forehead. He felt a sudden weariness, as if a great weight had settled on his shoulders.

"So my memories aren't my memories?"

"Well, now, that's the thing. We don't know for certain. Some of what you recognize as your memories may well be that. Some of them, alas, maybe not."

Christopher had a sudden vision of his mother. Flour in her hair. Her smile. The pang in his chest was back again, but this time it was fiercer, and this time he knew it would last.

"How do I know what happened and didn't happen? How do I know what was real?" he sobbed.

Blake stepped toward him and put a hand on his shoulder. "It's all right, Christopher. We'll find out together. I promise."

He could see Blake's face wobble and waver through his tears.

How can I cry? he thought again. The very idea of it seemed to be a mocking insult.

Blake shushed him and got him to settle back into the chair. Christopher felt ashamed and embarrassed as great gulping sobs convulsed him. He'd felt the urge to run earlier, but now he realized there was no point. And yet he also wanted to stay—he needed to know what were his real memories and what weren't. He needed to know who he was, and it frightened him.

"It could be a long process," Blake said softly. "You've been patched quite a bit. We have to separate the false memories from the true. It'll take a little bit of delving."

Christopher nodded and rubbed his nose with his hand. He tried his best to straighten up as Blake examined his skull. He stared ahead at the ceiling and thought again about the way life had changed for him, and about what was true and what was false.

CHAPTER 15

Jack watched Estelle as she sat up in bed and glowered. She was still wearing her overcoat, and she had her hands jammed deep into the pockets. He could see the muddy soles of her boots, which she hadn't taken off, even as she slept.

"Are you thinking, Estelle?" asked Rob.

Early-morning light was seeping through the window. Rob was sitting in a corner, while Manda, Jack, and Gripper all leaned up against the back wall.

"Yes," said Estelle, without taking her eyes off the wall.

"I knew it," said Rob. "I knew it because you were doing your frowny thinky face. I'm not as good at doing a frowny thinky face because I don't have real skin like you, but when I want people to know that I'm thinking, I sometimes stroke my chin, like this."

Rob narrowed his eyes and started to stroke his chin between his thumb and index finger.

"That way people can tell I'm thinking. Then if they want to ask me for advice they'll know it's a good time. I might be think- ing about something helpful, you see, something like how to—"

"Rob," Jack said gently, "this isn't helping."

Rob took his hand away from his chin and looked disappointed. Jack turned back to Estelle. "What are you thinking, Estelle?"

"The same thing I thought yesterday. I'm thinking he's not going to help us," said Estelle, still looking at the wall.

"How do you know?" asked Jack, trying his best to sound as if he didn't believe in the harsh truth of what she was saying.

Estelle gave him a look that was almost pitying. Jack was not impressed, and he felt a tingle of resentment.

"How do you know, Estelle? He might change his mind." Even Gripper turned to look when he heard the sharpness in Jack's voice.

"You said he refused to help, didn't you?" said Estelle.

"We can change his mind," Jack countered.

Estelle shook her head and snorted.

Jack sprang to his feet. "Well, what do you want to do, then? Do you want to give up and leave Christopher to the Agency?"

"No, of course not," said Estelle, leaping off the bed.

"Well then," said Jack, as if that was enough to settle the matter.

But Estelle wasn't going to let it rest there; she was about to shout something else when a bright cheerful voice interrupted her.

"Porridge?" it asked. "Or maybe boiled egg and soldiers?"

Everyone turned to see Egbert standing in the doorway. His fingertips steepled delicately together. He was smiling from ear to ear.

"What?" snapped Estelle.

"I was inquiring as to whether madam might like porridge for her breakfast, or perhaps boiled egg and soldiers."

Estelle looked at Egbert as if he had two heads.

"Perhaps madam would like both? What about honey for your porridge? And may I suggest—"

"No, you may not," snapped Estelle. "And it's miss, not madam. Didn't *Mister* Cormier teach you proper manners? Actually, no, forget I said that. Mr. Cormier and manners don't even go in the same sentence together."

A still smiling Egbert was unfazed, which sent Estelle into an even bigger rage.

"I'll bet he's a very obliging chap, Mr. Cormier. Or at least my friend Jack thinks he might be."

Jack clenched his jaw. "I was only suggesting—"

"What? That we get down on our hands and knees and beg, is that it, Jack? He's not going to help—why can't you get that into your thick metal skull?"

Jack took a step toward Estelle. "Don't. Don't you dare—"

"Well, actually, Mr. Cormier can be quite accommodating," said Egbert.

"Nobody asked you, skinny. Why don't you just shut up!" Estelle roared.

Egbert kept smiling. Jack started shouting at Estelle. Estelle screamed back at him. The shouting became fiercer, until nobody could distinguish who was shouting at whom or indeed what they were saying, until finally another voice joined in:

"I MISS CHRISTOPHER!"

All eyes turned to see Round Rob standing defiantly in the center of the room with his fists clenched.

"I miss Christopher," he repeated, looking fiercely at each of them in turn. "And we shouldn't be fighting. We should be doing the best we can to find him."

Jack turned back to Estelle, who looked shamefaced. She lowered her eyes to the floor.

"It's simple," said Rob. "We just do our best for him because he's our friend, and we miss him. We owe him our best. He'd do it for us."

Jack smiled and nodded in appreciation at Rob. Rob straightened up proudly and gave a little wriggle to get the stiffness out of his joints.

"Porridge," sighed Estelle, turning toward Egbert.

Egbert bowed. "Very good, madam."

They all trooped downstairs after Egbert. There was no sign of Cormier anywhere. The butler breezily informed them that: "Mr. Cormier will be with us after breakfast."

He led them to a dining room with a table so large it looked like it had been built for a giant. Estelle sat and hunched her shoulders forward, holding her hands between her knees. Jack thought she looked like someone half her age, and for the first time he realized that her anger was really just a mask to hide her fear. She was as worried about Christopher as any of them.

Egbert offered the mechanicals some oil. Everyone sat at the table except Gripper, who stood by the door, moving awkwardly from one foot to the other, because there was nothing big enough for him to sit on.

Jack was nervous. He could almost hear the crackle of tension in the air. He knew he only had one more chance to convince Cormier to help them before they were booted out of the house, and he could feel the responsibility weighing down on his shoulders. But he had to do it for Christopher. Rob had reminded them of that, and he turned to thank him for his outburst upstairs.

But Round Rob was missing.

Round Rob had always had what Absalom called "a curious streak" in him. He was always nosing in things and prone to wandering off whenever they went anywhere.

He'd felt the old impulse as they made their way down

Cormier's hallway for breakfast. The niggling feeling had crept up on him as soon as they'd left the room upstairs, and so it was that Rob had found himself looking around as the others receded into the distance, and he started to scan the walls, as if he might find something interesting there.

That's when he heard the skittering sound.

It came from somewhere to his left. Rob turned to look in the direction of the sound. If he had a heart it would have skipped a beat—a narrow doorway leading to another part of the house had been left ajar.

"What's that? Who's there?" said Rob, smiling in excitement.

The skittering sound came again, like tiny scampering feet on metal. Rob couldn't help himself. He took one final look at the others as they disappeared around a corner, and then he turned and stepped through the doorway.

The corridor on the other side was narrow and gloomy. It was bordered on both sides by stained gray paneling. It was the strangest hallway he'd ever been in—it seemed to zigzag one way, then another, with the ceiling dipping and rising at odd intervals. Rob heard scuttling in the murk up ahead. He started forward, feeling another tickle of excitement. He wasn't frightened. It was rare that Round Rob became frightened—as he saw it, the world was a reasonable place. If you had difficulties, there was usually a simple solution of some sort.

Like how Christopher had been taken from them—to Rob, it was all just a simple matter of getting him back.

He missed Christopher, and he could feel it somewhere in his being. It was a different feeling from the scratchy curiosity he felt as he followed the noise. This was a cold, lonely feeling, as if some part of him had been cut out—he knew he had to find that part again and put it back in.

Rob came to an open door on his left and heard a pattering

sound from within. The room was small, no more than a glorified cupboard with a tiny grubby window on the far wall. There were batteries and bits of scrap metal piled on top of one another. Rob looked around and frowned. He waited for a few moments but heard nothing, and was about to leave when something moved on the window ledge.

A small sheet of tin was edging forward bit by bit as if something was pushing it from behind. Rob watched it in fascination as it kept coming, until finally gravity took hold and it crashed off the window and down onto a pile of nuts and bolts below.

The thing that had pushed the sheet of tin looked like it was trying to get out the window. It was gray, disc-shaped, and as big as a man's fist. It had six legs and tiny, shiny black eyes. It scrabbled the needle-sharp points of its legs against the window, and they made a screeching, scraping sound. Rob stepped forward and wiggled his fingers in greeting.

"Hullo," he said.

The spider thing whipped around and glared at him with beady eyes. Its multi-jointed legs started quivering.

"I'm Round Rob. I'm a friend."

The spider thing regarded him suspiciously, and Round Rob counted its legs again and reminded himself that spiders have eight legs. Insects have six legs and spiders eat insects, so maybe this insect thing was afraid of being eaten. Round Rob looked over his right shoulder, as if expecting a large metallic spider to appear at any moment.

When he was sure nothing was coming he turned back to the spider. Or the *not a spider,* as he reminded himself. He thought for a moment and decided he couldn't call it "not a spider." Also, it didn't look like any insect he knew, so he made the most logical decision he could make and decided to call it George.

123

"George, here, boy," he said.

George sat up and pawed the space between them delicately with his front two legs, as if testing the air. Round Rob took George's response to his new name as a good sign, and he stepped forward and held out his forearm. George's legs clicked and clacked and made slow circular motions in the air, then they tentatively rested on Rob's arm.

"That's it, George." Rob smiled.

George placed two legs on Rob's arm, then four, then all six, and he sat there and looked up at Rob with his shiny eyes. Rob chuckled with glee, then, as if he couldn't quite believe his luck, a seemingly delighted George skittered up Rob's arm and nestled under his chin. Rob giggled.

Rob turned around and left the room. "Let's see what else we can find," he said to his new friend.

It didn't take him long to find something else. There was a door five feet down the hall to the right. It was slightly ajar, but Rob, being Rob, wasn't perturbed by the prospect of what might be on the other side of the door—he just pushed it open and ambled in.

The room was large and surprisingly neat. There was a big bed, a wardrobe, and a dressing table. A washbasin and jug were balanced on a stool near the bed. Rob scanned the room, and his eyes drifted to his right.

And that was when he found the most amazing thing of all.

CHAPTER 16

Estelle polished off her second bowl of porridge.

She caught Jack's eye as the spoon was halfway to her mouth. "What?" she said.

"Nothing," said Jack as he watched her lower her eyes to the bowl. "Well, just one thing."

"What?" said Estelle warily.

"Sorry," he said. "Sorry about earlier."

Estelle gave him a look of gratitude, and then she shrugged and gave a quick scowl, just in case Jack thought she might be getting too soft.

Jack grinned at her, and then felt a sudden daring impulse, as if he knew now might be the only moment for what he was about to do next. The words were out of his mouth before he knew it.

"Why did you leave home, Estelle?"

Estelle's head whipped up. She looked stunned by the question. Her lower lip moved, up down, up down, as if she'd forgotten how to speak, and then suddenly she rattled off an answer:

"I wanted to see the world. I wanted to better myself."

Jack nodded. He tried to frown to give the impression of understanding, but secretly he was strangely delighted, and he pressed his advantage a little more.

"What was your dad like?"

"Mean," snapped Estelle, and just as soon as she'd said the word Jack could tell that she regretted it.

"Mean? Like with money? Like Mr. Absalom?"

Estelle's head shook involuntarily ever so slightly, and Jack knew she meant the other definition of the word. She lowered her eyes and fixed them on her spoon as she stirred the porridge in her bowl.

"Dad taught me everything he knew," Estelle said with a wry smile. "Then I got better and better, and I began to teach *him* a thing or two. Most people would have been happy with the help. Most people would have had something nice to say about it once in a while, but not him."

Estelle jabbed her spoon into her porridge. Jack took it as a sign that the subject was now closed. She had raised her shoulders, as if she was trying to shield herself and was embarrassed by having said so much.

After breakfast was finished, Egbert came in and announced: "Mr. Cormier will see you now."

"What is he, royalty?" Estelle muttered.

He led them back along the hallway toward the room they'd first encountered Cormier in the day before. Manda held Jack's hand as they walked down the hallway. "Where's Rob?" she asked.

"I don't know," said Jack.

"I wouldn't worry," said Estelle. "He'll turn up. He always does."

They stepped into the room to find Cormier kneeling on the floor, viciously unscrewing something from an engine. He had a file clamped in his mouth and he was growling with the exertion. He gave them barely a glance, only nodding curtly at Egbert.

"Wuh ijit Egber?" he muttered through the file.

"Our guests, Mr. Cormier. You said you wanted to say good-bye to them before they left."

Cormier waved a dismissive hand at them and grumbled "Ubye" before turning back to his work.

"We're not going anywhere," said Jack, taking a step farther into the room.

Cormier took the file from his mouth and glared at him. "What?"

"I said we're—"

"I know what you said," replied Cormier, starting to file something on the surface of the engine.

Jack gave a bitter smile. "You obviously don't want to listen, but I'll tell you anyway."

Cormier sighed and shook his head.

"Our friend is one of your Originals. He might not even know it, but he has to be, and only you can claim him."

"All my Originals are accounted for. Like I said, I've just got my bits and bobs now," Cormier muttered.

"Are you sure?" said Jack.

"Course I'm sure," Cormier growled. "Anyway, let's just say this friend of yours is one of mine—how would you prove it? It's not like he has a stamp."

Jack looked at Estelle, confused. "Some models are stamped," she explained.

"I never stamped mine," said Cormier. "Stamping's for egomaniacs."

"He didn't have a stamp," said Estelle.

"Well, that means nothing." Cormier shrugged. "And anyway, you still haven't explained how you know he's one of mine?"

"He's a very good model," said Estelle.

Cormier grunted.

"The craftsmanship is excellent," she added.

Cormier considered this for a moment and nodded, as if both conceding the point to Estelle and taking the chance to appreciate his own genius—but then he went straight back to scowling.

"Appearance, articulation, movement; everything is top grade," said Estelle.

"Pah," said Cormier, concentrating on his filing.

"No one else could have made a model like it. He's one of yours," said Jack.

Cormier rose slowly into a standing position and very deliberately wiped his oil-stained hands with a rag. He jabbed a finger in the direction of Jack and Estelle: "Now you listen, and you listen well. I, Philip Cormier, the greatest engineer of this age, indeed of any age, am certain of one thing, and that is that my few remaining Originals are all accounted for. I have names, dates, locations, and ownership details. I would most certainly remember if there was one wandering about in a junkyard."

Cormier raised an eyebrow, challenging them to retort.

"You have to help us," said Jack quietly.

"I don't have to help anyone," said Cormier.

"You helped Manda and Rob when we first arrived here. You could have left us outside, but instead you called us in. Why did you do that?"

"I was bored," said Cormier, looking slightly flustered.

"I think you're a good man, Mr. Cormier. I think you care," said Jack.

"Nonsense!" roared Cormier.

Jack took Manda's hand and gently pushed her toward Cormier. "Well, then I'm wrong," he said. "You don't care at all, Mr. Cormier. That's quite obvious," he said, looking pointedly at Manda.

Cormier wrapped his hand around a wrench. His knuckles whitened. His arm was trembling with fury.

"Get out," he hissed.

"Mr. Cormier—" Jack began.

"I said get out!" Cormier roared, striking the engine so hard with the wrench that sparks flew upward. "Your tinpot friend is no concern of mine. The Agency can tear him up for scrap for all I care. They have machines in London, crushers. They'll pulp him right down into a cube no bigger than a fist."

Manda burst into tears.

Cormier looked both frightened and guilty when he looked at Manda, but he roared on anyway. "Yes, that's right. A tiny cube. That's all he's good for. He's no more one of mine than the air. He can go and hang for all I care. Now get out!"

Cormier stood there gasping, his chest heaving in and out with the effort he'd expended. Manda was still crying, and Gripper was holding his left forearm and looking forlornly at the ground. Even Egbert seemed shocked. Estelle glared at Cormier with contempt. She turned to look at Jack, who could see the flicker in her eyes that suggested she'd decided that this was now a lost cause. Jack felt an awful plummeting sensation. He nodded at Estelle, and they turned to leave.

A panting, shamefaced Cormier watched them as they made their way toward the door.

And that's where it would have ended, if Round Rob hadn't waddled in at that very moment, holding something aloft in his right hand.

He fixed Cormier with what, for Round Rob, was a very stern look and said:

"Why do you have a photograph of Christopher in your bedroom?"

CHAPTER 17

Christopher spent most of his first day in the Crag in the chair. Blake worked on him with the patches, always with an apologetic air, and with frequent interjections like: "This might sting a little" or "Brace yourself."

Often Christopher would see something from the past, its colors incredibly vivid—so vibrant it almost hurt to look at them. He could see Mr. Jenkins mopping the hall in the orphanage. The vinegar solution he was using was so strong that it stung Christopher's eyes and made them weep. Jenkins's dungarees, which were a faded blue, suddenly blazed with a brightness that made Christopher want to shield his eyes with his forearm. Jenkins looked up from what he was doing, and then suddenly, he, the shiny mahogany surfaces of the hallway, the sting of vinegar, everything was gone, as if it had all been sucked down a plughole with violent force.

"What about that one?" Blake asked.

"What one?" said Christopher.

"The memory with the caretaker, Mr. Jenkins."

Christopher frowned. "Who's Mr. Jenkins?"

130

Blake exhaled and wiped a sweaty hand across his brow. "Another false one," he said. He'd taken off his jacket and rolled up his sleeves. All he'd been doing was sorting through patches on Christopher's skull, gingerly touching them with tweezers, removing them gently, and asking him to recall specific memories. At this stage, he'd worked through most of Christopher's memories of the orphanage. Blake hummed as he worked and murmured, "These are good. I wonder where your friend Absalom got them."

"Mr. Absalom wasn't a friend," said Christopher. As he spoke, the orphanage garden blazed into light with yellows, whites, reds, and oranges, and then was gone. Christopher felt a sudden sharp sting that seemed to vanish almost as soon as he felt it.

"That was a good one," said Blake, holding the patch up to examine with his tweezers. "Smells, sounds, textures—everything."

He dropped it into a small kidney-shaped tray where it rattled with the others.

"Absalom was a liar," said Christopher, feeling a quiver of anger run through him.

"I'm sorry to hear that," said Blake. "There's nothing worse than a liar." He narrowed his eyes and scanned Christopher's skull. "What do you remember now?"

Christopher swallowed. There was the sudden flash of a kitchen, warm sunlight through a window, the smell of baking. "I can see my mother."

"Good," said Blake. "I think—"

"What?" snapped Christopher. He immediately felt guilty about the tone he'd used when he saw the look of surprise in Blake's eyes, but he couldn't help it. The tension was too much, and he could feel a creeping panic as each memory was removed. "Sorry," he said.

"Quite all right," said Blake with a smile. "I was just about to say we might be getting closer to your real memories."

Christopher nodded, but turned his face away so that Blake couldn't see the fear in his eyes. *What if my mother isn't real?* he thought. *What if she was just a patch-induced illusion too? Then what?* The fear was a cold, sore thing that he could feel growing inside him. It felt like a stone lodged in his chest, making it hard to breathe.

"Those tears too," said Blake, not noticing Christopher's mood. "They're quite the bit of workmanship. I could never do tears."

"And I eat," said Christopher. "And I drink too."

Blake gave a little grunt of effort and pried away another patch, which he held up in front of Christopher's eyes. "Not anymore you don't."

Christopher blinked.

"That's a rather clever patch right there. It gives you false memories that are a bit more current. What you ate for breakfast and lunch, that sort of thing. You've never had a bacon sandwich in your life. Which, when you think about it, is probably the cruelest mode of torture of all."

Blake smiled weakly at his own attempt at humor, and dropped the patch into the tray.

"I'm a Cormier, aren't I?" said Christopher.

There was a slight pause, as if Blake was considering what he'd said. "Most likely."

"Then why did he abandon me? How did I get to Absalom's?"

"Well, that's what we're here to find out, isn't it?" Blake said cheerily.

"Did you know him?"

"Who?" Blake dropped another patch into the tray.

"Cormier. Did you know him?"

132

Blake didn't reply. There was nothing but the gentle *tap tap* as he loosened the edges of another patch.

Christopher bit his lip and decided to press his advantage. "I heard he worked with your father."

Blake flung one of his tools into a tray, and it bounced off with a clang and hit the floor.

He came around to where Christopher could see him and wiped his hands and forehead on a towel.

"We appear to be done for the day." He smiled, but it was forced and didn't hide his anger. He pressed the lever on the chair with real venom, and Christopher was almost thrown out of it as he was brought up into a sitting position.

Blake strode over to the doors and shouted down the hallway. "If you would be so kind, Mr. Reeves."

He then went to a table and started writing in a notebook. Christopher realized he was attempting to ignore him. He thought about asking Blake about his father again, and could feel the squirming sense of animosity within himself, and the satisfaction he might gain from angering Blake some more. But the moment passed as Reeves and Dunlop strode through the double doors.

Blake gestured toward Christopher with his pen without looking up. "You may take him."

"Very good, sir. May I inquire as to how things are proceeding?"

"Barely scratching the first layer. We'll know more tomorrow once we see if it's affected in any way by the memory stripping."

Christopher felt a hot twinge of rage when he realized the "it" being referred to was him.

Reeves took him roughly by the arm and pushed him toward the hall.

"Wait!"

Reeves turned around with Christopher, and Blake picked something up from a table and walked toward the double doors.

"This is for you," he said to Christopher as he held the marionette out toward him.

Reeves was as surprised as Christopher was. Blake's anger seemed to have faded, but Christopher couldn't read his expression. Was that guilt he saw? He took the marionette from him.

"Thank you."

Blake turned on his heel and walked back to his notes.

Dunlop and Reeves escorted Christopher back to his cell. The sky outside was darkening to a deep blue. The clank of the door bolt made him start a little. Christopher placed the marionette on the floor and it stood there, looking up at him as if awaiting instruction.

"Sit," Christopher said.

The marionette sat on the floor.

Christopher climbed into his bunk and stared at the wall until the cell had darkened, the marionette becoming just a gray outline in the gloom.

CHAPTER 18

Jack reckoned he had never seen anyone turn as white as Cormier did in the moment Round Rob produced the photo of Christopher. He stumbled backward as if he'd been punched in the gut, and if it hadn't been for the engine on the floor behind him, Jack reckoned he would have fallen. All eyes in the room were on him; his mouth opened and closed, but no sound was forthcoming, and it seemed like an eternity before he could utter anything that resembled actual words. When he finally did speak, all that he could manage seemed little more than spluttering nonsense.

"How did . . . did you . . . Chris . . . he's . . . but that's . . . how did . . . that's not . . ."

He held the wrench in his hand and raised it in Rob's direction and continued in this vein for some time. Rob turned and looked querulously at Jack.

"Is he broken?" he asked.

Then Cormier cleared his throat, gave a growl, and was suddenly like an engine revving into life, cogs and wheels spinning with a mad fury. The color came back into his face, and his eyes started to blaze.

"Egbert, get everything ready," he bellowed.

"Ready for what?" asked Egbert mildly.

"We're going to London," Cormier spluttered, as if Egbert had just asked the stupidest question ever.

"Very good, sir," said Egbert, and he gave a little bow and exited the room.

"Why's he going to London?" Round Rob asked Jack.

"Because that's where the Agency is," Jack said with a grin.

Round Rob frowned for a moment and looked at the floor. A smile started to slowly creep across his face as he realized what this meant. He stepped toward Cormier and held out the photograph. Cormier had been pacing back and forth, running his hands through his hair. He turned to see Rob, and he blinked rapidly at him as if seeing him for the first time. Rob stretched his arm out farther.

"He still looks like that," said Rob. "Just so's you know, when we find him."

Cormier gently took the photograph. He looked at the photo, then he looked at Rob. A great grating chuckle started to build in the back of his throat. He started to laugh again, like a man gargling with gravel. Rob joined in. Estelle looked at Jack and raised an eyebrow as Cormier and Rob started another round of mutual laughter.

Soon Cormier was dashing around the house, shouting and flapping his arms, while Egbert ran hither and thither, collecting tools and bags in the hall, only stopping to bow and curtsy and utter a "Very good" at occasional intervals.

The others stood in the hallway and watched the frenzy. Cormier's head darted to and fro as he muttered to himself. Rob was the only thing that caught his eye amid the frenzy.

"What's that?" he said, pointing at Rob's neck.

"That's George," said Rob as an anxious George attempted to hide himself by huddling closer into his neck.

"George?" Cormier spluttered.

"That's his name," said Rob.

Cormier frowned and scratched his chin. "Don't remember giving him a name."

"He's a six-legged, not a spider," said Rob.

Cormier nodded, but gave the mechanical the kind of look that people reserved for lunatics, then he was off dashing down the hallway, shouting Egbert's name.

"I found him down that way," said Rob proudly, pointing toward the corridor.

"Right," said Jack, not sure what to say.

"Did you find anything else?" asked Estelle, reaching out to touch George.

Rob shook his head. George gingerly touched the tips of Estelle's fingers, and when he felt brave enough he scampered up her arm and onto her shoulder. Estelle laughed. Jack wheeled around to look at her, and Rob raised an eyebrow and instinctively held it in place. They both exchanged a glance. Neither of them had ever heard Estelle laugh before.

"What?" she said.

"Nothing," said Jack. Rob pretended to be busy looking at a particularly interesting speck of dust on the floor.

Cormier arrived back a few moments later. He was wearing sturdy boots and a long black leather jacket. He rummaged through the inner lining of his jacket, which had pockets filled with screwdrivers, wrenches, and various nuts and bolts. He patted himself down, and when he seemed satisfied that he had everything, he raised his shoulders and rolled his neck as if to release some tension.

"Right, then, let's be off," he said, rubbing his hands together.

"All of us?" said Jack.

"Of course, yes," barked Cormier. He frowned for a moment and looked at Manda. "Well, maybe you can stay."

Manda looked like she was about to protest, but Jack stepped forward.

"It's probably for the best, Manda," he said. "You need to get used to your new legs."

Manda pouted and squeezed Ted into the crook of her right arm. She glowered at them.

"Egbert will look after you until we come back," said Cormier. He looked at her, as if he was about to say something else, then seemed to think better of it, then seemed to change his mind just as quickly. He started to stammer:

"Earlier . . . I said . . . when I said . . . and you cried . . . well . . . that—"

"The normal way to apologize to someone is to say sorry," said Estelle, with a raised eyebrow.

Cormier glared at her, then turned back to Manda. "Sorry," he said huskily, before stomping through the front door.

The others followed him outside. Cormier made it all the way down the steps before he stopped and stared wide-eyed at the remains of the gate.

"Who did that?"

Rob pointed straight at Gripper. Gripper looked panicked.

"You can fix it when we get back," Cormier said, and turned away, before turning back and squinting at Gripper. "I might use one of your arms to strengthen the new gate."

The engineer chuckled to himself, while a nervous-looking Gripper rubbed his right arm.

When they got outside the gate the truck was there, but so were dozens of other mechanicals. Cormier stopped in his tracks and looked nervously at them as they peeked out from behind walls and lampposts and trees. He made a great show of clearing his throat, as if their presence didn't bother him, and strode toward the truck with his head down and his arms swinging by his sides.

He tried to open the driver's door, but it was stuck. Jack stepped up to help him, and out of the side of his mouth Cormier growled, "Hurry."

Some of the mechanicals had stepped out of their hiding places.

Jack put his hand on the door, then seemed to reconsider. He took a step back.

"What are you doing?" hissed Cormier as he rattled the door handle.

Jack saw Sam Six Legs standing nearby. He looked unsure about what to do or say, and he was looking at Cormier with an expression of complete awe.

"You should say something," Jack whispered to Cormier.

"What? No," Cormier spluttered as he yanked at the door handle ever more desperately.

"You need to say something to them," said Jack, nodding toward the mechanicals, who were drawing closer. He fixed Cormier with a sly look. "Then I'll open the door."

Cormier clenched his fist. "Right. Fine." He stood back and placed his hands on his hips and tapped his foot on the ground. "Right. Well. Now then," he began, rolling his eyes in exasperation. "I, Philip Cormier, would just like to say that I shall return." He pointed a finger in the air with a grand flourish.

No one said anything.

Rob was leaning against the truck, looking up at him. "And when I do I'll fix everybody," he whispered.

Cormier looked stunned by the suggestion. Jack smirked.

"Fine. And when I return I shall fix everybody," Cormier

shouted. He turned quickly to Jack. "Come on then, let's be off," he muttered, putting his head down.

Jack opened the door and a grateful Cormier climbed in. Jack turned to wink at Sam and Sam smiled.

"Remember, Mr. Cormier, a promise is a promise," said Rob as the truck sputtered into life.

Cormier just looked straight ahead and growled.

Jack couldn't decide whether Cormier was a better driver than Absalom or, in fact, a lot worse. The difficulty lay in his style, which seemed both wildly erratic and insanely confident. He wrestled with the steering wheel like a man trying to grapple a bull to the ground by its horns. He took corners with a great sweeping motion that involved turning the wheel at the last possible moment, while accelerating at the same time. The whole experience wasn't helped by the fact that Round Rob kept squealing "Wheeeeeee!" every time they took a corner.

Jack and Estelle tried to get more information from Cormier as they sped toward London, but his eyes were fixed on the road ahead at all times, and the best they got in return was a series of grunts:

"So, he's one of yours, then," said Estelle.

Cormier gave a grunt that could have been construed as a "Yes."

"How did you lose him?" asked Jack.

Cormier gave another grunt that could have been construed as a "Mind your own business."

"You're not really telling us very much," said Estelle.

Another grunt—this time a very definite, "No, I'm not, because it is none of your business."

Estelle folded her arms and leaned back against her seat. "Charming," she said to Jack.

The rest of the two-hour journey was passed more or less

in silence, but it was hard to repress their excitement when they arrived in the great city. Round Rob, for one, had never seen a "proper" city before, and kept reminding everybody of the fact. He "oohed" and "aahed" as they made their way through the streets, and kept pointing out things to George, who chittered amiably in response while nestled under his chin. The incredible height of the buildings alone dazzled them.

There were more cars than they'd ever seen before. Rob and the others were used to the country roads, where they would normally pass a horse and cart and not see an actual car for hours at a time. London was different. London was filled with cars. Many were driven by mechanicals while their owners sat in the back seat reading papers, or in some cases having papers read to them by the latest super-intelligent Harrison V5 model.

Other mechanicals stood on street corners selling newspapers or running fruit stalls. Rob's darting eyes were moving so rapidly in an effort to take everything in that Jack feared they might fall out of his head. They all watched in amazement as a mechanical boy casually made his way across the frantic hustle and bustle of Piccadilly Circus with a dozen baskets balanced precariously on his back. The beeping of car horns didn't seem to bother him in the slightest.

They stopped outside an imposing building fronted with huge pillars. Cormier leapt out of the van and stood looking at the building's facade with his hands on his hips. The others got out and stood by his side.

Jack had never seen so many windows on the front of one building. They were jammed together over five floors, and the building itself took up half the street. People in suits bustled in and out of the large revolving doors that led into a reception area. Most of them were serious faced; the men wore dark, sober suits and the women tweed skirts and jackets, sensibly buttoned collars, and businesslike hats. Cormier squinted at the large sign that adorned the center of the building. It was off-white with large black letters in relief that simply said THE AGENCY.

He headed straight for one of the revolving doors; the others started to follow, and a great clanking behind him alerted Jack to the fact that Gripper had climbed out of the truck and was eagerly heading toward the building with them. He turned to Gripper and told him to stay in the truck. A disappointed Gripper ground his jaws.

"No," said Jack, "because you just can't. Besides, we won't be long."

Gripper clambered back into the truck petulantly.

Jack followed the others inside and found himself in the center of a great marble atrium. The floors gleamed and sparkled, wood paneling shone, and droves of people bustled through the great cool space, lending it an air of elegance and efficiency. Three men in macs and trilbies strode past toward the exit. As soon as Jack saw them he felt a jolt of panic. For a terrifying moment, he was back in Absalom's junkyard on that awful night. He could see Christopher being dragged away; there were flashes of blue lightning. He had to resist the urge to grab Estelle by the arm.

There was a large reception desk facing the main door. Cormier strode toward it purposefully. There was a young man in a pale gray suit sitting behind the desk, scribbling in a ledger. Cormier rapped the desk to get his attention. The young man's face shot up, and he attempted a friendly but professional smile. He managed to curl up one corner of his mouth before his smile vanished and his face blanched to a milky white.

"Hello," said Cormier.

"You're . . . you're not . . ." stuttered the young man.

"I am," said Cormier.

The young man looked back over his right shoulder. There were six portraits high up on the wall behind him. All of them were of men looking imperiously outward at the world. The first, of course, was a painting of Runcible. The third one from the left was Cormier—a much tidier, younger-looking Cormier, but Cormier all the same. He was standing sideways, holding his left lapel, his eyes blazing with his typical mixture of belligerence and defiance.

"How . . . how can I help you, sir?" asked the man, adding, "Mr. Cormier, sir," in a panic.

"Hibbert," was all Cormier said. He laid his hand on his left lapel and drew himself upright, mirroring his stance in the portrait.

"Hibbert," repeated the young man.

"Hibbert," said Cormier.

They sound like a pair of frogs, thought Jack.

"Mr. Hibbert?" the young man almost shrieked.

Cormier leaned forward and gave a low, threatening growl. "Mr. Hibbert."

The young man swallowed nervously and looked around the top of his desk in a dazed fashion, as if he'd misplaced something. Finally, he managed to pull himself together.

"He can't see you, sir."

Cormier glared at him.

"He can't see you," the young man yelped, between nervous licks of his lips. "Not without an appointment."

Cormier nodded toward his portrait. "Who's that up there?"

The young man turned in his chair to look back at the portrait. "That's you, sir."

"And I am?"

The young man swallowed again, as if something had gotten stuck in his throat. "You're Philip Cormier."

"Top floor, office number seven. Am I right?" said Cormier.

The young man nodded, his face still white.

"Good lad." Cormier smiled.

He turned on his heel and headed toward the elevator doors.

CHAPTER 19

The elevator doors were dark and baroque and covered in an ornate tracery of varnished briars and branches. Cormier pressed a brass button and the doors parted to reveal a small boy standing inside the elevator wearing a brown uniform and a bellboy's cap.

They entered the elevator, and the boy piped up:

"Where to, sir?"

"Top floor, please," said Cormier.

The boy pressed a button and the doors rolled shut. There was a pause, then a clacking sound, a quick jolt, a sensation of rising, and they were off.

There was silence in the elevator for a few moments. Cormier cleared his throat and tried to stare straight ahead, but something was nagging him. He looked at the boy, then looked away. Then, as if he couldn't fight it anymore, he looked at him again.

"Pilkington, eh?" he said.

"That's right, sir," said the boy.

"Mark Four. Am I right?" said Cormier.

"You are, sir. Mark Four and proud of it, sir."

There was another moment's silence, broken only by the sound of the elevator's cogs and pulleys. Cormier lowered his head and sighed. He reached inside his coat and took out a wrench, and knelt beside the boy.

"May I?"

"Of course, sir," said the boy.

Cormier took the boy's right arm and raised it. He gave it a quick up and down motion and grunted, "Knew it."

He unbuttoned the boy's jacket and took out his right arm and tightened a nut on his left shoulder. Throughout all of this the boy just looked straight ahead. When he seemed satisfied, Cormier told the boy to lift his arm up and down. The boy did as he was told, and Cormier took a small can from inside his jacket and oiled the boy's shoulder and elbow.

"Now," said Cormier. The boy lifted his arm up and down without looking at him.

"Spotted it as soon as I came in," muttered Cormier, looking at the floor. He seemed almost embarrassed. The boy simply blinked and looked vacantly straight ahead as Cormier buttoned his jacket back up.

The elevator shuddered to a halt, and the doors opened.

"Fifth floor," announced the boy.

They all stepped out of the elevator, and Cormier gave a quick sharp bow and thanked the boy. As they walked along the hallway, Rob leaned into Jack and whispered, "Did you see that boy's eyebrows? They were well proper."

A small girl in a pale-gray dress glided past them carrying a tray filled with envelopes. Rob watched her go. Jack had to turn him around and gently nudge him along the corridor. They hadn't gone far when Cormier took a swift right to face a wooden door. There was a gold plaque on the door with the name EDGAR HIBBERT, CHIEF COMMISSIONER.

Cormier hammered the door with the heel of his fist; then, without waiting for a reply, he stormed straight in.

They entered the room to find a man sitting behind a large desk in front of a window. The man looked to be in his fifties. He was small, gray, and balding. He wore spectacles and a dark-gray suit, and he blinked at them in utter astonishment.

There were three chairs positioned in front of the desk. Cormier strode to the middle one, pulled it out, flapped his coattails behind him, and sat down. Jack and Estelle decided to sit on either side of him. Rob stood at Cormier's right shoulder.

Cormier grinned at the man, whose mouth was open in shock. "Edgar," Cormier said.

"Philip."

"Edgar Hibbert," said Cormier with a chuckle, slapping his thighs. "Good old Edgar Hibbert."

"Good old Edgar," said Round Rob, and he and Cormier winked at each other and chuckled.

"What are you doing here?" Hibbert demanded. His cheeks had taken on a pink tinge, and he wriggled in his chair in an attempt to appear in control, but only succeeded in doing a very good impersonation of a man who'd just found something uncomfortable in his pants.

"I came to say hello to an old friend," said Cormier, giving a hard smile.

"Well now," Hibbert huffed, and cleared his throat.

"You have my Type A," said Cormier. He threw the framed photograph of Christopher and himself on the table in front of Hibbert. "I want him back."

Hibbert picked up the photograph. It showed Cormier and Christopher standing side by side in front of a shed. They were both smiling and squinting into the sun. The top half of the photo was faded, so that things appeared to be disappearing

147

into the flared whiteness behind them. Jack had marveled at the photo back at Cormier's, not just because Christopher was in it but because he was amazed by the fact that Cormier appeared to be happy. His hand was resting on Christopher's right shoulder, and Christopher too seemed just as happy.

Hibbert placed the photo gently back on the table. He pushed his spectacles farther up his nose with one finger, and then clasped his hands on the desk in front of him.

"I'm sorry, Philip, but you lost him."

"Ha!" barked Cormier. "You mean you took him."

Hibbert allowed the ghost of a smile at the corners of his lips. "No, I mean you lost him years ago."

"You sent agents—"

Hibbert lowered his head and shook it vigorously. "Philip—"

"He wasn't lost. Somebody found him, and you sent agents, and they took him."

"We've been through this, and as your friend—"

"You sent them, they took him, and I want him back."

Hibbert raised a hand and looked at his desk as he spoke to Cormier. "You lost him, and admittedly it was a tragedy, but it was a long time ago, Philip, and you have to remember that he contravened Article Four."

Cormier exploded. "Article Five was written into law after he was created!"

"Philip—"

Cormier was having none of it. He bellowed at Hibbert, while Hibbert gave as good as he got in his own calm but unyielding manner. Jack didn't know exactly what was going on, but "Article Five" was bandied about a lot, along with stuff about the "governing principles of Basic Propulsion" and talk about various rules and systems, and the importance of "the Natural Law of Mechanics." Cormier slammed the desk with his hand so hard that Jack wondered which would break first. He exchanged a glance with Estelle and her cheeks ballooned as she blew air out in exasperation and folded her arms. Jack had also had enough.

"Excuse me," he said. "Excuse me."

Hibbert turned to him and did a series of tiny rapid blinks, as if reminding himself that there was someone else in the room. Cormier was still ranting, but he gradually became aware that Hibbert was no longer focused on him.

"Excuse me, Mr. Hibbert," said Jack, "but our friend Christopher lived with us in Mr. Absalom's junkyard. He was taken by men from your agency."

Hibbert frowned. "Who are you?"

"This is Jack," said Round Rob, before Jack could even open his mouth. "He's my bestest friend after Christopher. That's Christopher in the photo there with Mr. Cormier. This is Estelle. She makes skin. She's not registered, but she's never been bothered by that because she knows how good she is. Her father taught her how to make skin, he used to hit her, but one day she hit him back and he never hit her again and she left home. Estelle tells me everything. Isn't that right, Estelle?"

All eyes turned to Estelle, who had lowered her head and was looking at the ground in an effort to hide her burning cheeks. Round Rob turned back to Hibbert. "We're looking for Christopher. Do you know where he is?"

Cormier looked away from Estelle and shifted uncomfortably in his chair.

Hibbert cleared his throat. "I'm afraid I don't," he said.

Cormier glared at him. Hibbert held his hands up in a gesture of placation.

149

"It's true, Philip. As far as we're concerned, your Type A was lost several years ago."

"Christopher," said Jack.

"I'm sorry?" said Hibbert.

"His name is Christopher," said Jack.

Hibbert looked from Cormier to Jack and back to Cormier again. "Really, Philip, if we're to talk we really need to do so with proper—"

"If you use the P word again, I swear I'll leap across that desk and rip your throat out with my bare hands," Cormier growled.

Hibbert touched his throat gingerly and swallowed.

"The man who took our friend was called Mortimer Reeves, Mr. Hibbert," said Jack.

Hibbert frowned. "I don't know anyone by that name."

"Check your files," said Cormier.

"I don't need to, I know all my agents by name."

"Dunlop, then," said Jack.

"Who?" asked Hibbert.

"Dunlop was the name of the other man who took Christopher," said Estelle.

Hibbert turned to Estelle. "We don't have anyone here by those names. There is a Megan Dunlop who works in Stamping and Registration."

"You're lying," said Cormier.

Hibbert snapped his head to the right, his cheeks became flushed, and he drew himself up in his seat. "Now look here," he said, jabbing the air with his index finger, "I won't take that from anyone. We've known each other a long time, Philip, and you know me to be an honorable man."

Cormier leaned back in his chair and shrugged.

Hibbert sat back and straightened the hem of his jacket. He

was jiggling about now in an angry fashion, and Jack could see that the comment from Cormier had really stung him.

"Simply outrageous," Hibbert spluttered.

Cormier regarded him coolly. "Who signs off on the acquisition of Type As?"

"That would be me," replied Hibbert, giving a condescending nod.

Cormier raised an eyebrow.

"If you're asking if I signed off on the acquisition of your model, then the answer would be no. I never signed off on a mission like that—now, or before he was lost."

"You could check your files," said Cormier.

"I assure you I don't need to. There has never been a mission that has required such an acquisition."

Cormier sighed and slouched down in his chair.

"I have to find him, Edgar."

"I understand," said Hibbert sympathetically. "Unfortunately for you, Philip, there is no way of tracing him."

There was silence for a moment, during which Cormier looked up and gave a slow, deliberate smile. Hibbert saw the smile and started to edge back almost imperceptibly in his chair.

"There is one way," Cormier said.

Hibbert's eyes widened and he shook his head. "No, Philip."

"You could help me."

"No, Philip."

"You have one, I know you do. You could let me use it."

Hibbert looked completely flustered now, and Jack could swear he saw tiny beads of sweat on his forehead.

"Article Five states—"

"Oh, Article Five can go hang," shouted Cormier.

"Article Five was sanctioned by His Majesty the King

himself," Hibbert squealed. He was trying his best to project an air of authority, but Jack exchanged a glance with Estelle. They could both detect the note of panic in his voice.

"It is forbidden—"

"You haven't admitted that you haven't got one," said Cormier with a grin.

"We . . . we haven't. You could use your own."

"Which you know I destroyed," said Cormier.

Hibbert swallowed and slapped his palm on the desk. His voice became quite high-pitched. "We haven't got one, and even if we had we wouldn't allow you to use it. It would be illegal and just downright improper."

"Haven't got what?" asked Jack.

Hibbert opened his mouth, but it was Cormier who spoke first:

"A Diviner. It's a special device used for—"

Hibbert suddenly bounced up in his chair, wagging his finger. "The secrets of Refined Propulsion are not to be—"

"Oh, do shut up, Edgar. You're beginning to bore me now."

"What's a Diviner?" asked Rob.

Cormier leaned back so Rob could hear him.

"Philip! Don't!" Hibbert screeched. He was now half standing, with his bottom hovering over his chair. Cormier looked askance at him, as if considering something for a moment; then he sighed and leaned across the desk toward Hibbert.

"Sit down, Edgar," he said.

A pink-cheeked Hibbert regarded him for a moment with round frightened eyes, then slowly began to sit back on his chair. His shoulders sagged, and he stared at his desk.

"What's a Diviner?" whispered Round Rob.

"I'm not supposed to tell you," whispered Cormier.

"Why not?" whispered Estelle.

"Because it's terribly secret," whispered Cormier.

"It's a device that can help track down a Type A mechanical," said an exasperated Hibbert. "Mr. Cormier created the first one"—Hibbert paused—"and he also destroyed it."

The chief commissioner gave Cormier a meaningful look. Jack tried to read it, but he couldn't interpret what was passing between the two men.

"Why destroy it?" asked Estelle.

"Because it's dangerous," said Cormier, his eyes fixed on Hibbert's.

"How?" asked Jack.

Both men just looked at each other.

"Why didn't you use it to find him the first time you lost him?" asked Estelle.

"I destroyed it before that," said Cormier.

Jack was perplexed. Nothing they were saying made any sense to him, and he could feel his frustration building at the lack of information being offered.

"It's only used for tracking, but it's dangerous?" he said. He shook his head at the apparent idiocy of it all.

"I often suspected the Agency had created a Diviner of its own," said Cormier, looking back at Hibbert. "The first time he went missing, I came to them to ask for it. But your predecessor, Mr. Locke, refused to give it to me and had me thrown out of the building."

"He couldn't give what he didn't have," said Hibbert quietly.

"And there you go, still denying you've always had it, while I know better." Cormier gave a bitter smile.

Hibbert couldn't look him in the eye.

"Locke was a very stubborn and implacable man. He was always about rules and regulations," said Cormier.

"As am I," said Hibbert, jutting his jaw out in a defiant manner.

Cormier looked at him for a moment and nodded. "Yes. Yes you are." He gave a little groan as he stood up. "Time to go."

"What?" said Jack and Estelle simultaneously.

"We've done all we can here," said Cormier.

They left the room, an oddly guilty-looking Hibbert watching them go.

CHAPTER 20

Cormier marched down the hallway and pressed the call button for the elevator. Jack didn't even have to look at Estelle—he could feel her simmering fury. There was a moment in Hibbert's office when Jack thought they might be getting closer to Christopher, but that moment was gone. Like Estelle, Jack was feeling more and more angry, but with the anger came a horrid slipping sensation, as if something was falling away from him. He tried to picture Christopher, but that only made the feeling worse.

The same boy greeted them when they stepped inside the elevator. Cormier bent down on one knee. "How goes the arm?"

The boy swung his arm and grinned. "Very good, sir. Thank you very much, sir."

Cormier smiled and seemed to be about to say something when two agents stepped into the elevator. The engineer stood up, but as he did so he took the boy's cap off his head and ruffled his hair. The boy leaned forward slightly and pressed the button for the ground floor. The two agents stood with

155

their hands clasped in front of them, staring grimly ahead. Cormier still had the hat in his left hand, while he idly tapped out a tattoo on the boy's head with his right. The boy didn't seem to mind, and the only sound in the elevator was the tinny tapping sound as Cormier's fingers danced across his metal skull. Jack was bemused by Cormier's suddenly carefree attitude, and he exchanged a glance with a still-furious-looking Estelle.

When they reached the ground floor, Cormier put the cap back on the boy's head. "Thank you very much, sir," said the boy.

"No, thank you," said Cormier, giving a tiny bow.

Jack could see one of the agents give a slight frown at this behavior, before he and his partner briskly made their way out through the foyer.

Cormier walked toward the exit with a smirk on his face. Estelle was glowering. Jack couldn't take the tension anymore.

"What do we do now?" he demanded.

Cormier looked at him and picked up speed. "We go back to the truck." In a moment, he was skipping down the steps outside.

"What about the Diviner?" Jack shouted after him.

Cormier spun around and put a finger to his lips. "Don't worry about that," he said.

"I *am* worried," said Jack. "Christopher isn't here, we don't know who took him, and that Diviner thing might be the only way to find him."

Cormier said nothing, but he had stopped near the bottom of the steps to squint up at the building.

"Do you believe him? Do you think they don't have it?" asked Estelle.

"Of course they have it," said Cormier.

"Then we need to get it," said Jack.

"Of course we do," said Cormier with a smile. "That's why we're coming back here tonight to steal it."

Try as he might, Jack couldn't see how they were going to get into the building. They'd spent the rest of the afternoon a short distance away, watching it from a nearby street corner.

People started to trickle out just before five. There was a general rush just after five, and by six the flow of people was back to a trickle. At about seven o'clock, Cormier rubbed his hands together and said, "This is it. Nearly ready."

Jack still couldn't see how they were going to break in, but Cormier simply laughed and tapped the side of his nose. Gripper offered to go straight through the front door, but Cormier told him it wouldn't be necessary. Round Rob came up with a plan that involved him scaling the building, jimmying open a window, and, once inside, creeping around its various corridors "stealthy as you like."

"How are you going to climb that, Rob?" Jack asked, gesturing at one of the pillars.

Rob told him not to worry.

"Where's the Diviner, Rob?"

Rob frowned and scratched his chin. "Let me think about that," he said.

Estelle, arms folded and head held high, looked insolently at Cormier. "So how *are* we getting in?"

"Easy," said Cormier. "We're going to use a variation on Gripper's tactic and go right through the front door."

They waited another hour until the street was dark and empty, and then Cormier ushered them out of hiding and started strolling nonchalantly toward the Agency building.

"What's he doing?" hissed Estelle, rolling her eyes in exasperation.

Cormier skipped up the steps and rapped on the glass of the revolving door. Jack tensed, preparing to run. He could see Estelle crouching in readiness too. They hadn't expected this, and he now reckoned that Cormier had simply lost his mind. Jack was about to tell Rob and Gripper to come away from the door before they were seen when something small and dark shuffled across the foyer.

It was the bellboy, and he was holding a large set of keys. Without even looking at them he inserted one of the keys in the lock and turned it.

Cormier breezed in, while the others stood gawping at him from the other side of the door.

"Well, come on, then," he said, waving them in.

They pushed through the door, Gripper having to bend down and step in sideways. Jack was last to enter, looking over his shoulder toward the empty street as the door revolved. Once on the other side he looked at Cormier.

"How did you . . . ?"

"Simple," said Cormier. He took the bellboy's cap off and started tapping his fingers on his head. "Morse code. All Pilkingtons have a built-in understanding of it." He grinned and jerked his thumb in the boy's direction. "I just said thank you."

"You're very welcome, sir," said the boy.

Cormier chuckled and placed the cap back on the boy's head.

"What's your name?"

"William, sir."

"Well then, William, can you show us where it is?"

"That I can, sir."

William led them toward a large oak door set within an arched alcove. He took his set of keys and deftly selected one, which he used to unlock the door. He flicked on a light switch.

Bulbs flickered to life, dimly lighting the way ahead. "Follow me," he said.

Inside the door was a set of stone steps that led downward into the bowels of the building. The steep steps were almost too small for Gripper's feet—he supported himself by clamping his claws against the walls in order to wedge himself in place, and moved as carefully as possible. Jack didn't like the idea of having two tons of metal behind him, but they'd already started their descent and it was too late to go back now.

Cormier whistled as he followed William, like a man out for a picnic on a sunny day, but Jack felt uncomfortable—the way down was too long, the passage too narrow, and they didn't know where they were going or what to expect when they got there. The whistling was only making things worse. Estelle must have felt the same. Her eyes were burning holes in Cormier's back as she descended.

Round Rob, however, was fascinated.

"Can you teach me to do that?" he whispered to Jack, while nodding at Cormier.

Jack squeezed his hand. "Yes, Rob. Once we've found Christopher and all of this is over."

Rob grinned. Jack didn't have the heart to tell him that he would need breath to be able to whistle.

They finally reached the end of the steps and found themselves in a long exhibition space with a high ceiling. The walls were covered with paintings, and the room was nearly full of statues and display cases. In a glass cabinet, Jack spotted what looked like innards of a large and very intricate clock, its brass wheels and cogs glowing even in the dim light. On a plinth opposite was a long-limbed skeletal structure made from steel.

"It's a museum," said Estelle, her voice filled with wonder.

Jack followed Cormier as he moved along the display cases lined up against the left-hand wall. The cases held a strange variety of objects—everything from leather-bound books, bits of parchment, cogs, and gaskets to bits of wiring and hands and limbs made from metal.

Cormier stopped in front of one display and rested his chin on his chest, lost in contemplation. The painting directly above the case depicted Joshua Runcible and the First. The picture was slightly different and a lot more vivid than the one they were used to from Absalom's shed, but Runcible was wearing his customary scarlet jacket and cloak, ruffled cravat and breeches that stopped at the knees. He looked noble and aloof.

Jack stared at the painting. He paid particularly close attention to the First. His nose was a stubby thing plonked in the middle of a round head. His hair was painted on, and two bulbous nodules on either side of his nose appeared to be painted to resemble eyes. He was dressed in clothes much like Runcible's. He had a carved, lopsided mouth that made it look as if he was about to speak.

Estelle stood beside Jack and gazed in wonder at the painting.

"They burned the First, Estelle. Imagine." Jack shivered, unable to take his eyes off what was contained within the display case. "I wonder—"

"Shhh!" Cormier hissed in the gloom. He was now standing at the end of the room with his ear placed against a large wooden double door.

"Is this it?" he asked William.

"I don't know, sir," William replied. "They don't tell us about this part of the building. Nor do I have a key for the door."

Cormier grinned. "Then this is it." He beckoned Gripper forward and smiled up at him. "Mr. Big, if you would be so kind."

Cormier stood aside. Gripper looked at the door, then looked at Cormier.

"Well, go on then," Cormier growled.

Gripper looked questioningly at Jack.

"Do it, Grip," Jack said.

Gripper stepped toward the door and pulled his right fist back. Jack could see the coils and wires in his shoulder contracting and tensing. It never ceased to amaze Jack that for all his shortcomings as an engineer, Absalom had somehow managed to make an efficient machine out of Gripper. Indeed, it made him wonder if Absalom had any part in his construction at all.

Gripper held his arm in position for a moment, and then suddenly it sped forward in a gray blur. It was like watching the unleashing of an elastic band that had been stretched too far. His fist punched through the wood of the door with an explosive crash, then he stepped forward and grabbed the edges of the splintered hole with his claws and wrenched it apart until all that was left of the door were jagged pieces of wood and warped hinges.

CHAPTER 21

Gripper cleared the debris as Cormier squinted into the gloom that lay beyond. Light from the exhibition room seeped in but only reached so far. "It's in here," he said. "It has to be."

They all stepped over the threshold and Cormier turned to William.

"Do you know anything about this room?" he asked.

William shook his head. "No, sir. It's out of bounds to mechanicals and all staff members below Grade Seven."

"And I take it Mr. Hibbert is the only Grade Seven in the building?"

"That's right, sir."

Cormier chuckled to himself.

"I don't see anything," said Jack.

"It's dark in here," said Estelle. "Surely there's a light."

"Like those two green ones?" said Rob.

A puzzled Jack didn't have enough time to ask him what he meant, because something sharp and silver sprang out of the blackness and whipped Rob clean off his feet and back out through the door.

The air was slashed with a high, drilling shriek as a towering, mantis-shaped machine with green eyes rose up before them. It started to flail its scythelike forelimbs at the intruders.

"Damn you, Hibbert!" roared Cormier, before he was dashed against a wall.

Jack saw the mantis bearing down on him and was tensing his limbs when something hit him in the side and sent him sprawling beyond the creature's reach. He looked up to see Estelle, who had pushed him out of harm's way, raise her arms to defend herself. The sharp point of one of the mantis's legs was buried in a floorboard, and it was twisting this way and that, its five other legs scrabbling and slipping madly behind it in an effort to free it. With a great heave that almost threw the creature onto its ridged back, the leg was free. It brought it down again, but this time it was William's turn to be selfless. He threw himself in front of Estelle and the point tore through his belly. There was a jagged screech, and William wobbled on his legs and fell to the ground.

"Gripper? Where's Gripper?" Jack screamed. Then he saw him on the periphery. His legs seemed frozen in place, and he looked on, his head moving back in forth in agitation, as if he was unsure about what to do.

"He's useless," a voice roared. Jack turned to see Cormier scrabbling toward him on the ground. "There's no point," he shouted at Jack. "We need a distraction."

Cormier put two fingers in his mouth and gave a piercing whistle that made the mantis turn its head toward him.

Another flash of silver. This time from the wreckage of the door they'd all entered. George sprang through the air. Cormier's right hand shot straight up to catch the tiny machine, and the engineer whispered fiercely: "Jump!"

He threw George at the mantis just as it scuttled toward

him. Jack thought he could almost see curiosity in the creature's eyes, along with something else. Yes, there was something else in the green—a sensation of a rolling, panicked motion, as if something in there was trying to escape, like a trapped animal.

Then the eyes were covered and the creature screamed as George dug his legs into its neck. The mantis writhed frantically. It shook its head violently, but the tenacious George hung in there, and there was a terrible rending sound as he dug his legs in deeper. The mantis started to scrabble and roll madly in every direction. Jack had to scramble out of its way and narrowly missed being impaled on the point of one of its legs.

With a violent whiplash motion, George was finally thrown from the creature's neck and landed a few feet away on his back, his legs scrabbling at the air.

The creature's long neck convulsed up and down as it screamed with rage. Jack was too frightened to move and he could see Gripper's cowering shape in the gloom. Up and down went the creature's head as it continued shrieking, advancing toward William, who was the nearest target but was being pulled out of harm's way by Estelle. Jack saw the creature rear backward. He saw the look of defiance in Estelle's eyes. Estelle threw what looked like a door hinge at the creature's head and it clanged off it, causing the monster to shake its head and shriek some more. *That won't be enough*, thought Jack. *It's going to move in for the kill.*

That was when Cormier stepped forward.

He was holding a plank of wood he'd fished from the wreckage of the door. He stepped in front of the creature and its head snapped toward him. It gave one great dipping motion, and for a terrifying moment Jack thought it would collide with Cormier and send him straight off his feet.

But it was Cormier who connected first.

He brought the plank of wood down on the creature's head, and while it was stunned he swung it across in a broadside that hit the creature clean on the left side of its skull. That was the defining blow. The metal at the base of the creature's neck, which had already been weakened by George's assault, tore with an awful grinding sound as its head flew across the room and smashed into a wall, before falling on the floor and see-sawing there for a few moments until it came to rest. The lights in the creature's eyes dimmed and faded. Its body spasmed and jerked, its feet thrashed in and out like those of a skater scrabbling for purchase on ice, and then it too crashed to the ground.

The only sound in the dark was Cormier's panting. He looked at the creature's neck, wires like shredded veins peeking out from where its head should have been.

"Shoddy workmanship," he gasped. He wiped a hand across his forehead and gave a short sharp yelping laugh, and in that moment Jack hated him.

Estelle must have felt the same. With her head lowered, and still trying to catch her breath, she looked at him as if she'd decided he was the next most likely candidate to be struck with the plank. An oblivious Cormier was too busy grinning and feeling self-congratulatory to notice.

Jack picked himself up. His first thought was for Rob, but someone else was already ahead of him on that score. George flipped himself back up on his legs and skipped and scuttled through the wreckage of the door. He arrived back seconds later, nestled under the jaw of a dazed-looking Rob.

"Rob, you're all right," said Jack, running toward him.

"Something hit me," said Rob, blinking frantically as if trying to readjust himself to the world around him.

"It was that," said Jack, pointing to the creature's motionless body.

Rob stepped toward its remains and gaped at it. "Where's its head?"

"Over there," said Estelle, wearily pointing to the wall where Gripper was still cowering.

Cormier was attempting to help William back to his feet. There was a long gash in the bellboy's torso. Cogs and sprockets and wires gleamed in the darkness of his chest, and there was a low grinding sound as he got to his feet, like a motor trying to start.

"I think I might need some repairs, sir," he said to Cormier.

"I'll see to it that you're as good as new," said Cormier. He ruffled William's hair, and just as quickly seemed to forget him as he turned toward the rear of the room. He moved farther into the darkness.

Jack went to William and helped him straighten himself up.

Estelle felt along one of the walls and found a light switch. The lights blazed into life, and with them came a loud "Aha!" from Cormier.

He was at the back of the room standing before a black plinth. There was something silver placed on it. Cormier held his cupped hands forward and gingerly picked the device up. He stood there for a moment, his back turned to them, his head bowed. Nobody said anything until Cormier himself uttered a low, victorious "Yes." He spun around and marched toward the door.

"Right then, off we go."

"Wait," said Jack. "Is that it?"

Cormier turned to look at him. He was cradling the Diviner in his hands as if it were a newborn baby. It was a silver pyramid about six inches tall. Apart from its glossy silver sheen there was nothing even remotely special-looking about it.

"Yes," said Cormier, "this is most certainly it." He stood in the doorway and looked at them. "Well, come on, then."

Nobody moved. Jack in particular was having difficulty trying to come to terms with what had just happened. His mind was spinning. The terror of the thing leaping out at them from the dark. The awful fear as he watched Round Rob being thrown from the room. Gripper seizing up, as if he couldn't handle what was happening.

"Well?" said an impatient Cormier.

"What happened to it?"

All eyes turned to Rob, who'd asked the question. He was standing over the monster's head, looking perturbed. He glanced from the head to the body and back again, confusion written all over his face. Then he nodded to himself as if he'd just realized something. He turned around in a waddling motion so he could get a good look at Cormier.

"You killed it," he said; his tone was almost conversational, but there was no mistaking the look of accusation in Rob's eyes.

Cormier looked at him, his eyes narrowing reflexively in confusion.

"Why?" said Rob.

Cormier shifted on his feet. He looked distinctly uncomfortable with the question. "Never mind the why. We need to get going."

Cormier stepped out of the room, but Rob waddled back around to look at the head. He still looked perturbed.

"Come on, Rob," said Jack.

Rob looked like he was about to say something else, but then he ambled out the door after Cormier. Estelle helped William, and they were making their way through the display section when she turned back toward Jack.

"Its eyes," she said. "Did you see its eyes?"

Jack nodded.

For a moment, Estelle looked troubled. She paused and then

shook her head, as if she wanted to say something else but had thought better of it. She turned and headed for the stairs. Jack held back for a moment and stood in front of the painting of Joshua Runcible and his wooden boy. He looked again at the display case and the plaque above it that read REMAINS OF THE FIRST, and his eyes turned to the blackened and charred pieces of wood it contained.

CHAPTER 22

The marionette sat on the edge of a table in the lab with its hands under its legs. It looked like it was paying close attention to Christopher in the chair, despite not having any eyes. In the absence of Jack and Rob and the others, it was the nearest thing he had to a friend in this forsaken place.

"He was a good man, you know," said Blake.

Christopher was surprised by Blake's conversational tone as he picked at another patch.

"What?" said Christopher.

"My father. He was a good man," said Blake. "You asked about him. The mannerly thing to do is to give you an answer."

There was a pause as Christopher wondered how to proceed.

"He had this country's interests at heart when he did what he did."

"What was that?" asked Christopher, trying his best to sound innocent.

Blake gave a quick disdainful laugh. "Don't pretend you don't know. The results of that particular experiment are public knowledge and have been for quite some time. It's why Refined Propulsion is outlawed and why we have Article Five."

Christopher remembered the story Absalom had told him and the others. There was always a certain sadistic relish in the way he told it, as if he was deriving some pleasure from the failure and suffering of others. Perhaps he embellished it all a little, Christopher didn't know for sure, but what Absalom told them sounded horrific. The display had been carried out in the Royal Horticultural Hall. "Hope was in the air. We were told we would win the war in a matter of days," Absalom had said. He'd told them the sense of nationwide anticipation was overpowering. Hundreds of people had gathered to see what the prime minister was calling "Britain's crowning glory." Of those hundreds, dozens were killed. Absalom always tried to deliver this part of the story with a suitable air of sorrow, but his genuine glee at someone else's failure was unmistakable. "And he was licensed," Absalom would say smugly. "Imagine that. Licensed. It goes to show you, licensed or unlicensed, it all means nothing. All that matters is how good an engineer you are."

"Is it true that it spat fire?" Christopher asked Blake.

Blake gave a little chuckle. "Yes. It's true."

"Did you ever see it?"

There was a slight pause before Blake gave a hesitant "No."

Christopher was about to say something else, but Blake spoke first.

"I saw sketches, and I saw some components."

"And what were they like?"

"Magnificent," said Blake, with a very obvious tone of pride in his voice.

"Is it true your father designed most of it?"

"Yes," said Blake, sounding very pleased. "My father said

it would be the war machine to end all wars. It and its brethren would stride across battlefields, and men would be like leaves in the wind in their wake."

He came around and fetched an instrument from the table to Christopher's right. He could see the light in Blake's eyes as he reflected back on his father's achievements.

"You must have been very proud of him," said Christopher.

Blake stopped what he was doing for a moment, as if remembering something. A muscle twitched in his left cheek. "Yes, very," he said quietly.

"Even afterward?" said Christopher.

Blake's voice hardened. "Especially afterward." He stepped back behind the chair.

Christopher considered what Blake had said for a moment. There was something else he needed to know.

"Is it true it had a soul?"

There was a tense pause before Blake said, "Yes."

He was obviously uncomfortable with this line of questioning, and Christopher felt he'd gained some kind of advantage. He decided to press it.

"Why would anyone want to ensoul a mechanical?"

"Well, you're an inquisitive sort," said Blake, trying his best to sound lighthearted, but Christopher could hear the hint of steel in his voice.

"I mean, what's so important about Refined Propul—"

Christopher didn't get to finish his sentence. There was a *plik* sound, and he felt a whooshing sensation in his head.

Blake looked at the patch he held between his tweezers and said jauntily: "A small one, that. A vague memory of a spring morning. Useless, really." He tossed it into a tray, where it came to rest among the growing pile of patches. "How are you feeling?"

"I'm not sure," said Christopher.

He was lying, of course. The work to trace his original memories had continued, and with each false memory that was removed, Christopher felt as if he was being hollowed out. He wasn't frightened by this feeling anymore. The sense of loss he'd felt at the diminishing of his memories was something that was so short-lived he was almost used to it—the way someone becomes used to the quick, sharp bite of a needle. If anything, he was oddly calm about the whole process, as if the stripping away of layers was allowing him to feel more like himself.

He was also afraid to reveal too much about his state of mind, particularly since his experience in his cell overnight.

He hadn't told Blake yet, but since some of the patches had been removed, he'd felt something else change inside him. During the night, he'd experienced strange episodes that gave him a blooming sensation, as if new knowledge was becoming his, and the world was opening up before him. The feeling was both terrifying and exhilarating. He'd had several of these episodes during the night, some with images and some without. Each one was like opening a long-forgotten and locked room in an empty house. Christopher found himself getting utterly lost in these strangely invigorating moments.

He was reluctant to tell Blake because he really didn't believe that the engineer's main focus was on finding out how Christopher had ended up in Absalom's hands. Christopher had spent enough time around Absalom to know when someone was lying, and he could tell that Blake had some other goal in mind. Christopher was certain of it, but for now he thought it best to play along with Blake's charade.

They continued sifting through Christopher's memories for the rest of the day. More false memories were lost. A birthday party for a boy called Tom back at the orphanage. A day trip to a beach somewhere filled with sunshine and wheeling gulls and the feeling of warm sand between his toes.

"What does warm sand between your toes feel like?" Blake asked after removing the patch.

"I don't know," said Christopher, the memory of it completely gone.

Blake was working with his usual serene focus. The only sound was the *scritch-scratching* of tweezers and needles and the soft click of patches. Christopher had a thought.

"Have you ever been to the beach?"

There was the slightest pause as Blake froze for just that moment. It was enough to make Christopher smile inwardly, because he knew he'd sensed something. A weakness, perhaps?

Blake cleared his throat and recommenced working.

"Once," he said.

"With your parents?" said Christopher.

There was a long *scritch scratch scritch scratch*. Christopher heard Blake take a breath in.

"With my father. My mother died when I was very young."

"I'm sorry to hear that," said Christopher.

Another brief pause. Blake started again.

"Why did he do what he did?" asked Christopher.

He tensed as he sensed movement from Blake. There was a clatter as his instruments were thrown onto the workbench. The engineer came around to face Christopher, wiping his hands on a towel.

"Do you have any idea how many men died in the Great War?"

Christopher shook his head. He'd heard Absalom talk about the war, but only to mention his heroic exploits, despite the fact that Estelle had told them that she knew for a fact that

Absalom had spent the war cleaning toilets in a hospital some-where in London.

"Millions died. *Millions*. And so many more could have been saved if we'd been able to end the war earlier, and we could have if we'd had war machines."

Blake leaned on Christopher's chair.

"Mechanicals created for the purpose of war would not have only saved lives but would have made this nation great again. But the government stopped their manufacture because of one simple accident."

"People died that day," said Christopher.

"And many more could have been saved if we'd continued on that path," said Blake, his face tightening with rage. "My father did what he did for Britain."

"And what are *you* doing?" Christopher asked. Blake straight-ened up and stared down at Christopher. Christopher held his gaze. "You must have loved him very much to be able to ignore the mistakes he made."

Blake said nothing. Instead, he turned on his heel and threw the laboratory door open.

"Mr. Dunlop!" Dunlop stepped into the lab. "We're finished for today," Blake said, walking back in Christopher's direction while avoiding his gaze.

Dunlop took Christopher out of the chair and shoved the marionette at his chest. He dragged him out by the elbow, but Christopher turned to look at Blake.

Blake's swagger was gone. He was leaning on a table with his head bowed, looking away, perhaps thinking about another time and another place.

Christopher knew what that felt like.

CHAPTER 23

Cormier was back to being his usual, grumbling self.

He'd initially been ecstatic after they'd obtained the Diviner, and eager to get back on the road. So much so that Jack noticed his impatience as he'd patched William up inside the museum. Jack could see the delicate flash of irritation in the engineer's eyes, and the sudden downturn of his smile whenever William or any of the others spoke.

The story they concocted for William was that he had been overpowered by masked thieves during the night. Jack didn't think Hibbert would believe a word of it, but having seen the way he and Cormier had interacted, he knew the chief commissioner would be the kind of man who would lay the blame squarely at Cormier's feet. William would be of no consequence to Hibbert. He thought about this as they locked William in a cupboard. William thanked Cormier again and said goodbye to the others, even as Cormier grunted a half-hearted farewell and shut the door on him.

Back in the van, Cormier ordered Jack to drive and barked directions as they rattled through the city streets, still busy despite the late hour. The engineer spent the whole journey glaring out through the windshield, grinding his jaw and occasionally muttering to himself. After an hour or so they were about ten miles outside the city, and Cormier told Jack to turn down a side road. A little way down the road they came across an old disused shed. Jack parked the van by the side. Cormier jumped out and opened the shed's large door. The building had a rusty corrugated iron roof, one corner of which looked as if a giant had tried to peel it off, like someone trying to rip the lid from a tin of beans. The stone walls were stained and weathered, and gnarled, rubbery grass grew around its edges.

Cormier pulled on a cord and a bulb wanly lit up the inside of the shed as the others filed in. The interior was a jumble of old wires and piping, with rusted bits of engines and farm machinery strewn around the floor. It was dank and smelly, and Jack couldn't help but think of Absalom's shed, which didn't help his mood and only amplified the awful sinking sensation he'd been feeling since they'd left the Agency. He'd thought he'd be pleased that they'd obtained something that would help them find Christopher, but there was a muted feeling among the group since the creature had been killed and Cormier had gotten his hands on the Diviner. It was as if a strange simmering rage had now infected all of them. Jack had the feeling that the journey was somehow spinning out of their control.

Cormier moved briskly through the shed as if he'd forgotten they were there. His shoulder brushed off a metal mannequin that was strung from the ceiling with chains. It swayed and rattled gently.

Jack stood beneath it and looked up at it. It looked like a puppet that had been forgotten by its puppet master. It had no features on its domed head, and one arm was raised and stretched behind its neck. The other hung limply by its side.

Jack could see the soles of its feet were lined by the brown of corrosion, and a honeycomb of holes peppered one rusty side where the rain had run down after seeping through the roof. It made gentle squawking, moaning sounds as it swung in the air.

Cormier glanced toward the door for a moment and caught sight of Jack looking at the hanging body. "An Empty," he grunted. "This is an old workshop of mine. Haven't used it in years." He walked toward a bench that lay at the back of the shed.

Rob came and stood by Jack's side and looked up at the body. He was uncharacteristically quiet. He hadn't said a word since they'd left the museum, and as he looked the Empty up and down, Jack could see a kind of helpless sadness in his eyes. Rob turned to look at Jack, and for some reason Rob looked older and wiser, as if the melancholy that had taken hold of him had added to his years. He looked as if he was waiting for some kind of an answer from Jack. Jack felt as if he should say something to him, but for the life of him he didn't know what.

"What do we do now?" asked Jack, turning so that he was facing Cormier. He'd deliberately raised his voice in an effort to give the impression that he was in control. But Jack didn't feel in control at all.

Cormier didn't reply. He was too busy, hunched over the bench with his back to them as he inspected the Diviner. Jack exchanged a glance with Estelle, who was standing with her arms by her sides, her thumbs working against her index fingers, her jaw clenching.

"What does it do?" she asked Cormier, her voice tinged with resentment.

"Never you mind," came the response from Cormier, who didn't even bother to look at her.

Estelle started toward him, but Jack placed a restraining hand on her arm and shook his head. He cleared his throat:

"We were just wondering, Mr. Cormier—"

"Blast this thing! Blast it for being the piece of rubbish it is. Only a prototype. How am I supposed to work with something this shoddy? This is unacceptable."

Cormier turned the Diviner over and over in his hands, as if looking for something on its surface. In the light from the bulb, the metal surface of the Diviner looked flimsy and delicate. Round Rob frowned and moved toward Cormier, his hands down by his sides, his steps slow and steady. George nuzzled into his neck.

"You think they could put together something even remotely workable? But no, oh no," Cormier muttered as he held the Diviner aloft and shook it, before placing it roughly on the bench and leaning on his fists. He sighed and lowered his head. Nobody said anything. Round Rob stood behind him, that frown still on his face.

"Mr. Cormier?" he said.

Cormier turned around at the sound of his voice. His face softened slightly when he saw Rob, but Rob was still frowning. "Why did you have to kill it, Mr. Cormier?"

Everything stopped. For Jack, it felt as if the room was noiseless now except for the tiniest hint of something like hissing sand filling an hourglass. Cormier straightened up and looked surprised.

"What?" he said.

Rob's voice was firmer now. "Why did you have to kill it, that thing back in the basement? Why did it have to die?"

Round Rob shook his head in disbelief as he pondered his own question. Cormier looked at Jack and the others, and then at the door, as if looking for a means of escape.

Rob kept his eyes fixed on him. "You wanted it dead, and you made it dead, and it's gone now, and you did that. Why?"

The hissing sound in Jack's ears had stopped. There was no

sound now, not even the clanking of chains from the Empty suspended from the ceiling. Cormier's face, which had gone deathly pale at Rob's question, was now beginning to turn pink again. His mouth opened, but he said nothing. He finally pursed his lips, turned back to the bench, and bowed his head as he pretended to examine the Diviner. Round Rob kept looking at him.

"I don't think he's going to tell you," Jack whispered, leaning into Rob.

Rob was still looking sternly at Cormier's back.

"Once I get it working, it will help me track your friend and find him," said Cormier suddenly, spinning around and waving the Diviner in his right hand. They were all looking at him now, even Gripper. Cormier's cranky demeanor seemed to have been eroded by a creeping sense of shame. Jack could see the uncertainty in his eyes, and maybe even the tiniest glimmer of guilt.

"It will take some time," Cormier said quietly.

"But we'll find him?" said Estelle.

Cormier nodded and started to turn back to the bench. He seemed to consider something for a moment, and he looked back at Rob.

"We do what we have to," he said quietly.

Rob frowned and considered this. He looked at the ground and then nodded and stepped back toward the others.

Cormier turned away, but not before Jack caught the briefest glimpse of something on his face. It looked like pure agony.

For some reason the mood seemed to lighten a little after that. Round Rob in particular didn't seem to be as perturbed, and he reverted back to his usual jolly self. Cormier was still gruff, but he was slightly more amiable as he worked through the night, especially with Rob. That said, Jack couldn't help feeling there was still a slight edge to the engineer's exchanges, as if he'd been found out in some way, and felt angry about it.

Jack sat outside the shed, where Estelle joined him.

Estelle toed a tuft of grass with her boot. "He's hiding something," she said. "You feel it too, don't you?"

Jack nodded. He'd been suspicious of Cormier from the start.

"This Diviner thing." Estelle shook her head and chuckled bitterly to herself. "He seems to have an awful lot invested in it."

Jack said nothing. Estelle continued kicking at the tuft of grass. "Have you thought about where we're going to go after we find Christopher?"

Jack felt slightly off balance for a moment. The truth was he hadn't thought that far ahead. "I don't know. We'll need somewhere to live, I suppose."

Estelle pursed her lips and nodded as she contemplated the toe of her boot.

"You don't think . . ." Jack began.

Estelle looked back toward the shed, where Cormier worked in the barely lit gloom. "That he'll let us stay with him?" She shook her head. "And what if he wants to keep Christopher? What then?"

"Well, who says Christopher will want to stay with him?" said Jack, a little too defensively.

"No one knows what's going to happen. I'm not sure we'll even find him," said Estelle dolefully.

Jack shot her a look. "Don't say that, Estelle. Don't ever say that. We will find him. I'm sure of it."

Estelle expelled air through her lips and sighed. "That's if that fancy Diviner thing of his works in the first place. Even if it does, I doubt whoever sent Reeves will just hand Christopher over." She stood up. "I'm going to see if I can get some sleep. Wake me up if anything happens. Although I doubt it will."

Estelle settled down in the cab of the truck with her coat on, and a blanket, which she'd found underneath the passenger seat, wrapped around her tightly.

It was just before dawn when she felt Jack's hand on her shoulder. He roused her gently, and Estelle heard her name whispered—coming to her as if wafting down through the soft black layers of a dream. She turned her head and rubbed her eyes and saw Jack standing with the cab door open, a strange light pulsing behind him. She stepped out of the truck and wondered where the brightness was coming from because the sun hadn't yet risen, and the light illuminating the gloom was bright and blue—a shimmering sapphire glow that bathed everything. She turned to her left, to where Round Rob and Gripper were both gaping at the shed.

Cormier was standing just outside the door. He was holding his hands in front of him, like someone cradling a skein of wool between their fingers. The Diviner was hovering in the air between his hands. It was an even brighter silver than Estelle had previously thought, and tiny blue threads of lightning were arcing across its surface and making the air around them shimmer and waver in a gentle corona of light. The Diviner was revolving with a smooth, almost hypnotic movement. Glyphs were moving across its surface, appearing and reappearing like ripples on water. They merged and coalesced, divided and flowed liquidly away from each other, then rejoined again, smooth and serene.

Round Rob's face was the very picture of wonder and delight as he gazed at the Diviner. He turned to Estelle and smiled. "Estelle, look."

Estelle couldn't help but look. Cormier weaved his hands in the air and the Diviner rotated gently, throwing off genteel sparks of light while moving in a still liquid silence of its own making.

"What's it doing?" she asked, almost afraid to speak too loudly for fear of breaking the spell.

"Seeking," said Cormier.

He turned toward her as the Diviner still hovered in the air.

And then Estelle saw the most surprising thing of all.

She saw Philip Cormier smile.

CHAPTER 24

Dunlop pushed Christopher into the laboratory. As soon as he saw the smile on Blake's face, Christopher felt a cold chill, and he knew he was in trouble.

Blake beckoned him forward. He was beaming.

"Good morning, and how are you today, young Christopher?"

Christopher looked at the chair. There was a long metal arm protruding from the back, at the end of which was a dome-shaped object made from a latticework of metal strips.

"Do you like it?" said Blake, framing the device with his hands the way a magician might present a magic contraption to an audience. "I haven't thought of a name for it yet, but that will come with time." There was a vicious glint in his eyes. "Would you like to try it?"

Christopher turned, but Dunlop grabbed him by the elbows and forced him toward the chair. Christopher had no choice but to sit in it, the marionette still clutched to his chest. He could feel himself gripped by the beginnings of a wild panic.

Blake looked down at him. "You see, the thing to remember,

Christopher, is that memories are layered. It's like sifting through the sand at the bottom of a seabed. Sometimes the sands shift this way and that with the tide, and it's difficult to sift the false memories from the real ones. But down deep, down at the bottom, that's where the genuine memories are." Blake chuckled and shook his head. "But then you'd know that, wouldn't you, since you've started remembering all of your own accord?"

Christopher looked straight ahead, trying to keep his face expressionless.

Blake leaned down toward him. "The memories leave traces, you see."

Blake stood behind the chair's headrest and lowered the dome-shaped cap onto Christopher's head. Christopher squirmed, but he was stilled when Blake laid a hand gently on his forearm.

"It's best if you don't struggle."

Dunlop watched in nervous curiosity, his brow furrowed so hard he looked even more apelike and more stupid than ever.

Christopher was about to ask what was happening when there was a bright chiming *plik* sound that seemed to resonate inside his skull. It was followed by a sudden bright light, and then the past came flooding in.

Christopher was so taken aback he didn't have time to be afraid.

"What do you see?" asked Blake.

There was only one word to describe what Christopher saw. Only one word in the world did it justice.

"Home."

"It's working." Blake sighed with relief.

Christopher saw a long, low whitewashed cottage bordered by bushes of a deep green so lush and glossy he could almost reach out and touch them.

"What can you see, Christopher?"

"I see a house. I see my house."

"Can you go into the house for me, Christopher? There's a good lad."

Christopher was dimly aware that Blake was working away at the patches on his head. He thought about resisting, but he knew there would be no point. The truth was he was also desperate to see what he could find. It was almost impossible to resist. The bloom was as vivid as life itself.

There was a rush of sounds, scents, and colors, and he was almost bowled over as if by a wave. He lurched sideways.

"Whoa," said Blake, catching him by the shoulders. "Easy now."

A dazed Christopher turned to look up at him. Blake was smiling. Christopher could see that it was a nervous smile, almost like a child's. Shy and hopeful.

Blake's face began to fade as Christopher delved deeper into the memory. He heard a snatch of music—someone singing, a woman's voice from very far away. And something else . . .

The fire.

Part of the cottage roof at the back and to his right had caved in due to the fire.

He felt the flames rather than saw them. The smoke was the thing that he saw more clearly. Yellowing gray and acrid and choking. He could feel it at the back of his throat—a hot, searing, almost salty sensation.

"What is it? What's wrong?" asked Blake.

Christopher twisted in the chair.

"Nothing, it's just . . . the fire," he said. His eyes started to water. He wiped his hand across them, and then, as suddenly as it had arrived, the vision was gone.

He felt Blake lay a comforting hand on his right shoulder. "Be careful, Christopher."

Christopher closed his eyes again and looked at the hole in the roof. It was edged by a maw of blackened rafters. They looked like the tips of rotted teeth. The floorboards at his feet were dusty and smeared with dark streaks. There were scorch marks on the walls.

"Do you remember what happened after the fire?"

Christopher shook his head. "No, just some of what happened before."

"So, what exactly do you rem—"

And just like that, Blake's voice was gone as the gray house around Christopher suddenly glowed with a light that was a mellow golden brown. He heard a voice coming from somewhere to his left. He turned and found himself in the kitchen.

His mother was kneading bread at the kitchen table. Clumps of dough clung to her fingers, and she smiled at him as he came in.

Christopher's father stepped into the kitchen from a door to his left, and Christopher felt his heart leap in his chest. He was wearing a soldier's uniform and he was wiping his hands on a cloth. Christopher could see the oil on his fingers, the flash of his brown eyes. His father smiled at him. Christopher, whose head had already been spinning with delight, now felt himself consumed utterly by a new wave of euphoria. It felt as if the world were buzzing around him. It felt as if everything was right.

It felt like coming home.

The glow started to fade as the room grayed over again. Christopher leaned against the table and felt the warp and weave of its timber. He marveled at the touch of it, and the sensations it brought back.

"What do you remember?" asked Blake, stirring him from his reverie.

Christopher turned toward him. "My parents. I remember my parents," he said. "Both of them."

Christopher beamed, and Blake smiled encouragingly.

"Do you remember anything else?"

"Bits and pieces," said Christopher, mulling over the images that were crowding through his mind.

"Does anything in particular stand out?"

Christopher shook his head, and then smiled again. "No, just all of it," he said, and retreated into his mind's eye.

The light in the kitchen changed again. The sky outside darkened. It was evening. Early evening possibly. The kitchen was lit by low candlelight and there was someone at the table. It was an older boy, possibly in his mid-teens. Christopher felt himself hide behind the frame of the door. He was looking at the boy, hoping not to be seen. The boy had dark hair and eyes, and even his clothes were dark. He was using a screwdriver on what looked like a piece of clockwork. There was something cowed and beaten-looking about him. Christopher could see it in the way he sat with his shoulders hunched, and the way he looked furtively at the door to his right.

That's right, Christopher thought to himself, *he'd come here with* . . .

The thought eluded him. It was as slippery as a fish.

And he'd come to see . . .

This one evaded him too.

"What do you see, Christopher?"

It was Blake's voice. Soft and far away.

Christopher looked at the boy. He stared at him for a long time. There was something important about this. If only he could remember. Christopher was gripped by a sudden overwhelming certainty that this was something that only he must know about.

"Nothing," he said. "I don't see anything. It's just the kitchen."

There was movement to the boy's right. A shadow in the doorway, and then suddenly a figure moved into the kitchen. Christopher couldn't see a face, but he got the impression of a very tall, well-built man. The man came and stood over the boy, and Christopher saw the fear in the boy's eyes as he looked up at this visitor.

The man raised an index finger, as if making a point about something. Then his fist came crashing onto the table. The boy flinched and cowered.

Christopher couldn't hear anything. For some reason, he saw this happen before him in silence. The boy's lips moved as he said something.

That was when the man swept his hand back and dashed the clockwork piece the boy had been working on out of his hands. It flew across the kitchen and smashed against a wall.

The man left the room.

The boy started to cry. He lowered his head, and his shoulders shook as he sobbed uncontrollably. Christopher felt his devastation and took an instinctive step toward him, and the boy's head came up.

Their eyes locked.

Christopher gasped.

"What is it, Christopher?" came Blake's voice.

Christopher and the boy continued to stare at each other. Christopher looked at the way his lank dark hair hung down over his forehead. He could see the pain and sadness in the boy's eyes and he could feel the pity well up inside him. But there was also a moment of recognition that passed between them. Christopher knew him. He felt a sudden surge of energy. They knew each other. The boy was . . .

"My mother. I just saw my mother again," Christopher lied. The boy started to melt and fade.

The room changed and became a bedroom. Christopher smiled. Locking eyes with the boy had given him a strange burst of adrenaline, but now he felt himself coming down from it. His heart was beating slower. His body felt heavier, but there was still that sensation of light euphoria, especially when he saw this room.

"My room," he said proudly.

"Anything of interest here?" Blake said. His voice was clear again, and there was a hint of impatience in it.

"I used to sleep in here," Christopher said wistfully. "Proper sleep, you know, like . . ."

For a moment, the visions he saw and the joy he felt were crowded out by questions. *Proper?* He wasn't proper. How had he managed to have a family? Why couldn't he remember everything that came before? Why not after?

As if reading his mind, Blake asked: "What else do you remember? What about after the fire? Tell me about that. Try and go back before it too."

Christopher concentrated. After a few moments he shook his head. "There's nothing," he said.

Blake suggested he explore the cottage further. Christopher didn't need to be told. He traveled from room to room like a feather borne on a gentle breeze.

Everywhere he went he was surprised by the new memories and sensations that offered themselves up to him. His and his parents' laughter as they tumbled in through the front door to escape a wet and windy day, leaves scudding around their feet. Sitting by the fire in the sitting room, his mother wiping his wet hair vigorously with a towel. A story told to him by candlelight. The smell of strawberries, warm and full and ripe on a hot summer's day. Sunlight, rain, wind, snow. The low moan of the wind settling around the eaves at night as he bundled his blanket up to his chin. Moonlight through his bedroom window. Knitting all these memories together was a feeling of safety, and of home.

And yet, with all these happy memories, the one that remained the sharpest was of that boy and his eyes.

"You're absolutely sure there's nothing else?" said Blake.

"No, nothing," Christopher lied again. He could see the garden now, and there was something else—as if something was just at the periphery of his vision. For a moment, the garden seemed to flare with evening light, turning from dusky gray to gold, and Christopher's eyes widened. He felt the hand again . . .

There was another *plik* sound and everything started to blend into a brown soupy consistency. Christopher instinctively tried to brush the brown fog away from his eyes.

"Just relax, Christopher," said Blake.

Christopher could tell by his tone that he was clenching his jaw.

"What are you—"

"Relax," said Blake. "Let the cap do its work. You just need to go deeper. I need to know more."

"More about what?" said Christopher. He was starting to panic now. Things were getting darker now rather than clearer. He could smell smoke, and somewhere he heard someone shouting his name.

"Christopher," Blake growled.

"I can't . . ." Christopher's eyes were stinging, and the smoke had wound its way insidiously down his throat. "I can't . . ."

"Listen to me, Christopher," Blake roared.

And the fire roared too, and crackled, and wood popped

and cracked as the flames took hold and Christopher couldn't see or breathe. He tried to scream, but nothing came out.

"Christopher!" came the cry, and it was two voices now, intertwined. One from the past, and Blake's in the present.

Christopher's hands went to the cap and he wrenched it off with all his might.

Blake gave an inarticulate roar, but Christopher didn't care. He flung himself from the chair and headed straight for the door. The marionette had fallen from his chest and was now picking itself off the ground. The cap was fizzing and sparking behind Christopher. In front of him was the great, hulking, stupid-looking Mr. Dunlop, whose piggy eyes were now blinking in incomprehension at the scene that played out before him.

"Grab him!" Blake snarled.

Dunlop nodded and lumbered toward Christopher. He grabbed him by the shoulders and turned him back around in the direction he'd come from.

Now Blake was bearing down on Christopher, his face twisted and red with fury.

"Why won't you help me?" he screamed.

Christopher was angry too. "I *am* helping you."

Blake raised his arms. His fists were balled, and he tried to compose himself.

"I need you to be truthful with me, Christopher. I need you to remember back to when you first woke. I need to know the circumstances."

"Circumstances?" Christopher's mind was a whirl. He had no idea what Blake was talking about.

"You must remember something. What was it like? Who was there? What glyphs might have been used? I'm looking for a mechanism . . . a means . . ." Blake squeezed his eyes shut and tapped his right fist against his forehead in frustration. "You have to tell me everything."

"I *have* told you everything!" Christopher protested.

"You're hiding it from me!" Blake shouted.

"I don't even know what you're looking for!" Christopher's response earned him a clip on the back of the head from Dunlop.

Blake's eyes widened. He was almost pleading with Christopher now.

"Do you have any idea how important this is? Do you? I need those memories. I want them all. We can't go forward without them. I need you to remember how you woke. I need to create . . ."

Blake stopped himself and ran his hand through his hair in frustration.

You need to create what? thought Christopher, biting his lip, knowing that to ask the question might risk more rage. Out of the corner of his eye he saw Dunlop's stun gun, in the same place he always put it. He felt the sudden urge to lick his lips, and he fought it.

Blake looked as if he was ready to explode. He looked around desperately, as if seeking something to take his rage out on.

And he found it.

The marionette was standing on a table. There was something gormless about the way it looked in their direction, even though it had no features. Blake ran toward it and, sensing it was in danger, the marionette tried to make its escape across the table.

But Blake was too fast. He scooped it up and wheeled around to face Christopher.

He was panting, and his face was scarlet. "Will you help me? Will you tell me everything I need to know and stop hiding things from me?"

Christopher looked at the marionette, squirming in Blake's fist, trying to squeeze its way out. He shook his head. "Don't, please . . . I've been trying . . . I've told you everything I know."

Blake smirked and headed toward the hydraulic press Christopher had noticed the first time he'd entered the lab. The marionette redoubled its efforts to escape. Christopher shouted, "NO!"

Blake pressed a button, and the press whirred into life. He pressed another button, and the hydraulic hammer came down with a *WHAM!*—so hard that it sent vibrations across the floor, up Christopher's legs, and right into his jaw.

Blake turned to look at him.

"Will you help me, Christopher?"

Christopher could feel the tears coming. *I won't cry*, he said to himself. *I won't.* He tried to turn his head away, but Dunlop grabbed him by the hair and forced him to look.

WHAM.

Christopher tried to look defiant.

"Will you help me, Christopher? I'm asking you nicely," said Blake.

WHAM.

Christopher tried to nod, but Dunlop held his hair so tight that it was hard to.

"What's that?" said Blake.

WHAM.

"Ye-yes," said Christopher.

WHAM.

Blake cupped a hand to his ear.

WHAM.

"I'll help you, yes! I'll tell you everything I know," said Christopher, the tears coming freely now.

Blake closed his eyes and breathed out with relief. He nodded in appreciation and lowered the marionette. "That's all I wanted to hear, Christopher. Thank you."

Then he turned and placed the marionette in the hydraulic press.

The hammer came down.

WHAM.

And again.

WHAM.

And again.

WHAM.

Christopher was on his knees. He tried to look up but found that he couldn't. By the time the press had finished its work there was barely anything left.

Blake walked toward Christopher with a fragment of metal in his hand. He hunkered down to his level and waggled it in front of Christopher's face. "I just want your help, that's all," he said reasonably.

Christopher looked at him, breathing hard. Blake just smiled back at him.

"You could lose a hand in there," chuckled Dunlop.

"Indeed one could," said Blake, without taking his eyes off Christopher. He tilted his head and tried to look sincere. "Will you help me, Christopher?"

Christopher nodded his head. Blake smiled and ruffled his hair. "There's a good boy." He took a moment to examine Christopher's face, his eyes filled with genuine awe. "Tears. I still can't quite believe it. What exquisite workmanship." Then he turned away and headed back toward the chair. He threw the piece of metal away and it landed somewhere with a clang. "Take him down, Mr. Dunlop. We'll let him rest up until tomorrow."

Dunlop dragged Christopher toward the door as Blake inspected the cap.

I'll help you all right, Mr. Blake, Christopher thought to himself. *I'll help you, don't you worry.*

His grief was forgotten for a moment, and as he was dragged back to his cell, his mind was a torrent of rage.

CHAPTER 25

They'd been driving most of the day and had decided to camp for the night in a forest. Cormier had acted as navigator as he was busy interpreting the light from the Diviner. Jack was driving. They'd kept to the back roads for fear agents from the Agency would be looking for them. The driving was sporadic and halting. They frequently had to stop for long periods while Cormier grumbled and hunched over the Diviner, moving his hands over it as if trying to align it like a compass. Despite the frustrating stop-start nature of their journey, all of them felt a mixture of fear and excitement.

It was decided the best thing to do to avoid detection was to hide in the forest. Jack had been keen to stress the word *camping* if only to reassure the likes of Rob, who he thought looked a little frightened. Rob's mood had immediately changed to one of delight. Jack smiled as he watched him scurrying about behind Gripper as they looked for firewood. Rob had never been camping before. Jack knew this because Rob had already told them all at least a dozen times.

As soon as the fire was blazing, Gripper took up a position

on the edge of their camp to keep watch. Rob stood in front of the fire rubbing his hands together and holding them toward the flames.

"What are you doing, Rob?" Estelle asked.

"Warming my hands," said Rob.

Estelle gave a small smile and winked at Jack. Jack smiled in response, then he went back to looking at Cormier, who was sitting opposite them with his back against a tree trunk. He was inspecting the Diviner and stroking it gently. It looked like he was whispering to it the way one might whisper to a cherished pet. The soft blue light was shining on his face. Cormier looked up briefly and caught Jack and Estelle looking at him.

"He's not far. Shouldn't be long," he said, and he went back to looking at the Diviner.

Jack watched Cormier, and he decided to ask the question that had been plaguing him ever since that night back at Absalom's yard:

"How does Christopher have a soul?"

The delight fizzed through Jack when he saw the look on Cormier's face. It felt as if he'd loosed an arrow and it had gone straight to its mark. He smiled to himself as a clearly shaken Cormier tried to adopt his typically gruff attitude.

"Never you mind," he said, pretending to look at the Diviner.

"It's a fair question," said Estelle, giving Cormier an insolent look.

Cormier glared at her. "The principles of mechanics are very complex. And besides, you only make skin. Explaining such matters to the likes of you would take too long."

"Try me," said Jack.

Cormier's head whipped around and he licked his lips. He had a hunted look about him, and Jack felt more of that deliciously victorious sense of rage.

"You?" he said, giving a nervous laugh. "You're too young to understand. I mean, look at you. When were you constructed? You're little more than a baby."

"I'm twelve," said Jack defiantly.

"Bits of you are," whispered Rob.

"Christopher remembered having parents," said Jack. "How can he have had parents if he's one of us?"

"Don't know," grunted Cormier. "Don't care. Why don't you ask your know-it-all friend there?"

Now it was Estelle's turn to blaze with fury.

"I know plenty," she said.

Cormier raised an eyebrow. "Do you now? An unregistered skin-maker, with probably only the most basic of skills. I bet you even have ambitions to become an engineer."

Estelle's cheeks flushed red.

"Aha! You do, then. Bless you. You know that girls are forbidden from becoming engineers and have been since Runcible handed down his edicts?"

"You sound like my dad. He was an idiot too," said Estelle.

"And what about your mother? Did foolishness run in the family?" Cormier grinned.

Estelle stood up with her fists by her side. "You take that back," she said.

Even Gripper turned at the tone in Estelle's voice. Rob forgot he was warming his hands and let them hang by his sides as he looked at Estelle. The only sound was the crackling of sticks in the fire.

Cormier shook his head and smirked at Estelle. "You're a very silly young lady."

"I said, take it back." Estelle was quivering now, and her eyes were dark.

Cormier had a half smile on his face, but it was the nervous smile of someone who knows they've overstepped the mark and is too stubborn to back down. He seemed to reconsider for a moment, and he looked down and flapped a hand at Estelle.

"Tell us about your mother."

Estelle swallowed hard, and she kept her fists clenched by her sides. "Why?"

Cormier looked up at her with a conciliatory expression on his face. "Just tell us."

Estelle looked around nervously. Jack could feel the tension in her, the anger, the uncertainty.

"My mum was the most important person in the world to me. She's the reason I make skin. She's the reason I'm as good as I am because she always said, *Estelle Wilkins, whatever you do you must always do your best.* So I do, to honor her."

"What happened to her?"

"She died."

"How?"

Estelle's head shook for a moment, and she grunted as if stifling something and turned her face away. She shook her head and looked out into the darkness.

Cormier nodded in sympathy.

Estelle turned back to glare at Cormier her steely composure reasserting itself for a moment.

"My mum taught me everything. She knew knowing your history was important. She told me how those who followed Runcible made people of copper and steel and how it changed everything. She told me about the first adult mechanicals and how they were banned because people were frightened of them. She told me how they made children then who could work in factories and go up chimneys, and when I left home I used to watch all the engineers, even rubbish ones like Absalom, and I learned. I did all this because she told me I had to find my place in the world, and I'd already decided that my place was going to be with mechanicals, and making them someday, illegally or not. I know all this because a person needs to find their place in the world." Estelle shrugged. "But then again, what do I really know? I *only* make skin."

Estelle sat down and clasped her knees up to her chin and glowered at the fire.

Jack had felt the surprising urge to run over and hug her, but he knew that would probably involve him getting a smack in the face, so he resisted it.

There was silence. Gripper shifted his weight slightly, still eyeing them all curiously. Rob raised his hands toward the fire again, but he kept looking from Cormier to Estelle and back again. Cormier said nothing and simply sat there running his fingers over the Diviner. His gruffness was gone, and his mouth was half open as he shaped silent words.

It was Estelle who spoke first.

"See, the thing is, you don't get to lord it over anybody and you don't get to understand anything until you've lost somebody." She looked at Cormier defiantly. "Who have you lost, Mr. Cormier?"

Cormier gave a sad half smile, and he continued stroking the Diviner. When he spoke his voice sounded cracked and broken: "I've lost everyone."

He stood up and cleared his throat. He cradled the Diviner and held it to his chest and walked off into the forest.

Rob looked from him to Estelle and back again rapidly. He was as gobsmacked as the others. Nobody else said anything until Cormier had disappeared from view.

It was Rob who broke the stunned silence:

"You made him cry, Estelle."

CHAPTER 26

Broken was how Christopher felt. Broken and alone.

When he was brought back to the lab in the morning, he'd only been able to sit slumped forward in the chair. He never looked up from the concrete grayness of the floor, and the constant pain that hummed in his head and limbs never left him. He wanted to cry, but it felt as if the grief and pain were just lodged in his throat. The cold gray pain grew and grew and consumed him.

Until the anger returned.

Blake was still tinkering away with patches, all pretense of civility gone as he pushed Christopher's head this way and that. Blake never spoke to him, but he spoke to Reeves, who was occasionally present during this new session.

Blake referred to Christopher as "it" now, saying, "It would reveal its secrets soon" while he spoke about something he called "deep excavation," which he said would help him uncover Christopher's memories. It would take a little longer than he'd expected, he said, but the outcome would be "splendid."

Christopher kept himself in check and looked at the ground, feeling the dark vortex of anger whirl within him. The more Blake spoke about him as if he weren't there, the faster the vortex of fury within him spun.

His anger gave him strength and hope. He had made his decision. He was going to escape, and there was nothing they would be able to do to stop him.

The next couple of days brought the same thing. Dunlop escorting him to the lab. Blake working on the patches, questioning Christopher incessantly about his first moments of consciousness. Was there any special machinery present? Did Christopher remember any special symbols or glyphs? The same questions were asked over and over, with Christopher giving evasive answers as he waited for his opportunity to escape.

It came at the most unexpected moment.

Blake was tinkering with the cap when the new bloom hit Christopher with the force of a tidal wave. It was so strong he almost threw himself forward off the chair. He gulped deep as he tried to catch his breath.

The laboratory disappeared, and he was in the kitchen of his home again, and the boy was there. He watched him as his eyes roved hungrily over the small piece of machinery in his hands. This time Christopher saw the light in his eyes, the simple joy of someone working on something he loves. Christopher smiled at the boy, and the boy looked up and returned his smile.

It felt strange this time. Christopher wasn't just an observer. It felt as if he'd traveled back to this moment and was visiting with the boy.

"Hello," he said.

"Hello," said the boy.

He was a little older than Christopher, but something about the boy—the way he carried himself, the way he spoke and smiled—made him seem younger somehow.

"What are you doing?" Christopher asked.

The boy held up the piece of clockwork for Christopher to see. It was an intricate piece filled with dozens of cogs and wheels.

"I'm making a machine," said the boy. "I like making machines. Machines make the world a better place. That's what my dad always says." He seemed very proud of his creation. "Would you like to see?" he said, handing the piece to Christopher.

"Yes," said Christopher. He reached his hand out, but as he was about to touch the contraption his vision wavered, and the world started to shimmer, then darken . . .

Christopher was back by the door now, observing the boy. It was the same scene he'd witnessed before, when Blake had placed the cap on his head. This time he could hear sounds. It was gloomy in the kitchen, and rain was sizzling down outside.

The boy looked toward the door as before. The man entered and stood in front of him. The boy was clearly terrified. The man bellowed at the boy:

"What have I told you before about playing with toys?"

The boy mumbled something to the man, and that was when the man slapped the piece of clockwork machinery from the boy's hand.

"They're secrets for a reason, boy!"

Christopher could feel his chest and throat tighten. It was as if all the air had been sucked out of him. He gave a strangled gasp, and he sat forward in the chair.

He was back in the laboratory, and Blake was fussing around him.

A wide-eyed Christopher looked at him. He was still stunned by his realization, but examining Blake's face now he couldn't believe how he'd missed the evidence of his first bloom. He had the same dark eyes as the boy, and the hair might have been more tightly cut, but there was no mistaking the fact that Blake and the boy in his vision were one and the same person.

He blinked rapidly and found he had to bite back his words. And then, as if by pure instinct alone, Christopher let his eyes glaze over and looked around as if dazed.

A strange sense of inner calm descended upon him as he took in his surroundings, realizing that this was his moment. Why else would he have had that particular vision? He felt the inexplicable urge to laugh, but he fought that too. Instead, he said:

"I can see . . . I can see . . ."

Blake was in front of him now. "What is it, Christopher? What do you see?"

Christopher narrowed his eyes, as if concentrating on something that no one else could see.

"It's something important . . . I know it is . . ." he said woozily.

Blake was wringing his hands expectantly. "Go on, Christopher. Tell me what you see."

Christopher waved him away with his hand and signaled that he needed to get off the chair. Blake helped him down. Christopher looked around like someone seeing his surroundings for the first time, but really he had already taken in what he needed to know.

Dunlop was leaning against a table and eating his sandwich. Blake had become so engrossed in his work that he'd forgotten to ask him to take his lunch outside. Dunlop had briefly cast an eye over what was happening and then returned to gobbling his sandwich.

Christopher started to wheel around, as if he was lost in one of his visions and was seeing things no one else could. Blake was following a few feet away from him, entranced, and almost too terrified to interrupt him lest he lose some valuable insight. And all the time Christopher was moving circuitously toward Dunlop.

That was the other thing about Dunlop. As well as his stupidity, and his inability to realize that there was anything else going on in the world besides his sandwich, there was also his predictability.

It was this predictability that meant he came in at the same time every day, put his coat in the same place, and scratched his backside and his chin before settling himself against the same table for the morning.

And it was the very same predictability that meant he left certain items in the exact same place every day.

Christopher reeled backward, then made a great show of doubling over, as if in agony.

"I can see it! I can see it!" he roared.

"See what, Christopher?" Blake cried.

"I can see . . ."

Christopher straightened up and twirled around. He'd judged it just right. Dunlop was still munching his sandwich a few feet away and staring into it as if it had some great secret to impart. Christopher was by the table and he saw exactly what he needed. He took his opportunity.

He leapt for the stun gun and grabbed it.

"NO!" Blake roared.

Christopher had just enough time to flick the switch as Dunlop bore down on him. He still had his sandwich in his right hand, and its contents—lettuce, tomato, chicken—flew through the air as Christopher plunged the stun gun up and into his breastbone.

Dunlop stiffened with his arms down by his side, shuddering like a child trying to contain a tantrum, his eyes bulging in disbelief and pain. Then he started to flop forward. Christopher could suddenly feel the weight of him press down on the tip of the stun gun, and he had just enough time to whip it around to point it at Blake before Dunlop hit the ground with a great big wet slap and spasmed for a few moments before becoming still.

"Christopher!" Blake shouted, his hand clawed and outstretched.

"Don't come any closer," said Christopher. He shoved the stun gun forward, and pressed the button for good measure. Blue sparks crackled along its tip, and Blake took a step back with the palms of his hands raised.

"Christopher, listen to me," he said quietly.

Christopher shook his head and gave a nervous bark of laughter. "No, you listen to me."

"Christopher, I'm warn—"

"'They're secrets for a reason, boy!'" Christopher roared.

The effect of those words couldn't have been any more dramatic than Christopher actually using the stun gun on Blake. The engineer looked as if he'd been slapped in the face. His mouth opened and his eyes widened in terror. It was real terror that Christopher saw, and he gained some delicious satisfaction from it.

"I know you. I saw you in my house. I know who you are, Richard Blake. I spoke to you. You made clockwork toys. I've known you since you were a child. You told me you wanted to be like your father."

Blake shook his head in disbelief. Christopher looked in his eyes, and he saw the same pain and incomprehension that he'd seen in those same eyes all those years ago.

"You and your father came to my house. Why?" Christopher demanded.

"Christopher . . . I . . . Christopher, please . . ." Blake inched forward.

"Don't!" Christopher snarled.

He looked at Blake and saw the pleading expression on his face, and for a split second he again felt pity.

Blake must have seen it on his face, because his own expression hardened, and he took the opportunity to lunge forward.

Christopher sidestepped his flailing arms and thrust the stun gun upward just underneath Blake's chin. It made contact, and there was a *FRRZAAK* as Blake's eyes rolled in his head and he collapsed onto the ground inches from Dunlop.

Dunlop was moaning and trying to get up. This time Christopher shoved the stun gun into his throat. Cords sprang out on Dunlop's neck and it was as if all the flesh on his body was tightening to one single point. Inside his head, Christopher roared *That's for Jack!* and he gave a bellow of exultation. As soon as Dunlop went limp again, Christopher bent down and took the key chain from his belt. His hands were trembling and he dropped the keys twice. He stood up and took some breaths to steady himself, then he took one last look at Blake, contorted on the floor in a fetal position, before he made a run for it and exited the lab.

It seemed to take forever to get to the first door, and with each step he took he expected Reeves to jump out and grab him. He was holding his breath the whole way and when he reached the door he had to unlock it while holding the stun gun between his knees, his hands trembling all the while. The key jittered in the lock, and the door opened with a squeal that made his eyes water. He stepped through to the other side and tried to close the door as slowly and quietly as possible, but it still groaned in protest. With that door locked he headed down the corridor toward the outer door.

The corridor was cold and seemed somehow larger and more threatening than when he'd first walked its length. He could scarcely believe it when he reached the outer door, and he fumbled in a panic at the key chain when he realized he couldn't remember which key he needed. He tried one that was too large, and the second he picked was the same one he'd already used on the inner door. He cursed himself and then took a deep breath. *Calm*, he said to himself, *calm*.

He picked another key. He put it in the lock.

It turned.

Christopher wrenched the door open and sunlight flooded in. He felt as if his legs would only do a shuffling motion to get him outside, as if they were afraid to respond to the most basic commands. He walked a few feet into the courtyard and felt the sun on his face. He couldn't help himself giving a nervous giggle as he turned toward the gate.

But Reeves stepped in front of him, blocking his way.

Christopher felt as if someone had thrown a bucket of ice water over him. He stumbled back, fumbled for something, and realized with shock that he'd dropped the stun gun on the other side of the door.

Reeves smiled. "Well, well, aren't we the clever one."

Christopher looked toward the gate. He leapt forward, but Reeves grabbed him by the lapels of his jacket.

"Oh no you don't!"

He'd already grabbed the keys and bunched them in his fist. For one terrifying moment, Christopher thought Reeves was going to hit him, but instead he pushed Christopher back toward the door. The henchman's grip loosened while he fumbled with the lock. Christopher twisted left, then right, and suddenly he was free once more.

He ran toward the gate, but Reeves lunged, snagging Christopher's arm. It was enough to knock him off balance, and there was a clang as his head hit the ground. He blinked, raising his head, vaguely aware of Reeves towering over him. He glimpsed movement behind him and felt icy coldness in his guts as Blake stumbled through the outer door.

"Mr. Reeves!" he shouted. "Leave him."

Reeves lifted Christopher by his shoulder, and Blake almost sent his henchman flying as he pushed forward and grabbed Christopher by the lapels and started screaming in his face. What shocked Christopher most of all was the fact that Blake was crying.

"You don't know! You don't even know! You're the key to everything, it all comes down to you."

Blake looked ashamed, and he twisted his head left and right as if he was unable to look Christopher in the face. Finally, with a huge effort, he turned to him and snarled.

"Nothing is going to stop me now. The project is too near completion. Do you hear me? Nothing will stop me!"

Christopher was aware of the tiniest pause, as if the whole world were holding its breath, as if everything in creation but them had suddenly realized something was about to happen.

There was a great concussive rumble. It was a sound like thunder.

All eyes turned toward the main gate, which was still vibrating from the impact of something hitting it on the other side.

And then the whole gate exploded in a storm of shards and wood splinters, and Gripper lunged into the yard.

"Grip!" Christopher shouted.

Gripper beat his chest with one fist and gave a victorious roar.

A tall bearded figure in a long leather coat stepped in through what remained of the gate. He stood with his hands on his hips, taking in the destruction Gripper had caused. Then finally the stranger spoke:

"I've come for my grandson."

CHAPTER 27

"What did he say?" asked Rob.

Jack, Estelle, and Rob had just stepped through the shattered entrance to take up positions beside Cormier.

"*I've come for my grandson*," said Estelle, her voice sounding dreamlike and far away. She turned to look at Jack, her face white, and the incomprehension in her eyes was so complete it looked like she'd never blink again.

"Mr. Cormier has a grandson?" said Rob.

"Yes, Rob . . . that's . . . yes," Jack stuttered, completely at a loss for words. His mind was whirling. Did Cormier mean . . . ? But how could that be? Christopher was a mechanical. Admittedly he was a very high-grade mechanical, but he still wasn't proper. Maybe it was a pet name Cormier had for him. Maybe . . .

His next instinct was to run, to run faster than he'd ever run before, because he could see Christopher across the courtyard.

"Christopher!" he shouted, and made to rush forward.

It was Cormier who stopped him. His arm was around his

neck in seconds, and Jack's heels skidded on the ground as he tried to wrestle himself free, feeling idiotic as his world slipped beneath him and he found himself looking up at the sky.

"Let me go!" he roared. "It's Christopher!"

"I know!" Cormier bellowed in response, and he looked both angry and frightened. That was when Jack realized something was wrong. Jack turned to see a man mirroring Cormier, with his arm around Christopher's neck.

Before Cormier had made his demand, Blake had seized Christopher and was pointing the stun gun directly at Christopher's neck.

"One step forward, go on, take it," said Blake.

Jack felt a sudden pulse of rage, and it took all his reserves of willpower to fight the urge to leap out of Cormier's grasp.

Estelle advanced forward.

"Ah ah," said Blake, waving his index finger at her and smiling.

Estelle clenched her jaw, but she took a step back.

"Let him go, Richard," said Cormier.

"It's good to see you too, Philip. How have you been? I've been very well, thank you. I thought you'd shuffled off to Iron-haven to die, but happily you seem to be very much alive. So, what have you been up to recently? Go on. Tell me everything."

Blake fixed Cormier with a crazed grin. Cormier looked at him and took in a deep breath as he raised himself up to his full height.

"I thought you were dead too, Richard. Wait, no, hold on, let me go back and substitute the word *hoped* for *thought* in my previous sentence."

Blake's smile wavered ever so slightly. Jack could see the sudden flash of anger in his eyes. He looked surprisingly hurt by Cormier's statement. Blake spoke, but it seemed difficult for him, as if his teeth were too bared and some animal part had taken control of him. Jack couldn't help but picture a cornered dog with its hackles raised.

"Isn't it marvelous that the two most celebrated engineers of the age—the amazing Cormier and the ingenious Richard Blake—can have a reunion like this? The greatest and the second greatest."

"I presume I'm the former while you're the latter," said Cormier.

Blake gave an almost hysterical bark of laughter. "Oh, Philip, dear dear Philip. What a droll man you are. Droll and old and completely irrelevant."

"I feel a speech coming on," sighed Cormier.

"Don't stop yourself on my account," said Blake.

"After you," said Cormier.

"Stop it! Stop it, both of you," shouted Estelle. She took a step toward Blake. "Let my friend go," she snarled.

Blake looked coolly at her, then his eyes flicked back to Cormier.

"She's quite feisty, isn't she? Not one of yours, I take it. Slightly more fragile than your creations too, I'd say. She needs to step carefully."

A bedraggled and stunned-looking Dunlop stumbled out of the Crag. When Blake saw his henchman, he grinned.

"Well now, the odds, which were poor for you to begin with, Philip, are getting even poorer."

Cormier simply stared Blake down. "Let him go," he said quietly.

"Or what, Philip? You'll set your ragtag troupe of mechanicals on me?" Blake shook his head. "We both know that's not going to happen, don't we?"

Cormier had loosened his grip on Jack now. There was a moment when he seemed to tense, then Cormier's arm simply sagged, and Jack heard him give a low sigh.

"What did you think was going to happen when you came in here?" said Blake. "Did you think I'd just hand him over and that would be that?"

Blake took the stun gun away from Christopher's neck but kept his left hand on the boy's shoulder, like a kindly uncle posing for a picture with a favored nephew. He casually waved the stun gun in the air.

"I'm about to change the world, Philip, and you don't even know it yet."

"Whatever it is you're doing, I'll stop you," said Cormier.

Blake chuckled. "You won't." He turned toward his henchmen. "Mr. Dunlop," he shouted. He threw the stun gun in the air, and a now fully recovered Dunlop caught it without taking his eyes off Cormier and the others. Blake pushed Christopher toward Dunlop, who gripped him by his collar. Jack felt the urge to race forward again, but he could see the murderous look in Dunlop's eyes, and he willed himself to stand still.

Blake reached inside his jacket pocket and took out a small silver box that had a tiny lever sticking out of its surface, along with some gray buttons and switches. He held it out by a limp wrist for all to see.

"I haven't decided what to call this yet. It's quite a clever invention, even if I do say so myself. But enough of my prattling. Let's get down to it, shall we?"

Blake smiled and pressed a button. Immediately there was a great whirring that sounded like thousands of spinning gears. The whirring cycled upward and upward to an angry roar. The courtyard became filled with the sound. Blake gave Cormier a great, vulgar grin.

"Behold, Philip, my greatest achievement, and the instrument of Britain's transformation."

The weather-beaten gray tarpaulin in the center of the

courtyard started to bulge in places. Christopher had assumed, when he was led past it by Reeves when they'd first arrived, that it was simply covering scrap metal and junk, but now it was rising as the roaring grew louder. Rob covered his ears and Jack looked toward Cormier, as if he might give him some comfort, but for some reason Cormier's head had dipped. He looked old now, old and weak, like a man resigned to some terrible fate.

The tarpaulin started to tent in two places. At least half a dozen pegs, which were holding ropes in place, started to ooze slowly out of where they'd been spiked into the ground. Blake was still smiling, and Reeves had an insane gleam in his eyes and was starting to giggle.

"What is it?" asked Jack fearfully.

Blake heard him even over the noise. "The future!" he shouted.

The air was suddenly rent with the ear-shredding shriek of a buzz saw. Threads on the tarpaulin started to pop explosively, and a long tear was ripped in it by a serrated blade that was whirring around with a dizzying speed as it appeared through the wound. The tarpaulin's threads exploded, and the whole shroud convulsed as the first figure emerged.

It stood at least two feet taller than Gripper, and its body was barbed with vicious-looking spikes. It shone a brilliant silver, and its dead black eyes gazed emotionlessly at its audience. It snapped its clawed right hand, and the blade that it had used to cut through the tarpaulin snicked back into a recess near its wrist. Blake flicked a switch and the metal creature slammed its fists together with such force that they raised sparks. Another, almost identical, figure had also emerged from under the tarpaulin, and it took up a position beside its companion. It too clanked its claws together, and the pair towered above everyone and everything in the courtyard.

For a moment, nobody said anything. The great whirring noise had died down, and now there was just a low, tension-filled hum. Blake raised a hand toward his creations, like a particularly pleased ringmaster at a circus.

"I call them Berserkers. Aren't they wonderful?" He waved the small silver box in his hand. "I control them with this. A crude device. It's a temporary measure that allows me to bypass some of their standard limitations." He gave Cormier a meaningful look.

"What is this?" said Cormier, his voice torn and husky.

"This is how we change the world, Philip. This is how we make things better."

On the word *we*, Cormier flashed Blake a look, his face contorted into a snarl. "You can do what you like with your tin-pot toys, but I'm not leaving without my grandson."

He took a step toward Christopher. Blake flicked a switch, and the first Berserker advanced toward Cormier and brought its fist down on the ground in front of him. The force of the blow was almost enough to throw Cormier off his feet. The second Berserker lumbered forward and took up position behind the first.

Jack watched the Berserkers moving toward Cormier. He looked at Christopher, with Dunlop's arm jammed around his neck, and a fury from deep within took hold of him. He looked at Estelle. She nodded.

They both ran toward Christopher. Jack was vaguely aware of Rob shouting his name. Gripper had also launched himself forward, and Jack could hear him clanking behind him. For a moment, he didn't feel any fear. For one deliriously optimistic moment Jack thought that they would rescue their friend, just as they'd planned.

When it came, the clawed hand simply scooped him up and sent him hurtling through the air. He had a glimpse of Estelle half running, half contorting herself as she tried to avoid a similar blow. She sidestepped enough to avoid the full force of the giant hand, but the effort involved meant she lost her balance, and she fell heavily. Jack tried to call her name, but the world was tumbling over and over, and he hit the ground with such force that he bounced before finally coming to rest in the dirt. He heard a great metallic *CLANG*, and somehow he managed to twist himself around and raise himself up with his hands. That clanging sound chilled him to the core. He scanned the courtyard. Cormier was standing with Rob beside him. Estelle was lying on her side, her face smeared with muck, her eyes blinking with shock and horror. Cormier was standing with his arms hanging by his sides, his chin almost on his chest. Dunlop had decided to loosen his grip on Christopher, who had stumbled forward to gape at the stricken figure in front of him. Jack saw Christopher's mouth form one word:

"Grip?"

Gripper was down on one knee, trying to raise himself up. The first blow from the Berserker had almost sheared off the left side of his jaw. Wobbling there on one knee, one arm raised, he looked like he was pleading for mercy.

But Grip wouldn't do that, Jack thought, *because Grip is brave and Grip is strong and Grip—*

He didn't know which was louder, the splintering punch that the second Berserker dealt to Gripper's head or the howl of anguish Christopher gave when he saw the punch connect. Gripper wheeled backward and tried to right himself by flailing his arms, but fell on his back. He lay still for a moment, then raised himself up on his right elbow. One of the Berserkers grabbed his head with a clawed hand and started to drag him up. The other Berserker tilted its head and watched. When its companion had raised Gripper into a semi-standing position, it drew back a clenched claw and punched Gripper with such force that its fist came out the other side of his torso. The shriek of torn gears and twisted metal filled the courtyard, along with Christopher's screams. Jack heard another sound too. Someone pleading "Stop." It was moments later before he realized it was his own voice.

"Fight back, Gripper. Fight back!" he screamed.

The first Berserker had a hand resting almost tenderly by Gripper's shoulder blades, as if trying to help him up. The second one gripped Gripper's right arm. The first one grabbed his left. They pulled.

There was a sudden shrieking and a shower of blue sparks as Gripper's right arm was torn out of its socket. The left one was hanging by some wires. Gripper, who had been silent up till now, gave something like a groan before collapsing face-down in the dust. The second Berserker looked at the arm in its claw, then tossed it into a mound of scrap.

Jack tried to get up, but it seemed as if all his strength had left him, and the world flared to a vividness that hurt his eyes. He saw Round Rob gawping at the scene. Christopher was scream-ing and trying to get to Gripper, but Dunlop was pulling him back. Estelle was crying.

Gripper was trying to crawl away, but his arm was useless and his legs only propelled him so far. It was like trying to watch a fish survive on dry land. Jack saw the grin on Blake's face as he pressed a button and turned the lever on his pad. He saw the first Berserker reach for a metal spike from the scrap that seeped out from under the tarpaulin. He gave a pleading "No." It was more a moan of preemptive grief than a plea for mercy.

The Berserker walked slowly toward Gripper and stood over him. It raised the spike up with both hands, then brought it down with all its might. There was a sound of metal being shorn, and torn, and split. The bitter tang of sparks filled the air. Round Rob took tiny tottering steps forward, then two steps to his left, then his legs went out from under him and he fell to the ground.

There was no other sound in the courtyard now, apart from Estelle's sobs and Christopher moaning the word "No" over and over again. Jack turned back just in time to see the Berserker twist the metal spike one way, then the other, before finally pulling it from the ruin of Gripper's head.

CHAPTER 28

The cell was dark and hot with the stink of fear and defeat.

Cormier sat slouched in a corner, his knees pulled up toward his chin, his head down. Estelle sat on the wire-mesh base of an old metal bed. She leaned her head back against the wall, her mud-splattered face streaked with the pale tracks her tears had made. One hand was clasped to her hip, which she'd bruised when she'd fallen. Her eyes stared up through the ceiling.

Jack was on his knees by the door. It seemed to be the only thing he could do, the only thing that was right and proper in their current circumstances. He wondered if Estelle had the right idea, that maybe staring blindly through walls and ceilings might be best—because the only thing Jack could see, no matter how hard he tried, was Gripper's face. He looked at the floor, he looked at the walls, he looked up at the bars on the window, but it was useless. Gripper's face was everywhere. Gripper's eyes were everywhere, and whenever he saw them he saw the light bleed out of them.

"Jack?"

The sound of Rob's voice was gentle in the dark. Jack looked up to see Rob looking down at him with a look of concern on his face.

"Yes, Rob?"

"Is there something wrong with your legs?"

Jack tried to smile. "No, Rob. My legs are fine."

But his legs weren't fine. No part of him was. If he was proper it would have felt as if his limbs were on fire, as if every part of him ached. As it was he found that he just couldn't move. Like all the others, he hadn't struggled when Blake and his men had dragged them into the prison. There was nothing they could do then. There was nothing they could do now.

Nothing.

"When are we escaping?" said Rob.

Jack raised his head and looked up at him. Rob was looking down at him with a slight frown. His right eyebrow was hanging off.

"Rob, I don't . . ."

"It'll be soon, won't it?" He turned to look up at the barred window. "Maybe if we could cut those bars, and I could squeeze out the window." He looked down and frowned again, then he turned back to Jack. "Gripper's gone, isn't he? He's not coming back."

Jack was momentarily stunned by Rob's matter-of-factness. "Yes, Rob," he said huskily.

Rob frowned again and nodded. "Just like Proper Edward. He won't be coming back either, I know that now. But when somebody goes away the best way of keeping them alive is to remember them. Christopher told me that after Proper Edward went." Rob leaned closer and dropped his voice to a whisper. "Me and Manda planted a flower for him at the back of the shed. Estelle helped us." Rob nodded curtly in a "there you go" fashion, and straightened up proudly. "You should always remember your friends when they're gone. And the best way to remember Gripper is to rescue Christopher and for all of us to be together again."

Rob turned and waddled over to Estelle. He took her right hand in his and pulled gently. "Come on, Estelle. Let's get out of here."

But Estelle didn't move. The only thing she could manage was to turn to Rob and give him a blank look. Rob huffed and folded his arms. He started to tap his foot. He looked at the barred window. "I could climb up there, I could climb up there and try to squeeze through."

"Rob," sighed Jack.

"I could," said Rob.

Nobody said anything. Rob looked around him and finally sat down on the floor and hung his head. "I could," he said quietly. The silence went on for a moment, and then Rob, as if forgetting his momentary funk, said brightly: "How is Christopher your grandson?"

Cormier said nothing. He moved slightly, as if retreating away from what little light there was in the cell.

"Leave him, Rob," said Jack. "There's no point."

"It doesn't make any sense," said Rob.

"Nothing does anymore," said Estelle.

Rob snapped his head in her direction. He shuffled over to her on his knees and reached out and took her hand again.

"We'll get out of here, Estelle. You'll see," he said earnestly.

This time Estelle looked down at him and gave him a trembling smile. Rob returned it with a big grin, and for now that was enough.

In the morning, as a pallid gray light filtered through the cell window, Dunlop arrived to escort the group to the lab. Here they found Blake sitting in a chair, nonchalantly twirling a long wrench. Reeves was standing by the door, looking the very picture of smug obedience with his hands clasped in front of him.

"Welcome, welcome, one and all," said Blake, springing up from his chair.

Christopher was sitting in a dentist's chair. For the first time since their imprisonment, Jack saw Cormier react. He took an instinctive step forward but was stopped by Dunlop's firm hand on his chest.

"Don't worry, Philip, he's quite all right," said a smarmy Blake.

Christopher didn't look all right to Jack. There was pain in his eyes as he looked at his friends.

"No, he doesn't remember you, Philip," said Blake, shaking his head and sighing in mock sorrow.

"Let him go," said Cormier.

Blake smiled and reached inside his jacket. He took out the Diviner and held it aloft.

"When I heard your grandson had been found, I knew that if I took him I would have one small piece of the puzzle. I thought I could delve into his memories and extract the information I required. But this"—Blake stroked the Diviner—"this is so much more. Thanks to this I have the necessary mechanism for Refined Propulsion. All I need to know now is how to use it . . ."

"I'll be damned if I'm going to help you," Cormier spat.

Blake hoisted himself up onto a steel table, swinging his legs like a child. He looked around and took in the whole room.

"I'll tell you what, how about a little history lesson? Would everyone like that? Good good," he said, without waiting for an answer.

"Let us consider this, shall we? We have Philip Cormier, a

great man, a superlative engineer who has discovered a new and more efficient means of animating mechanicals: Refined Propulsion. Meanwhile, war rages across Europe. As a nation we are suffering heavy losses, so our government decides to call upon Cormier's services, and those of his friend Charles Blake."

At the mention of his father's name Blake looked at Cormier and they locked eyes. Blake smiled bitterly.

"My father and Mr. Cormier worked on a prototype for a war machine that would've ended the war and saved the lives of thousands. Unfortunately, due to errors on the part of Mr. Cormier here, many people were killed at the first demonstration, including my father, and the scheme was abandoned." Blake's nostrils flared, and the look he gave Cormier was one of pure icy hatred.

Cormier didn't flinch. His tone was calm.

"The errors that led to that tragedy were all of your father's own making."

Blake shook his head. His lips were thin and white with fury.

"Your father was a great engineer," Cormier continued, "but he was ruthless and calculating, and he would have risked anything to lay claim to greatness. You of all people should know that."

Blake sprang off the table and covered the distance between himself and Cormier in seconds. He had the wrench in his hand and he raised it up toward Cormier's face.

"My father was a good man," he said, trembling all over.

Jack exchanged a worried glance with Estelle.

Cormier looked coolly into Blake's eyes.

"If you hit me with that now, Richard, then you're no better than he was."

Blake drew the wrench back. Cormier gently closed his eyes

and nodded. Jack was stunned to see tears brimming in the younger engineer's eyes. The hand gripping the wrench shook violently.

Suddenly Blake threw the wrench across the room. He wiped his eyes and stood in the center of the lab, one hand on his hip, his right foot tapping agitatedly on the floor. His eyes fell on Rob. He clicked his fingers and signaled for Rob to step forward.

Rob duly obliged and waddled forward, looking up guilelessly at Blake. Once again, Jack felt that awful premonition that something awful would happen. He tensed.

"You, my fat friend, how do you go? Tell me," said Blake.

"By Basic Propulsion," said a frowning Rob.

Blake looked down at him and gave him a warm smile. He even ruffled Rob's hair. Rob continued to look up at him as Blake lifted Rob's hair slightly and traced the glyphs on his skull.

"What were you before this, my little friend?"

Rob looked perplexed for a moment, and then answered, "Nothing."

"Not entirely true," said Blake, wagging a finger. "First you were the basic raw material. Then that material was given the form of a rudimentary. Then through craft and the manipulation of magical glyphs and the bringing of light you were given life. You became a standard example of the animation of the basic system."

Rob thought about this for a moment, then said, "Thank you."

Blake gestured toward Christopher. "Then of course we have the animation of the refined system. An altogether more complex and difficult process that requires a special type of genius. Am I right, Philip?"

Cormier refused to look at him. He caught Christopher's eye for a brief moment, with a look of guilt and shame, before looking away again.

Blake seemed pleased with himself. He rocked back and

forth on his heels. "The refined system has so many special advantages."

Blake clicked his fingers again, and this time he beckoned Reeves toward him, while keeping his eyes on his audience.

"If you would be so kind, Mr. Reeves."

"Certainly, sir," said Reeves, moving smartly toward his appointed position. Blake stood behind Reeves, grasped his shoulders, and moved him into place. Reeves smiled, and Blake patted him on the shoulder and walked away. Reeves continued smiling, but there was a brief flicker of uncertainty in his eyes.

Without saying a word and without turning around, Blake tossed the stun gun toward Jack. Jack caught it without thinking and looked at it in revulsion as he gripped it between his fingers.

Blake half turned toward Jack and raised an eyebrow. "Well, go on then."

"What?" said Jack, confused.

"He has been a cruel and callous man. His treatment of your good friend has gone beyond the bounds of what is acceptable. Stun him. Stun him and I shall let you and your friends go. You have my word on that. My solemn promise. You will all go free."

Blake gave them all a magnanimous look.

Jack looked at Blake as if he'd lost his mind. He looked at Christopher, hunched over in the chair. He looked at Cormier, whose head was bowed, and he looked at Estelle, whose eyes were sparkling with an eager and angry light.

"My word, my bond as an engineer." Blake nodded toward a very nervous-looking Reeves. "Hurt him. He deserves it. He deserves everything he gets."

Jack gripped the stun gun. There was something horrid about holding it, as if he were holding something malignant and alive that was pulsing like an eel. He looked at Reeves, who eyed him with a strange half smile of disbelief. Jack stepped toward him and Reeves recoiled slightly.

Jack stood in front of Reeves, who licked his lips nervously. Jack looked at him in horror, not because he felt disgust for him, but because he felt a strange disgust for himself. He looked at the stun gun again, and it felt as if the whole room were throbbing around him, sending a dark vibration through his skull. He tried to move the arm that held the stun gun but found that he couldn't. It was as if his arm had become leaden and dead. He turned to Blake, whose eyes glittered with a feral joy. Jack was aware that everyone else was looking at him now and his own voice sounded tinny and far away, even to himself.

"I can't," he said.

The clang he heard was the stun gun hitting the ground. It had slipped from his fingers without him even noticing. Blake was wheeling around and clapping his hands with delight.

"You see? You see! The one great flaw in the machine. The defining weakness of the basic animated mechanical: the complete inability to do harm." Blake scanned all their faces. He was grinning, and a sheen of sweat was forming on his forehead. "And the solution? Why, to make something more than machine."

He turned toward Christopher. That was the moment Estelle lunged for the stun gun. She scooped it off the floor and hurtled toward Blake without breaking stride. Dunlop was too slow to react, and it was Reeves who threw himself between Blake and Estelle before she could reach his master.

Estelle roared in anger. She plunged the stun gun at Reeves, burying it in his midriff. Reeves doubled over, his whole body constricting as he readied himself for the inevitable explosion of sparks.

CHAPTER 29

Nothing happened.

Estelle's eyes widened and she thrust the stun gun forward again. Reeves flinched, but only slightly, and a sly grin started to form on his face. Dunlop rushed Estelle and disarmed her with ease. She struggled and kicked as he pinned her arms behind her. Blake bent down and picked up the stun gun.

"Of all the things in British engineering history, surely the safety switch is the greatest invention of all," said Blake. He gestured toward Estelle. "Unlike a mechanical, violence is part of her nature, as it is with all humankind. And yet what is that essential element that separates us from the beings of metal? What is it that makes us capable of the most heinous acts, while they find themselves confined and constricted by petty notions of morality and civility?" Blake flashed a full-toothed smile, but his eyes were dark and filled with malice. "It must be the one thing we possess that they do not. It must be our very souls."

Blake turned ever so slowly, and all eyes followed him as he looked at Christopher. Christopher raised his head up now, and he looked at Blake with unmistakable hatred. Blake made a grand sweeping gesture in his direction and turned to his audience.

"Witness it, then. Witness the product of Refined Propulsion. The hate of one who has been ensouled."

Christopher's eyes widened in astonishment. "Who am I?" he screamed.

"You're my grandson," said Cormier, glancing up with a look of agonized guilt.

"I don't remember . . ." said Christopher. He couldn't finish speaking as his body became wracked with sobs.

Blake twirled the stun gun in the air, caught it, and twirled it again. "Mr. Reeves."

"Yes, sir?" said Reeves, who was making a *yuk yuk* sound of pleasure as all of this unfolded.

Blake pointed the stun gun at a spot on the floor just in front of him. "If you would be so kind."

Reeves frowned but did as he was told and stepped in front of Blake. Blake smiled.

Then he swung the stun gun and smashed it into the side of Reeves's face.

Everybody in the room except Cormier recoiled. Reeves fell instantly and went down on one knee, one hand clutching the side of his face, the other clawing blindly at the air. He didn't have time to make a sound.

"I thought I might continue the demonstration," said Blake airily to the room.

He swung the stun gun again. This time Reeves was flung on his side. There was an audible clang and Jack was the first one to see the flesh hanging from Reeves's face, and the shining chrome beneath his cheek.

"Oh no, Mr. Reeves, it would seem that you contravene a specific legal article. How terrible. How is it phrased again?"

Blake tilted his head to one side and began to recite: "'It is for-bidden to confer life and sentience upon any raw material that conforms to the standard agreed dimensions of an adult or "proper" human being.'"

Reeves twisted on the floor, attempting to right himself while he tried to press the skin back onto his cheek with the trembling fingers of one hand.

"But then again," said Blake, "I am one of the great engi-neers of the age, and it is the prerogative of genius to do as one pleases. Isn't that right, Mr. Reeves?" Blake brought the stun gun down on Reeves's head. Jack winced at the clang. "I said, isn't that right, Mr. Reeves? Why don't you defend yourself?"

Blake hit him again. "What's wrong with you? Why don't you fight back?"

Blake brought the stun gun down and across the back of Reeves's head. There was another smashing, clanging noise, and this one was followed by the groan and judder of small gears as Reeves's arms and legs spasmed in and out.

"And there we have it. Not only is the standard basic system unable to initiate aggression, it is also powerless to defend against it." Blake threw the stun gun aside. He walked over to Christopher and laid a kindly hand on his shoulder. Christopher recoiled, but Blake didn't seem to notice his reac-tion; instead, he searched Christopher's eyes and smiled at him.

"What do you want, Richard?" asked Cormier.

Blake turned around.

"I want to finish what my father started. I want to give him his rightful legacy. I want to take back what was once ours and to defend this nation against the barbaric hordes that would do it harm. Do you know how many men lost their lives in the last war? Do you know how many we could have saved if our government had had the simple courage to permit the use of Refined engines?"

"It won't work," said Cormier, shaking his head in disgust.

Blake strode toward Cormier with purpose, his voice cracking with emotion.

"War is coming, Philip, and we need to be ready. Don't you see? While our prime minister twiddles his thumbs and spouts lies about maybe someday repealing Article Five, our enemies are gathering their forces."

Cormier fixed Blake with a look of absolute fury. "It's wrong, and it's dangerous, Richard, and you know it. I won't tell you how to use the Diviner."

Blake took a step back and looked flabbergasted. He gestured back toward Christopher. "Look at him, Philip. Look at him. Was it wrong to rescue your own grandson's soul from the void and place it inside this metal shell?"

Cormier tried to look at Christopher, but again the look of shame passed over his face.

"That was different," he said, his voice almost a whisper.

Blake shook his head. "No, Philip, it was a miracle and this is the age of miracles. It's time to embrace that fact." Blake stared at Cormier for a few moments. His voice was gentle when he spoke again. "I know why you helped my father. I know you lost your son in the Great War. Think of how many more could be saved if we act now and finish what you and my father started. You're going to show me how the ensouling mechanism works."

Blake looked dispassionately at Reeves, who had managed to get himself onto his knees by clutching the side of a table. "If you don't cooperate, I'll see to it that your grandson dies a second time."

The look he gave Cormier was chilling. Jack could see the

grief and rage on Cormier's face. He was trapped with nowhere to turn and he knew it.

Blake stuck his chest out. "I intend to march on London with my new army. Both our pathetic government and our weak monarch will bend the knee. Then and only then can we make this nation great again. No one will be able to withstand us, and you're going to help me."

Jack had thought he couldn't have possibly felt any worse, but the episode in the lab had taught him otherwise. When they were all herded back into the cell, Cormier lay on one of the bunks in a fetal position and turned to the wall. Jack should have been angry, but instead he felt sick and lost. He could see Estelle's eyes burning into Cormier's back as she sat across from him.

"Tell us," she said. "You have to tell us."

"I don't have to tell you anything," came the muffled reply from Cormier.

Estelle leapt off her bunk, her fists clenched with fury. "You have to. He may be your grandson, but he's our friend, and you owe it to us."

Cormier turned slowly and half propped himself up on his left elbow. He looked at Estelle for a moment and seemed to consider his options. Eventually he sighed, and began:

"There was a fire. It happened a long time ago, after I lost my son in the war. His wife and my grandson . . ."

Cormier squeezed his eyes shut as if trying to block out the pain.

There was no pity in Estelle's gaze, and she pressed Cormier even more. "How did you ensoul him?"

Cormier looked even more pained. "There was a rumor, a story that had been passed down through Runcible's time, that it might be possible to ensoul a machine. I initially created the Diviner to see if I could improve mechanical systems—Charles Blake was part of that effort. He and his son, Richard, visited my workshop regularly, and we spent many months working through the possibilities before I discovered the solution. But after Christopher . . . after Christopher . . ." Cormier was struggling now. He clenched his fists and closed his eyes. "I just wanted to see him again. He was everything to me, and I'd already lost so much." Cormier looked at them all now with tears welling in his eyes. "I was . . . I was . . ."

"Broken," said Round Rob matter-of-factly.

Cormier looked at him.

"So you decided to fix yourself," said Rob brightly.

Cormier gave him a wan smile and continued. "The Diviner became a means of bridging the gap between our world and the afterlife. There are lines, you see, fractures in the world that souls can be brought through. I found one of these cracks and I brought my grandson back."

"And did he know?" asked Jack.

Cormier nodded. "Yes."

"But now he's forgotten," said Estelle.

"I'd gone to Ironhaven after the war machine experiment— Charles had pressured me into it, and after the disastrous result, I was sick of my own kind. I could only bear to be around Christopher. Hibbert knew he existed, but he let us be. I used to fix mechanicals. They came from all around, discarded and deserted and broken." Cormier shook his head and chuckled bitterly. "Imagine that. They came to me." He swallowed and straightened up. "Christopher used to help me and always insisted that we could do more, but I refused to let him work on his own. Always he kept at me; we could do more, he kept saying."

Cormier lowered his head and closed his eyes.

"One night he sneaked out. He just wanted to help others. I presume scavengers snatched him. A group of them had already been to the town and stolen some fuel and parts. They must have had an accident with the fuel, because there was an explosion on the road. Egbert and I found them." He paused and shook his head. "What was left of them. I thought Christopher had been destroyed."

Jack spoke up. "Absalom said he found him in a ditch."

"He could have been there for years. Just lying dormant," said Estelle.

A ripple of anguish crossed Cormier's face at the thought of it.

Jack felt sorry for Cormier, but he was still a little angry about all of this. Particularly about Cormier keeping so many secrets. "So you had a Diviner and you destroyed it, because you were afraid other people would use it?"

Cormier nodded.

"But the Agency made their own," said Jack.

"Presumably on the off chance that someday Article Five might be repealed, and that the military would be permitted to create ensouled machines for fighting any future wars," said Cormier.

"So in the absence of the Diviner, Blake took Christopher in the hope he might help him unlock the secret to Refined Propulsion," said Estelle.

"Your friend Absalom obviously wasn't discreet enough. Word of Christopher's accident must have gotten out—you said he was hit by a car? As soon as Blake heard his description he must have known who he was," said Cormier.

Nobody said anything for a moment, as they all took everything in.

"So, when are we escaping?" asked Rob.

He looked around at their faces and frowned at the gloomy expressions he saw.

"We are escaping, aren't we?" he said.

Cormier sighed again. The effort of talking seemed to have sapped the energy from him and he lay back on his bunk. Estelle gave him a look of contempt, then she turned back to Rob.

"We are, Rob. Most definitely."

CHAPTER 30

The next morning they were taken down a grimy tunnel and out beyond the prison walls, into the graveyard.

Blake was waiting for them. Reeves stood behind him, hunched and cowed, looking like a whipped dog. His trembling right hand covered the exposed metal beneath his cheek. In his left hand he held the dormant Diviner.

About a dozen Berserkers encircled the graveyard. Their silver bodies gleamed in the pearly light. Each body was spiked and serrated, a combination of steel muscle, blades, and guns.

In contrast, the graveyard was a small, squalid, cramped place with a broken wall. It was filled with lichen, moss, and squat gray tombstones that looked like they'd been hammered deep into the earth. The surrounding area doubled as a scrapyard. Metal sheets and piping were littered everywhere. There were various Empties and the heads of dozens of discarded Mutes scattered around.

A raised platform loomed over the site. It was a solid-looking construction built from steel girders. A ten-foot metal spike stabbed upward into the sky from each of its four corners.

"Welcome, welcome, one and all," Blake said, spreading his arms wide.

Cormier shook his head ruefully as he looked at the platform. "I see you've constructed a power node for amplifying the Diviner's energy."

"It's the best method for achieving psychonic adhesion of multiple vessels," said Blake.

"I'd like to say I'm impressed, but really I think you're insane, Richard, truly you are. Is this where you mean to harvest your souls?"

"Absolutely," smiled Blake. "Where better than the Crag's graveyard? A graveyard for the most violent degenerates society has to offer. What type of soul could be more suited to the art of war?"

Estelle looked at the graveyard and the Berserkers with disgust. "I don't understand."

Cormier turned to her. "When it comes to extracting souls, the best place for it is a place of rest. It's here where the barrier between life and death is at its most permeable."

Blake smiled, but it was a thin-lipped smile, and he suddenly seemed to be struggling with some dark emotion. "It's at moments like this that I think of my father." Tears started to well in his eyes. "Sometimes I think if he were here now, if he could see what I've accomplished, how proud he'd be," he said, his voice cracking momentarily.

Cormier shook his head. "There's still time to stop this, Richard."

Blake wiped his eyes with his sleeve and chuckled. Jack looked at him, and for one brief moment, despite everything, he seemed almost worthy of pity.

Blake took a deep breath in through his nostrils and tugged at the edges of his waistcoat. He stood as erect as possible. "I'm sorry, Philip. It's too late to go back now." His eyes settled on

Christopher, and the simmering anger that had momentarily evaporated from them returned. "I look at him, Philip, and I think—*why was it you who could bring someone back. What made you so special?*"

Cormier raised his chin. He had no answer for him.

At his master's signal, Reeves handed the Diviner to Blake, head bowed. In the early morning light the shining sides of the instrument looked as fragile as tissue paper, as if there were no way such a delicate device could hold so much power.

Jack took the opportunity to edge closer to Christopher. He smiled at him, despite it all.

"You came for me," whispered Christopher, a statement that was almost a sob.

Jack was still smiling. "Yes, we did."

"Thank you, Jack," said Christopher.

"There's no need to thank me," Jack said. "We'd have done it anyway, no matter what."

Christopher gave a brief smile, then Jack saw his eyes fill with grief as he looked toward Cormier.

"I don't remember him," said Christopher. "I don't remember any of it."

"That's all right," said Jack, "it'll all come back to you."

Christopher's eyes lit on Blake. "We have to stop him," he hissed.

"We will," said Jack, and as he smiled he hoped the confidence he was faking was enough to convince Christopher, if even for just a moment.

"Stop your yakking," growled Dunlop.

After conferring, Blake handed the Diviner to Cormier, who looked at his grandson with pain-filled eyes. Cormier's shoulders slumped, and he sighed as he closed his eyes and moved his right hand over the Diviner. The instrument started to pulse with light. Blake took the Diviner reverently and mimicked his movements. As Blake moved his hand over it, new glyphs started to solidify in the light. Blake's eyes were hungry as he watched them form.

These were different glyphs from the ones they had seen on the Diviner before. They were jagged, ugly symbols and they moved across its surface with an angry restless energy, like ants ready to devour something.

Blake motioned for Cormier to step toward the platform with him. Cormier followed him over, his leather coat billowing behind him in the cold wind. The two men stood under the platform, gazing upward. Blake held the Diviner in the air, and then let it go. It hovered at eye level and he closed his eyes and mouthed something. The Diviner levitated upward, rising toward the center of the platform. Both Cormier and Blake craned their necks as they watched it finally settle and hover a couple of feet above the center of the platform. Suddenly the Diviner's light flared sapphire blue. Four tendrils of blue lightning exploded outward from its surface, each one intertwining around one of the four spikes that thrust upward into the sky. The Diviner itself blazed brighter and started to revolve slowly.

Cormier lowered his head.

"We haven't got long, have we?" said Christopher, standing by Jack's shoulder.

Jack gazed up in wonder and fear and shook his head. He felt a flickering sense of hopelessness.

Round Rob, who was standing close to Jack, flinched suddenly. Jack saw his shoulder convulse and heard a loud chittering from George.

"Stop it, George," said Rob.

George's legs were spasming and he was making a high-pitched shrieking sound now, dashing around Rob's neck.

"Shut that thing up!" roared Dunlop.

"His name is George!" Rob shouted.

Dunlop advanced toward him, waving his stun gun, but was stopped dead in his tracks by a sound that made all of them turn.

It was a low hum, building in volume. All eyes turned to the horizon and the hill that swept down toward the graveyard.

The background hum suddenly became a metallic shrieking. It sounded like thousands of knives being sharpened simultaneously. Dunlop clutched his ears and everyone else followed suit as the shrieking intensified. The only person not clamping their hands to their ears was Cormier. He was too busy grinning.

Over the horizon came hundreds of metallic spiders, streaming down the hill toward the graveyard in a great wave of liquid silver.

Chittering, shrieking, gleaming—they came in a furious torrent. A steady rumble of tiny legs. A wall of vicious gleaming eyes. George shrieked back at them in response.

Blake stood there with his mouth open in shock.

Jack smiled.

Cormier turned toward Blake. He reached inside his coat and took out a small black box with buttons. "I call it 'remote control,'" he said. "Just to let you know, I get dibs on the name."

There was a thunderous metallic crunch as the spiders hit the low wall, then they were tumbling over it like floodwater.

That was the moment Blake seemed to regain control of his senses. He ran straight for the platform. "Protect the Diviner!" he shrieked. Reeves didn't move, paralyzed by terror and indecision. He turned slowly, as if trying to remember how to use his legs, and followed his master. Jack had been so busy watching the spiders he'd forgotten Dunlop.

It was a drilling shriek behind him that reminded him that

the thug was there. Jack turned to locate the source of the animalistic sound, and his eyes widened when he saw a silver-limbed figure twisting manically across the graveyard in a doomed effort to escape. It was Dunlop being consumed by a swirling mass of silver spiders.

Another seething mass of spiders rushed toward the platform, and Jack gave silent thanks that they were on his side. He nodded at Estelle, Rob, and Christopher, and they all followed Cormier to the foot of the platform.

"He's doing something with the Diviner," said Rob, squinting upward.

At the summit of the platform, Blake was inscribing symbols in the air in front of the Diviner. Nothing seemed to be happening, until suddenly it flared to a brightness that almost blinded them. There was a tremendous crack, like the sound of lightning ripping through air, and a great beam of blue light shot out from the Diviner, coming to a stop just over the center of the graveyard. There was a thunderous whirring sound like that of a giant drill boring through the earth, and great blue luminous fractures started to radiate out from the spot where the shaft of light terminated.

All the air around them seemed to roar and rush to that one point. It felt like a hole was being punched through the world.

"It's fully activated. He's going to initiate psychonic adhesion," said Cormier fearfully.

Rob turned and looked at him, bemused.

"He's going to ensoul his machines," Cormier simplified.

The air was split by a new sound—a terrible howling. It sounded like a creature in torment and it reverberated across the graveyard, making the air itself tremble with its anguish.

"Look," said Rob, pointing toward the source of the fractures.

Something black and smoky was pulsing along one of the veins of light. It spiraled around the twisting bolt, and then, as if propelled by some unseen force, it accelerated straight for one of the Berserkers standing at the edge of the graveyard.

The air vibrated, and there was a sound of shearing metal. The shadow made a *whoomph* sound as it passed through the armored chest.

The Berserker twitched. Its eyes glowed an icy blue. And it convulsed into life.

The creature lifted its arms and gazed at its clawed hands, then it threw its head back and roared at the sky.

Jack spotted another shadow curling around a blue tendril of light. He pointed at it, unable to speak.

"We don't have much time," said Cormier.

"What can we do?" Rob shouted over the din and roar.

Cormier turned and looked up at the platform, his face grim and determined. He whipped his head back around when he heard a great metallic groaning—the first Berserker was swiveling toward them. As it started its advance, there was another *whoomph* as the second soul found its mark and another Berserker started to waken.

Cormier put two fingers in his mouth and gave a whistle so piercing it made Estelle's eyes water. He clicked his fingers, snapped his wrist, and gestured at the spiders. The great mass split in two, and a silver swell flowed toward the first Berserker. Those at the forefront were crunched under the Berserker's feet. Those behind climbed over their fallen comrades and started to crawl up the Berserker's legs, chittering and shrieking as they ascended.

Jack frowned at Cormier. "You didn't use your remote control thing. How can they attack like that?"

Cormier nodded, and waggled his remote control. "This only calls them."

"So they have souls?" said Christopher.

"That's right. How do you think they could take care of

242

Dunlop?" said Cormier, his eyes lighting up as he watched his charges go to work.

"Where did you get so many souls?" asked Estelle.

"Rats," said Cormier matter-of-factly.

Estelle went slightly pale and held a hand to her mouth.

"Come on," said Cormier. Giving a great sweeping motion with his arm, he grabbed a steel rod from the pile of scrap and charged toward the platform.

Some of the spiders from the second group were already climbing the struts, spinning upward in ferocious lines. Cormier reached the ladder and had just touched the side of the frame when the whole platform crackled with energy and lines of blue lightning arced and fizzed along the metal. The engineer was thrown backward and a rain of silver spiders fell around him as they too were blasted from the platform.

Christopher was first to Cormier. He grabbed him by the wrists and they both looked at the red, raw bumps of wet flesh that now lined Cormier's left palm.

"It's nothing!" he shouted above the noise, and despite his pain his eyes were filled with hope as they met Christopher's. "The platform . . . it doesn't like Flesh."

"What do we need to do?" Jack asked Cormier, Rob at his side. Christopher helped Cormier sit up.

"You have to destroy the Diviner," said Cormier. "Once the pillar of light is broken all souls that have been released by it will be sucked back where they came from. The Diviner itself can contain great power, but its surface is essentially fragile. You'll have to smash it with something metal."

He handed the steel rod to Christopher, who nodded and slipped it through his belt.

"What are you going to do?" asked Jack.

As he got to his feet, Cormier fixed Jack with a grizzled look and smiled. "We're going to stand and fight," he said, winking

243

at Estelle. He started to laugh his big gravelly laugh. Rob joined in, and soon they were both egging each other on. Jack rolled his eyes, but despite everything he found he couldn't help smiling.

"Now go!" shouted Cormier.

They didn't need to be told twice. Jack led the charge toward the platform, with Christopher following and a wild-eyed Rob bringing up the rear.

CHAPTER 31

The day had darkened, as if the Diviner was sucking the light out of the world. *Or perhaps the world is filling with shadows*, Jack thought as they reached the ladder at the foot of the platform. A crumping sound followed by an angry bellow told him that another Berserker had been ensouled.

The platform was under assault from a new wave of spiders. They pounced and leapt—some of them thrown back, fizzing as the coruscating energy hit them. A few had reached the lip of the platform but were being kicked back over the edge by a frantic Blake. One look at them suddenly jogged Rob's memory.

"Where's George?" he shrieked, feeling around his neck.

"Never mind that now," Jack shouted. "We'll find him later."

But will there be a later? Jack wondered. He pushed the thought away and gripped the first strut. He could feel the energy bolts course along his arm and through his body. The ladder itself was also shaking, and he didn't like the way the hooks that held it in place at the top of the platform were hopping with the vibrations.

"We can do this," he shouted through gritted teeth.

He prayed that he could hold on and started to climb. Christopher followed him, then Rob.

Jack could see the graveyard laid out below him as he climbed. Three Berserkers were now fully animated. Two were crawling with spiders, and they were flinging them off in all directions. The weight of them on the legs of one Berserker made it look as if it was wading through mud. It howled in protest. Another was having more success and was stamping and smashing its way toward the platform. A fourth Berserker was stirring and turning to look at the platform.

They finally reached the top. Christopher and Jack helped Rob over the edge. They were just in time. A sudden pulse of energy ran through the whole platform. The vibration was enough to throw them all off their feet and rip the top of the ladder from its mooring. They watched, helpless, as the ladder tumbled to the ground. They got to their feet and Jack tried his best to look confident as he exchanged glances with Christopher and Rob.

Blake was standing some distance away at the opposite edge of the platform. Some spiders were scrambling over the edge, but the crazed engineer was kicking at them and swiping with an iron bar. Reeves was standing a few feet behind him, his arms hanging by his sides, his head lowered forlornly. Jack had never seen anyone look so wretched and defeated.

"Come, then! Do your worst!" Blake roared as the spiders swarmed onto the platform. Jack felt a bolt of fear as he heard the now-familiar roar of another waking Berserker.

"What are we supposed to do?" Rob asked desperately.

Christopher stepped forward. "I'll distract him. You two have to destroy the Diviner."

Jack nodded. Christopher signaled for Rob and Jack to go

left while he was going to attempt to go right and creep up on Blake.

"What about him?" said Jack, pointing at Reeves.

Reeves was looking at them now, with that same defeated expression on his face. He didn't look like he could move even if he wanted to.

"I don't think he's going to be a problem anymore," said Christopher.

Christopher hunched down and started moving toward Blake. Jack took Rob's hand and they moved to the left. All around them they could hear the wind roaring, the skittering and shrieking of spiders, and the howl of Berserkers. The world was gray and filled with smoke and sparks, and it seemed to take them forever to move forward.

Jack saw Christopher heft the steel rod he'd carried up with him. He smashed it against the platform and Blake wheeled around and snarled like a dog when he saw him.

"Oh no," he said, wagging his finger. "Oh no, not now. Not now."

Blake advanced toward Christopher and grinned as he raised his own bar. He brought it down in a great swooping motion. Christopher managed to sidestep just in time, wheeling backward, almost losing his balance.

Blake ran an agitated hand through his hair and lifted his bar again. Jack shook himself and nudged Rob on toward the Diviner. It hovered before them, the light thundering out of it while a strange gossamer aura of calm pulsed around its core. They could feel the pressure of the light that came from the Diviner pushing them backward. It was like trying to walk into the wind. They managed to get within inches.

Jack reached out for the Diviner, while a nervous Rob placed a hand on his shoulder.

The sudden shock of what he felt almost sent him reeling.

"What is that?" moaned Rob.

"I . . . I dunno, Rob . . . I . . ."

I think it's warmth, Rob, he thought to himself. *And I think it's cold. I think it's feeling.*

Jack blinked as the sensations rushed through him. The warmth, the cold, the joy, the sorrow. He looked at his hand. Some of the skin had been peeled off and he could see the gray steel of his fingers poking out. He looked at Rob.

There was a sudden shriek to their right, and both of them turned to see a crazed Blake shouting at them. Christopher was tottering back from him after narrowly avoiding another blow. He was just regaining his balance as Blake drew symbols in the air with his free hand and then pointed a finger at the Diviner.

In response, the Diviner blazed with a ferocious blue-white hotness, and Jack and Rob were thrown to the ground by a sudden blast of energy.

Blake gave a howl of triumph—which became a howl of pain as Christopher hit him across the shin with a mighty crack. Blake collapsed on the floor and Christopher moved in. He stood over Blake as the engineer held his hands up to defend himself. Rob and Jack were trying to get back to their feet. They were momentarily stunned and the world was spinning, but Jack had enough of his wits about him to realize what Christopher was about to do. He could see the rage in Christopher's eyes. He was starting to bring his weapon down for what would be a killing blow.

"Christopher! No!" Jack shouted.

As soon as he called out he regretted it. Christopher looked at Jack for barely a second, but it was enough for Blake. He grabbed the steel rod and wrenched it from Christopher's grasp with such force that it threw the boy backward across the platform. Christopher skidded to the edge and barely stopped

248

himself from going over. He could only watch as his weapon flew over the edge and disappeared.

Blake clambered up and limped toward him. Christopher tried to get up, but Blake was already upon him and raising his own rod for a blow that would surely smash Christopher's skull in.

Jack tried to say something, but only a strangled yelp came out.

Blake roared as he started to bring the rod down.

And, amazingly, he was stopped in mid-swing.

Blake swung around and twisted as the rod stayed right where it was, gripped tightly in both hands by Reeves.

"Let go!" Blake screamed.

Reeves remained impassive, his eyes fixed on his master's face.

"I said let go!" Blake roared again.

Reeves didn't even flinch. His grip on the rod remained viselike.

Blake had gripped the rod with both hands now and attempted to drag it away from Reeves, only succeeding in dragging the mechanical himself across the platform. Both of them were almost on top of Christopher now, the rod held between them as Blake wrestled for it, while Reeves simply held it in his clawed hands.

No matter how he tried, Blake couldn't release it from his servant's grip. Sweat was pouring down his forehead now as he gave one last animalistic roar of fury.

That was the moment Reeves let go of the rod.

Blake went tumbling and screaming off the edge of the platform.

His right hand fumbled blindly and snagged Reeves's coat. Reeves went slipping off the platform, as if not caring, mutely surrendering to the inevitable.

And then both men were gone.

For a moment, Jack, Christopher, and Rob gaped at the space where Blake had been.

Christopher was up first. He ran toward Jack and Rob and helped them to their feet. All three of them turned toward the Diviner, and all three felt the same sinking sensation.

The Diviner was blazing with such ferocity now that they could feel the waves of light pushing them even from this distance.

Jack made his decision in an instant.

"Take Rob back down," he said to Christopher.

Christopher shook his head. "Jack, no . . ."

"Take him down, Christopher, and go with him."

"You can't do this on your own, Jack," Christopher protested.

"Do what?" asked Rob, looking from one to the other and back again. "Do what? What's he talking about?"

Jack lowered his eyes and gently started to push Rob away. Rob frowned for a moment, then he looked at the Diviner and his eyes widened.

"No, Jack! No!"

Jack sighed. "Rob—"

"No, you can't. It'll explode and you won't come back, Jack. You won't ever come back, just like Proper Edward and Gripper, and then what will I do?"

Jack leaned in to Rob. He spoke gently to him. "I have to do this on my own. Christopher can't, because he has his grandfather."

"Then I'll do it. I'll destroy the Diviner," said Rob petulantly, and he started to barrel his way toward it.

Jack grabbed his arm. "No, Rob."

Rob tried to wrestle his way out of Jack's grip, but Christopher held him now as well.

"Why can't I?" Rob sobbed. "Why does it have to be you?"

Jack smiled sadly. "It doesn't, but I couldn't forgive myself if it was you or Christopher, Rob."

Rob's lower lip wobbled. He looked at the ground for a moment, then half looked at Jack, slightly ashamed and guilty. "Okay, but just know that I hate you for it. Just know that, Jack. I hate you," he wheezed.

Jack was still smiling, but it was a sad, resigned smile.

"What are you going to do?" Christopher asked Jack.

Jack smiled wryly despite his predicament. "I suppose I'll just have to crush it with my bare hands. Cormier said it was fragile enough."

Jack held up his hands, and Christopher saw the skin had been ripped off them. Jack quickly lowered them.

"What will it do to you?" Christopher asked.

Jack shook his head as if it didn't matter. "Nothing, I'll be fine."

A worried Rob looked from Jack to Christopher.

"I'll be fine, Rob," Jack said. He smiled, but deep down he knew that wasn't true.

"Come on," said Christopher, pointing to the edge of the platform. They followed him across and they all looked down over the edge.

The first thing they saw was Blake lying there, arms and legs splayed, a dark wet patch just below his left shoulder where the steel rod had pierced him through his back. Reeves was a few feet away from him, lying still.

"Climbing down isn't an option, but we should survive something like that," Christopher said to Rob.

Rob looked over the edge and nodded. "It's far, but not far for a mechanical. I should know. I've been rolled down enough hills." He turned to the others and smiled. "Am I right?"

Both Jack and Christopher smiled in response. When all

else failed, no matter what, they both knew they could rely on Rob to look on the bright side.

Rob grinned broadly at both of them.

Then he shoved Christopher into Jack and watched as they both went spinning off the platform.

CHAPTER 32

Rob's first response was to feel guilty. But he quickly shook it off as he reminded himself that it was for the best, and that at least his friends would be safe. That made him happy. The truth was, there was nothing more important in the world to Round Rob than his friends, and he was going to make damn sure they survived this.

He walked away from the edge and started to ponder his next move. He looked at the gray sky veined with blue lightning. He saw the Berserkers moving inexorably toward the platform. Almost all of them were animated now. At least two had collapsed under the weight of Cormier's spiders, and three more were fighting what remained, but there weren't enough spiders to stop them all. He looked at the sylphlike shadows that scudded out of those fizzing blue fractures. He looked at the Diviner blazing like a star, and he thought about the best way forward.

I'll have to crush it, Jack had said.

Rob nodded to himself. Jack was right. If anything was going to work, it was crushing the Diviner, and Rob reckoned he had a better advantage than most in that department. He stuck out his chest, tapped it, and listened to the hollow echo.

Rob turned to face the Diviner. He could still feel the waves of energy pushing him backward—like being in the teeth of a gale.

He knew he wouldn't have much time. "Best make the most of it then, Rob," he said to himself.

He held his breath. Then he laughed—he didn't have any breath to hold. He raised a hand to hold his eyebrow in place and advanced toward the Diviner.

The waves hit him in the chest, but Rob pushed forward. Strips of skin started to peel off his face, but he kept going. On he pushed, getting closer to his goal, his eyes fixed on the blue pulsing light, until finally he stood over it.

The energy roared off the Diviner and now the skin on his hands was being flayed. Rob didn't mind. He was too busy thinking about more important things. He thought about the day he'd woken in the junkyard and found Christopher and Jack looking down at him. He thought about the day Estelle had given him his face and how he'd caught her smiling with pride, even though she thought he wasn't looking at her. He thought about looking out over the junkyard at the top of one of the biggest piles of scrap, holding Manda's hand while the sun was setting in the west. He thought about Gripper.

Rob reached out with both hands and held the Diviner. He felt the strange cold and warmth again, the heat and iciness, the sound and fury, the sorrow and the pain, but he didn't mind it. His mind was on other things.

He held the Diviner to his chest and squeezed with all his might. He closed his eyes and pictured his friends' faces and whispered their names. Jack, Estelle, Gripper, Manda, Christopher. Then he fell forward onto the Diviner.

Round Rob smiled.

And the world exploded.

CHAPTER 33

Jack and Christopher had just gotten back on their feet when the force of the explosion from the platform threw them to the ground. There was the dreadful screech of wrenching metal. Jack felt Christopher grip his shoulder and scream: "Come on!"

Christopher dragged Jack away from the platform as its struts and pylons collapsed outward. Chunks of metal fell through the air and embedded themselves in the earth. Rivets rained down and clattered against Jack and Christopher. Jack's first thought was for Estelle. She and Cormier had somehow managed to drag Blake some distance away. He could see her lying on the ground, her face buried in her hands. Cormier was lying across Blake in an effort to protect him. A large supporting girder had collapsed and crushed poor old Mortimer Reeves.

The steel rain seemed to finally abate. There was a momentary lull, then a low rumbling. The great beam of blue light started to scream.

How can light scream? thought Jack.

The light contracted suddenly and viciously and the ensouled

Berserkers howled in unison. There was a sudden inrush of pressure, as if all the air was being squeezed from the world. The brittle fractures of blue light were sucked into the shrinking pillar.

The black souls followed. As quickly as they'd been shot into the metal bodies they were now ripped out of them. The Berserkers fell to their knees and collapsed. Shrieking tatters of blackness spiraled and streamed out of them and were sucked into the narrow pillar of light and back into the void. As each Berserker fell they sent tremors through the graveyard, until finally no more were left standing and the emptied silver shells were silent.

The pillar of light winked out of existence, leaving only threadlike veins of wispy light in the air.

There was nothing but silence.

Somebody coughed. Jack turned to see Blake attempting to rise. Blood was pooling at the corners of his mouth. It was a dark, mucky red, like the blood on his shirt.

"Philip . . . Philip . . ." he wheezed.

Cormier squeezed his arm. "Rest now, Richard. You must rest."

Despite his pain, Blake grabbed Cormier's arm with both hands. "I was trying my best, Philip, that's all," he hissed. "You won. You won, and in the process you've destroyed everything."

"It wasn't about winning, Richard," Cormier said wearily.

Blake smiled. "He would have been proud, Philip, wouldn't he? He would have been so proud."

Cormier seemed to struggle inwardly with something, then he nodded sympathetically, as if he'd decided there was no harm in what he was going to say next. Especially now.

"Yes, Richard. He would have been."

Blake smiled at Cormier. Then his smile started to fade and

his eyes glazed over. He gave a final sigh and went limp in Cormier's arms.

Cormier let him go, just as something smoky and black rose from Blake's chest.

"What's happening?" said Estelle, recoiling.

"It's the last vestiges of the Diviner's energy. Any dying souls caught within its radius are sucked into the next world."

They all watched in horrified fascination as Blake's soul drifted on the air like a spiderweb blown in the breeze. The soul came up against the tiniest glimmer of a fracture, but with a barely audible crystalline sound the fracture shattered like fine glass. The soul hovered for a moment, then started to dissipate and fade, making a sound like hissing sand, until soon there was none of it left.

"What happened to it?" asked Estelle.

Cormier shrugged. "It vanished. Simple as that." He turned away.

Estelle squinted out across the jumble of scrap the soul had passed over. Her look was one of deep suspicion and distrust.

"Rob," Jack moaned.

He turned around and started to run for the wreckage at the base of what was left of the platform. The others followed. Jack was frantic. He started to throw bits of metal aside, oblivious to those around him. "Rob!" he shouted, over and over again.

He found Rob's body moments later. There was no mistaking it. It was cracked and jagged where it had been torn open by the Diviner. The metal was blackened and burned at the edges. Jack dragged the body out from under the detritus and held it tenderly. There was no sign of Rob's head. A great hush fell, broken only by Jack's sobbing. Christopher fell to his knees by his side, one hand on his friend's shoulder, his eyes wide with shock and disbelief.

Jack looked at Christopher. "He's gone, Christopher. He's

gone," he sobbed. He held Rob's body and sobbed, rocking back and forth. No one said anything, until a familiar voice suddenly piped up:

"You said you'd teach me how to whistle when all this was over."

It was like being hit by lightning. It was Rob's voice, clear as day. Estelle shrieked and ran forward. She pulled aside a sheet of metal, and there was Rob's head looking up at them, battered and a little smoke-damaged, but it was unmistakably his head, complete with wonky eyebrows.

"You're alive!" Jack screamed.

"Course I'm alive," said Rob.

Jack grabbed his head and squeezed it to his chest. Christopher did the same and Estelle snatched him away from both of them and held him fiercely.

"How?" Cormier asked.

"Dodgy workmanship," said Rob. "Mr. Absalom gave me a loose head. I can run around without it and everything. It got blown off just before the big explosion." Rob made a face. "I just did a shrug there, but you probably didn't notice because I don't have any shoulders."

Estelle squealed and peppered Rob's face with kisses. Rob made sounds of disgust, but Estelle kept doing it anyway.

"You did it, Rob," said Christopher. "You saved us. You saved everyone."

Blake woke in darkness.

He had a moment of panic. He remembered falling. He remembered the pain.

He became vaguely aware of his surroundings, even in the dark. He felt a sudden rush of relief.

I'm alive, he thought.

His second thought was a murderous one. It took some effort

for him to calm himself, but when he did he felt suffused with a cold, joyous fury.

I will destroy them, each and every one of them, he thought.

He could see old wooden shelves, cobwebbed test tubes, and dust-covered bottles. He saw a sliver of light in the ceiling above. It was the opening of a door with steps leading up to it. He was in a cellar.

Blake felt the overpowering urge to rush to the light.

Then Estelle stepped in front of him.

Blake almost flinched, then castigated himself for his lapse. This girl was nothing to him. *I will kill you*, he said. *I will make you pay for what*—

"I don't think you can talk, which I suppose is a pity for you, seeing that you love the sound of your own voice," said Estelle.

She regarded him coolly. *How dare she*, Blake thought, *I deserve respect, fear . . .*

How dare you, he screamed at her. *You will be made to suffer.*

Estelle shook her head. "No, can't hear you, unfortunately."

She turned away and started to rummage on a shelf.

When she turned back she was holding something rectangular.

"I suppose I first became suspicious when your soul vanished, just like that. I thought to myself, *Surely there must be someplace for it to go*. Then I thought I saw something in the scrap heap, so I came back outside just to be sure."

Estelle winked at him. She turned the rectangular object toward him. It was a mirror, dirty and cracked, but with enough clear surface for him to see . . .

"The miracle of Refined Propulsion in action," said Estelle, and she smiled.

He was looking at a head on a table. Little more than a

mechanical mold. A scuffed brass head with rolling eyes. A sickening rudimentary without a mouth. A Mute.

How am I . . . ? Where am I . . . ?

Blake blinked and the head blinked in response.

That was when he started screaming.

Estelle sighed. "I think your soul found the nearest available empty object. Probably something to do with the Diviner." Estelle frowned. "I suppose Cormier would know, but then I'm not going to mention it to him. Ever."

Blake cursed, he swore, he screamed again. He promised to make her suffer, but of course Estelle heard none of it.

She leaned her elbows on the table and cupped her chin in her hands and gazed at him.

"You're stuck in there now. For a long time. Maybe even forever." She stood up. "Time enough, I suppose. Time enough for you to learn the lesson that no one hurts my friends and gets away with it."

Estelle turned away and started to walk up the stairs. Blake screamed at her again. He started begging when she was halfway up. He was sobbing when she put her hand on the door. She turned back to give him one last look.

"I don't know what's going to happen to you. Maybe you'll die again, maybe you won't. Maybe you'll just be like this forever. A stupid ugly metal head rusting in the dark." Estelle shrugged. "But then again, what do I know? I only make skin."

She turned away and went through the door. The square of light narrowed to a sliver. The sliver disappeared.

Blake screamed in the darkness. The scream became the darkness, until both were indistinguishable from each other, and finally for Richard Blake there was nothing but darkness.

And the darkness became forever.

CHAPTER 34

Ironhaven gleamed in the sunlight as they pulled up in the van. A rumble-tumble heap of metal and rivets, it shone with bright patches of copper and bronze and silver. Despite its haphazard nature, Christopher reckoned he'd never seen anything so beautiful.

"It'll be all right, you know," Jack said.

"What?" said Christopher.

Jack nodded without looking at him, as if reassuring himself more than Christopher.

"It'll be all right, you'll see. It'll all come back to you."

"Is that a new gate?" Rob piped up.

Cormier chuckled in appreciation. "Good old Egbert. Reliable as always."

As they neared the shining new entrance to Cormier's compound, a dozen or so mechanicals stepped falteringly into the light and watched them as they passed. Christopher noticed that most were in various stages of disrepair. He saw one girl look mournfully at them as they drove by. She had one eye, and the skin was missing from her right arm. He saw a boy carrying his own head and two more boys with their arms wrapped around each other's shoulders. They only had one leg each, and this accommodation they had come to seemed to be the only way they could both move around.

As they got out of the van, Christopher turned to see a boy with five legs approaching them with a hopeful look on his face.

"Jack," the boy said. "You came back."

"Of course we did, Sam," Jack replied. He turned to Christopher and gestured at Sam. "This is Sam Six Legs."

Sam smiled at Christopher. "I know you."

"Right then, shall we get inside?" Cormier said, a little too loudly, rapping on the gate while refusing to look at any of the broken mechanicals.

Christopher frowned at Sam. "You do?"

Sam nodded. "Of course."

"I don't remember . . ."

"That's all right," said Sam pleasantly.

"Right, everybody in," shouted Cormier.

"Welcome home," said Sam, and he gave Christopher a hesitant, almost apologetic smile.

Home, thought Christopher. *Is this home?* It didn't feel like it, and he wasn't sure how to respond to Sam.

The new gate swung open smoothly and Cormier shouted again for everyone to get inside, and they all started to move toward the entrance. Sam took a tentative step forward and looked over Christopher's shoulder in the direction of Cormier. Christopher couldn't help notice the nervous, hopeful expression on his face. It was the look of someone almost too afraid to hope, the kind of look you see in someone who's been let down once too often.

"We'll talk, Sam," said Jack.

Christopher could hear the note of reassurance in Jack's voice. Sam looked grateful. More mechanicals were arriving behind him and Christopher spotted the girl with one eye again. He turned and stepped into the courtyard, unable to forget the images of the mechanicals he had seen.

Cormier stood in the center of the courtyard and held his arms aloft. "Home!" he shouted.

The main door of Cormier's little citadel opened, and Manda dashed out and ran down the stairs toward them. Christopher was pleased to see that she ran on legs that were now admirably even in length. Her face had been touched up, and she now had new eyes, both of which were the same size.

"You're back," she squealed. She grabbed Christopher first and squeezed him with all her might. Christopher laughed. "I knew we'd find you. I knew it!" she shouted. When she was finished with Christopher she hugged each and every one of them. She grabbed Rob's head from Jack and spun around with him held at arm's length.

"Where's the rest of you, Rob?" she asked, after finally stopping.

"About a hundred miles back that way," said Rob, arching one eyebrow, which promptly fell off.

Christopher picked it up and pocketed it. "For later, Rob."

"I don't want it later," said Rob. "I want new ones, fancy ones. Like a gentleman. Isn't that right, Mr. Cormier?"

"That's right," said Cormier, ruffling Rob's hair. He stole a quick glance at Christopher and hurriedly looked away.

"Where's Gripper?" said Manda.

They all looked at one another. Nobody knew what to say. It was Jack who took her aside and quietly explained what had happened. Manda howled when she heard the news. It took a few minutes for her to calm down, and she was still sniffling when she turned to Christopher.

"But he got you back, Christopher. That's what matters, isn't it? You're back, and that's because of Grip."

She hugged Christopher again. This time she held him a lot longer.

"Right, then," said Cormier, gesturing toward the house. "Shall we?"

Christopher heard the sound of the gate swinging shut. He turned around to see Sam Six Legs standing on the other side. There were more mechanicals standing behind him, all looking in forlornly as the gate continued to close. Sam raised his hand, and Christopher and Jack raised theirs in salute. The gate closed. Christopher looked at Jack. Jack looked as if he wanted to say something, but then thought better of it. They turned and followed Cormier into his house.

Once inside, Egbert served oil in the dining room and Cormier drank something that seemed to make him extremely happy. The sound of bubbling laughter and chat filled the room, and there was a palpable sense of relief and joy. Cormier watched them all as they chattered to one another, and a faint smile started to appear on his face. Christopher caught his eye, and Cormier's smile wobbled, then disappeared completely. He turned away quickly and asked Egbert for another glass.

Christopher looked around at his friends. Everyone was happy. He felt safe for the first time in an age, but he didn't feel as if he was home.

He wondered if he ever would.

CHAPTER 35

Christopher watched Estelle in her new workshop. After the first week at Cormier's, she'd taken a shine to a small shed at the side of the house. She'd cobbled together some tools and had gotten straight to work. Cormier was happy to leave her to her own devices. Christopher saw the change in her straightaway. Her eyes were bright and she was possessed with a real sense of purpose as she moved fluidly around her work space, stirring pots, checking beakers, stretching sheets of skin. Christopher knew that this single-minded intensity was Estelle's version of happiness.

Jack sat in a corner tinkering with a piece of metal. He also watched Estelle, and exchanged a knowing smile with Christopher. Christopher tried to smile in response, but his effort was wan and unconvincing and he looked away before Jack could detect anything might be wrong.

They'd been here four weeks now, and Christopher had never felt so happy. Even so, there was still that nagging sense of something missing. Cormier had started working on his patches the first day after they'd arrived. He'd been strangely nervous about it and almost apologetic. At first, Christopher felt and shared his tentative sense of hope, but as each day passed Cormier seemed to become more quietly despondent, despite his best efforts to appear cheerful.

It got to the stage where he now seemed to be actively avoiding Christopher. He even went so far as to almost turn and run the other way whenever he saw him coming. Now he seemed to have given in to despair, and had stopped working on the patches altogether. Earlier that day, Christopher had turned a corner outside the house and almost bumped straight into him. Cormier had been all apologies, and that was the most unsettling thing of all. He seemed to be constantly remorseful in Christopher's presence. It was all there in the strange, furtive glances he gave Christopher when they were in the same room, and in the tentative smiles that vanished almost as soon as they appeared. The once great and garrulous Philip Cormier now just seemed mournful and ashamed.

Christopher felt strange about it. On one level, he didn't remember this man, and yet on another he felt a curious sense of absence, as if he was lacking something. He tried his best to remember but try as he might, nothing ever came back.

He was thinking about all of this when he felt a strange, watchful silence in the shed. Jack was looking at him intently, and Estelle was looking at him too, wiping her hands on a rag with a half smirk on her face.

"What?" said Christopher.

"What do you want to know?" asked Estelle.

"What do you mean?" said Christopher.

"Why are you here?" said Estelle.

A guilty-looking Christopher glanced from her to Jack and back again. "I like to watch you work, Estelle . . ." he said, giving a weak shrug. He looked at his hands for a moment, then looked up to see Estelle still eyeing him with a faintly amused expression.

"I want to know when you think I might start remembering," he said quietly.

Estelle laid her rag on the tabletop and sighed. "I don't know, Christopher. I can't answer that."

Christopher nodded. He tried his best not to look crestfallen.

"But I do know one thing," said Estelle. "I know that you *will* remember. You mark my words. When you least expect it, the memories will return."

Christopher nodded in appreciation of the sentiment, and yet he still felt that strange emptiness. "He won't even look at me," he said.

Estelle considered this for a moment. "He can't," she said. "He feels guilty because he hasn't helped you remember yet. Then there's the fact that he brought you back in the first place."

"You mean from the Crag?" said Christopher.

Estelle shook her head. Christopher knew exactly what she meant, but he was afraid to admit it.

"Bringing your soul back—that couldn't have been easy for him. He's probably wondering if it was the right thing to do. You remind him of that choice."

"What do you think, Estelle? Was it the right thing to do?"

"You're here now, that's what matters to me."

"But how do you think *he* feels?"

Estelle looked thoughtful. "He missed you and he wanted you back." She paused for a moment, narrowed her eyes, and nodded to herself. "He misses you now, and he still wants you back, no matter how he acts around you."

Christopher shook his head. The idea all seemed so complicated to him. He could remember his parents, but to him Cormier was a complete stranger. So why didn't he feel whole?

He was back with his friends, and for him friends meant home. But why didn't he feel complete? What was missing?

There was the sound of clanging from outside, and swearing could be heard in the distance. Cormier was obviously working on something. Christopher smiled at the sound, but he also felt an odd sadness.

The evening sun was seeping in through the half-open door, throwing a golden blob of light along the back of the shed. Christopher was mesmerized as he watched it shimmer and move, and he felt something—a stirring in his chest. His reverie was broken by the sudden flicker of a shadow within that light.

"Evening all," said a voice behind him.

They all turned to find Round Rob leaning nonchalantly against the doorjamb.

Although "Not Quite So Round Rob" might have been more accurate. Cormier had given him a new body, a slim-line one that was made out of proper metals that could accommodate his cogs and gears. Round Rob had tried to be blasé about all of this, but Christopher couldn't help smiling at the new attitude it had brought out in him.

Rob stepped into the room with big strides, his hands on his hips. He patted his new eyebrows delicately and cleared his throat.

"Thought I'd just come out and give you all a tune," he said.

Rob puckered his lips together and started to whistle.

The latest addition to Rob's new body was a small bellows that Cormier had constructed and placed in his chest. It allowed him to sigh, to exhale, and, best of all, it allowed him to whistle.

Christopher and Jack smiled as their friend whistled. The sun was sinking lower in the sky and in the distance they could hear Cormier hammering away.

Rob rubbed his hands together. "A whistle and a walk. Who wants to come with me?"

Jack grinned and raised his hand. Rob looked inquiringly at Christopher and waggled his eyebrows. Christopher laughed. "All right, Rob."

Rob raised his eyebrows even more and looked at Estelle.

"I've got work to do, Rob," she said.

Rob shrugged. "Your loss, Estelle."

He strolled out through the door and Christopher and Jack followed him outside. Christopher grinned at the way Rob strutted with his thumbs hooked into his belt. It was something he was particularly proud of because, as he put it: "I'm all skinny now and I need a belt to keep my trousers up like a proper person."

A golden droplet of sun was spilling over the lip of a cloud. Christopher felt that tremor again, and he shivered. Jack gave him a questioning look but Christopher ignored him. Rob was chatting away to no one in particular, his thumbs still hooked into his belt, swinging his legs with great alacrity as if all the world were his.

Rob stopped walking for just a moment. He kicked a stone and then turned to Christopher and Jack. He looked perturbed, almost guilty.

"What is it, Rob?" asked Christopher.

Rob lowered his eyes and looked at the ground. When he looked up again at Christopher and Jack he appeared slightly ashamed.

"I stood on a snail yesterday."

There was a moment of silence, during which Jack smirked at Christopher.

Christopher spoke gently. "Did you squash it, Rob?"

Rob nodded quickly. He bit his upper lip.

"Did you mean to?" asked Christopher.

Rob shook his head and refused to look at Christopher. "Does it mean I'm like a refined engine? Does it mean I'm like one of those Berserkers?"

Christopher smiled. "No, Rob, it doesn't. It was an accident. Besides, you can't harm anyone or anything intentionally. You don't have a soul. You don't need one. You're not proper. You're better than proper."

Rob looked taken aback. "Better than proper?"

"Yes," said Christopher. "You're pure, Rob. There's no malice in you." He looked at Jack. "There's no malice in any of you."

Rob seemed to consider this for a moment, then he smiled. "Better than proper," he whispered to himself. His smile suddenly vanished. "But being proper means having a family too, Jack said. I don't have a mum and dad."

Jack raised his head and looked proudly at Rob. "You're my family, Rob. You and Christopher and Manda and Estelle."

Rob beamed at this. He looked from Christopher to Jack and back again, and Christopher thought he would burst.

Rob's grin started to fade, and his brow furrowed as a new thought crossed his mind.

"A promise is a promise, isn't it?"

Jack nodded. "Of course it is, Rob."

Rob stuck his hands in his pockets and looked at the gate.

"Then why hasn't he done anything yet?"

Jack scratched his chin and shook his head. He had no answer.

"It's not fair," said Rob. "And Estelle says she's seen more of them, and more are coming every day." Rob looked disgusted. "It's not fair at all."

Christopher heard a clang behind him, and he turned to see an oil-stained and sweaty Cormier peering under the hood of the truck. He shouted something to Egbert and the butler stepped forward and handed him a wrench. Manda was sitting on a stool in the background, playing with a rag doll.

Cormier was in the process of reaching for the wrench when he caught Christopher's eye. His irascible air melted away almost immediately, and his eyes became filled with a pathetically hopeful look. He half raised a hand in greeting, then seemed to think better of it and turned away and pretended to examine the engine.

Christopher followed Jack and Rob. Rob's mood had lightened and he was now alternating his whistling with some excited babbling. It seemed he couldn't decide on which he wanted to do more. When he wasn't doing either of these things he was flicking the index finger of each hand over each of his eyebrows with a little gentlemanly flourish. Jack caught Christopher's eye and winked at him, jerking his head toward Rob. Christopher chuckled.

As they walked on, Christopher looked at the burnished golden light that washed through the sky. He found himself thinking about his parents. His mother's face, her blue eyes, her shining hair. He saw his father grin at him, and for one brief shocking moment it was as if his breath had caught in his chest.

"What is it, Christopher?" asked Jack.

"What?" said a dazed Christopher. He was aware that Rob was also giving him a funny look.

"You just stopped dead still and said something about a garden," said Jack.

"I did?" said Christopher, more for his own benefit than theirs.

Rob and Jack exchanged a look. Christopher shook his head.

"Nothing, it was nothing," he said.

He could hear the distant ringing of metal on metal in the background.

"Not to worry," said Rob. "Would you like to see my new walk? I've been practicing. It's a bit fast and it looks really good. Old Rob couldn't have done it, but I'm new Rob now." He raised an eyebrow and looked very pleased with himself as he raised his right leg. "And I think you'll be well impressed with—"

And somehow Rob managed to kick his left leg out from under himself. His arms spun furiously as he tried to keep his balance, but it was too late and he hit the ground.

He gave a little panicked squawk as he fell, which only made Christopher and Jack laugh all the more.

Christopher stepped forward and offered his hand to Rob.

He heard that clanging again, but it wasn't coming from behind him. Now it was like something heard in a dream. He was dimly aware of Rob's hand coming closer. And that sound, warm and resonant, like a distant echo.

Rob took Christopher's hand and Christopher pulled him up. He looked up to see the sun going down, the clouds tinged with gold, and he smiled, and he remembered . . .

It was his mother's voice that he heard first.

He's in the garden, she said. *Making something with your father.*

In his mind's eye, he was in the kitchen. His mother was kneading bread. She smiled at him.

Go on, then, she said with a chuckle.

Christopher turned to the door. It was open. There was light, evening light, mellow and golden on green grass. He heard the familiar ringing. He ran.

Out in the garden his father turned to him. He was standing in front of someone else. Someone who was kneeling down in front of a metal frame, a hammer raised in their fist. The clanging sound again, like a bell calling him home. His father smiled.

Christopher saw the hand raising that hammer, and his heart started to pound. He ran faster.

The world tilted.

Falling, I was falling. How old was I? Eight?

Christopher tottered backward as if he'd been slapped.

Jack looked concerned. "Christopher? What is it? What's wrong?"

I was in the garden. It was summer and Mum was in the house and Dad was in the garden, and I fell, and Dad was there with . . .

Christopher saw his mother's face. He saw his father's face. He was dimly aware that Jack was saying something, and now Rob was looking at him with real concern.

I tried to get up, and there was a hand and I took . . . I took the hand and I . . .

He was in the garden again, but this time it was different. This time as he saw the sun's golden light fade across the green he felt a new sensation. It was a feeling of home, but stronger and more powerful than it had felt when he'd had visions of the house in the Crag's laboratory. And there was something else too. He heard a voice call his name and he felt himself look up.

The figure wielding the hammer had stood up and was coming toward him.

The face, when it loomed into view, was familiar now in a way it hadn't been when he'd seen it for what he thought was the first time four weeks ago. The hair, more gray in the memory than white, the blue eyes, the wrinkles at the corner of those eyes when he smiled. When his . . .

When his . . .

Christopher ran.

He ran to where he could hear the clanging. Jack and Rob ran after him, calling his name, but he didn't care. He ran in the fading sunlight, just like he had run that evening in the garden. He ran for all he was worth, past Estelle, who had come out to see what all the fuss was about. He ran right into the yard and Cormier was there, his head buried in the engine of the truck. Egbert was still standing beside him holding some tools. Manda was sitting on the stool playing with her doll, but now she looked up.

As if sensing something, Cormier raised his head. He wiped his hands and looked at Christopher, and when he saw Christopher's eyes his own eyes widened.

Christopher looked at him.

"You used to make me toys. I had a clockwork mouse once and you used to make tiny cars that moved."

Cormier stumbled back slightly and had to support himself by placing a hand on the van's hood. His chin started to tremble.

"A clockwork bird for Mum. A train for Dad. A mouse for me. You made them all one Christmas. And I used to help you make things. I used to help you fix things, because you said there was no nobler thing in the world to do than to create and to take care of precious things."

Christopher felt the tears stinging his eyes, and the lump in his throat that made it seem harder for the words to come. There was one word in particular he was afraid to say, as if saying it might shatter the sensation he was feeling now. That warm sensation. The sensation of coming home.

Christopher tried to speak, but he was sobbing. He swallowed hard, and he somehow managed to say the word.

That one word that meant everything.

"Grandad," he said.

He ran toward him and Cormier took him in his arms and held his grandson tightly and started to cry.

Jack, Rob, and Estelle stood by the shed and watched them

embrace. Estelle folded her arms. "Told him so," she said, and she smiled.

After a while they separated. Christopher wiped his eyes and looked up into his grandfather's face with a look of determination. He took his hand.

"Come on," he said.

Cormier went with him, meek as a child. Christopher nodded at Rob and jerked his head toward the toolbox, which lay nearby. Rob gave him the thumbs-up and he picked up the toolbox. The three of them headed toward the main gate. Estelle, Jack, Manda, and Egbert followed them.

They stood before the gate. Cormier looked nervous. Christopher squeezed his hand and gave him an encouraging look.

"A promise is a promise," said Rob.

Cormier took a deep breath and motioned with his hand in the air in front of the gate.

The gate opened.

Christopher smiled when he saw what was waiting for them. He led Cormier outside, and the others followed.

The sun shone golden as it sank in the west, just as it had in a garden all those years ago. Christopher Cormier knew then that he was home.

And he and his grandfather set to work.

ACKNOWLEDGMENTS

A heartfelt thanks to all the Chicken House crew, to Barry Cunningham, Rachel Leyshon, Rachel Hickman, Jazz Bartlett, and everyone else who has helped shepherd *Tin* through what was a really enjoyable process. An extra special thank you to the brilliant Kesia Lupo, whose storytelling instincts have helped make *Tin* the best book it can be. I have been blessed and honored to have Kes as my first editor. Thank you also to Fraser for the copyedits and his lifesaving attention to detail.

I'd like to thank Sam Palazzi and the US Scholastic crew for their generosity and care in ensuring this version of *Tin* was in the best possible shape.

I want to thank my agent, Sophie Hicks, for her constant support and for always being brilliant every step of the way. Thank you, Sarah Williams, for stepping in and helping when needed. Thanks also to Katy Day for getting the ball rolling.

My thanks also to Katie Hickey for a wonderful cover that still takes my breath away every time I look at it.

For the goodwill and support I'd like to thank my family, extended family, and friends. A special thank you to my parents.

Also, a big shout-out to Catherine, Fran, Paul, and Jean—remember I'm the eldest so it means I'm in charge.

Conor, Clodagh, Ella, Huey, and Sam, never forget to remind the above who's in charge. Pauline, Gibbo, and Mike, thanks for your support, and again, as I said in the previous sentence . . .

Thanks to Robert Williams for his pep talks and support, even though I know he'll scribble on the book when my back is turned.

Thank you, Nana Marie, for all your help down through the years.

Thank you to Caroline for putting up with me, to Lochlann and Sadbh for reading the first draft, to Tadhg for Ironhaven, and to Teagan for being an excellent proofreader and making me laugh.